ISLAND INHERITANCE

An Isle of Man Romance

DIANA XARISSA

❀ Created with Vellum

AUTHOR'S NOTE

This book is set in the incredibly beautiful Isle of Man, which is located between England and Ireland in the Irish Sea. While it is a Crown Dependency, it is a country in its own right, with its own currency, stamps, language and government.

This is a work of fiction. All of the modern characters are a product of the author's imagination. Any resemblance to actual persons, living or dead, is entirely coincidental. Similarly, the names of the restaurants and shops and other businesses on the island are fictional.

The historical sites and landmarks on the island are all real (Castle Rushen, Peel Castle and Rushen Abbey), as are the Manx Museum, the House of Manannan and the Wildlife Park, however, all of the events that take place within them in this story are fictional.

The Manx History Institute does not exist, but Manx National Heritage is real and their efforts to preserve and promote the historical sites and the history of the island are extraordinary. All of the Manx National Heritage staff in this story, however, are fictional creations.

The historical characters mentioned within the story (the Seventh Earl of Derby and his wife) did exist.

While the Isle of Man has its share of ghosts, spirits and Little People (fairies), to the best of the author's knowledge the ghost of Charlotte de la Tremouille does not haunt Castle Rushen. That's fiction, too.

"I'm sorry, say that again? Granny wants me to do what?" Carly Munroe was sure that she must have misunderstood her mother, but the laugh on the other end of the phone told her that she hadn't.

"Granny wants you to go to the Isle of Man and sort out her inheritance," Carly's mother, Anne, repeated herself. "She'll pay for everything, or rather the estate will. She thought you'd be excited at the thought of having a foreign vacation. And apparently she doesn't trust the lawyer there to deal with things on his own. She wants someone she trusts to handle the matter."

Carly took a deep breath, her mind racing in ten directions at once. "I have plans for the summer," she reminded her mother, thinking longingly of the neat pile of paint cans in her garage.

"I know you do, honey," her mother answered. "Shall I tell Granny that you can't do it or will you go and talk to her yourself?"

Carly tried not to sigh too deeply. Her mother clearly wanted her to go and talk to Granny herself. That was obvious from her tone. But Carly also knew that she would struggle to say no to the older woman. Not only did she love the older woman enormously, Granny rarely asked anyone for any favors. Carly did sigh now as she spoke again. "I'll go and talk to her tomorrow after school," she told her mother reluctantly.

"Thank you, darling." Anne sighed herself now. "I didn't really want to disappoint her myself," she admitted with a laugh.

The two women chatted easily then, talking about their jobs and a cousin who was getting married that weekend, before wrapping up their traditional nightly conversation.

"Sleep tight, mom." Carly's closing line was always the same.

"You too, darling," was the inevitable reply. "And give Granny my love tomorrow," Anne added, subtly reminding her only child of her earlier promise.

Carly hung up the phone and sighed again. Why on earth would she want to spend her summer vacation dealing with legal matters halfway around the world? She made her way into her garage and looked happily at her paint collection. She had spent the last month trying out dozens of paint samples and making her selections.

Every room in her small house had at least one wall dotted with sample colors. Carly had agonized over every decision for every room, but she was confident that she'd made the right choices. Now she just had to wait out the last two weeks of the school year and then she could start painting.

She shut up the garage and walked through her living room. She loved the tiny house that she had bought six months earlier. It was fairly new, less than ten years old. She was only the second owner of the single-story dwelling. Now that she had finally unpacked, it was time to make it all her own.

She walked from room to room, checking her paint choices one last time. The front door opened into the small living room that had openings into an even smaller dining room and the fairly spacious kitchen. Off the kitchen was a narrow hallway with doors to the three bedrooms. The largest bedroom, Carly's own, had its own bathroom with a whirlpool tub that felt like the height of luxury to her.

A second half-bathroom had been squeezed between the other two bedrooms on the opposite side of the hall. Carly used one spare bedroom as an office and the other as a guest bedroom, though she hadn't yet had any overnight guests. A door on the other side of the kitchen led out to the single car garage where Carly rarely bothered to park her car. There was a small driveway where her car fit quite happily and just enough of a yard at the back to give Carly room to try a little gardening if she ever felt like doing so.

Carly smiled to herself as she surveyed her modest property. Her college friends had finished school and headed off to various big cities to make their fortunes. Carly had been born and raised in Meadville, Pennsylvania. She'd done well at Allegheny College, a prestigious liberal arts college in her own backyard, and she had been delighted when the local elementary school had offered her a teaching position as soon as she'd finished her degree.

While her friends had teased her about her lack of ambition, she couldn't imagine being happier. She was still dating her first boyfriend. They'd met in third grade and she expected that he would propose at some point in the not-too-distant future. For a while she had resisted purchasing a home, wanting to wait until she and Tom were married, but her mother had urged her to buy while interest rates were low and it was a buyer's market. She could always sell her little house and move once she was married if they wanted more space.

None of her friends living in those big cities had managed to buy a home yet, which gave her a small sense of satisfaction. Instead of throwing away money, month after month, to rent a tiny and anonymous apartment in Pittsburgh or Washington, D.C., Carly could see her mortgage getting smaller all the time. She could decorate however she wanted, she had plenty of space, and she didn't have to worry about who might be renting the apartment next door. Carly smiled again as she patted a splotch of paint on her living room wall. Whatever Granny said, she was spending this summer decorating her house, not traveling around the world.

The school days seemed longer than normal during the last few weeks of the year. Carly grinned at her group of restless seven-year-olds, knowing exactly how they felt. She was looking forward to the end of the year as much as they were.

"Right, everyone back in your seats and let's play 'Math Race' for the last few minutes of the day," she told them, ignoring the handful of groans from less enthusiastic members of the class. They only had time for a few questions before the bell rang and the bus numbers began to be called.

Carly sat back in her chair and watched the children file out slowly in their turns. She'd decided to head straight to her grandmother's from school, wanting to get what might be a difficult meeting over with.

Granny Madison greeted her warmly when Carly arrived at the nursing home. She was still able to look after herself, so she lived in a large and comfortable apartment in the section of the home for independent residents. Unfortunately, she'd taken a bad fall a few weeks earlier and she was temporarily almost bedridden, which she hated.

Before Granny's fall, Carly would have had to call in advance to make an appointment to see her, because Granny lived a very active life. Now that she was unable to get around much, however, Carly could just drop in at her convenience. Carly felt terrible when she realized that she hadn't visited in over a week. She was going to have to try harder to spend time with Granny, at least while Granny was recovering from her injuries.

"I need to tell you a story." Granny said, once she had fussed over Carly's new haircut and admired all of the paint samples that Carly showed her.

"I love your stories." Carly answered at once. Granny enjoyed telling Carly all about her life, regaling her granddaughter with stories about her own and her mother's childhood. Granny was nearly seventy, but age hadn't dimmed her mind one bit. Carly especially loved the stories about her mother's early years, delighting in learning that her mother had had a naughty streak as wide as Carly's had been in her younger days.

"This one goes back a bit further than my usual stories." Granny answered. "This one goes back to before I was born and it isn't a very happy story."

Carly was intrigued. "Go on then, tell me," she demanded.

Granny laughed softly. "No patience, your generation," she complained and then grinned. "I know that in the twenty-first century it's hard to imagine the early days of the twentieth century, but that's when my story begins, in 1915 or thereabouts. A small family, living on the Isle of Man, decided to make a new start in the New World. They were going to move to America and make their fortune." Granny paused for a moment, as Carly made a face.

"Granny, Mom said that you wanted me to go to the island to sort something out for you, but I already have plans for the summer." Carly spoke quickly, wanting to get the disappointment over with as quickly as possible.

"Your mother has a big mouth," was all that Granny said in answer. "The Isle of Man is a British protectorate in the middle of the Irish Sea," she continued, ignoring Carly's statement.

Seeing Carly's uncertainty she pulled a book of maps from the drawer near her bed. "See, if you look at the map of England and Ireland, the Irish Sea is here. It runs between them," Granny pointed on the map. "And there, in the middle of the Irish Sea, is the Isle of Man."

"I'm sure it's lovely," Carly murmured, wanting the conversation to be over.

"Anyway," Granny continued. "America was the New World, full of new opportunities, a new way of life and seemingly unlimited prosperity. William Cubbon's brother had made the trip five years earlier and he sent back letters full of glowing reports of jobs readily available and generous pay. He also sent money, enough money for William and his wife and two daughters to make the journey."

Carly shifted in her seat and then grabbed a cookie from the box she'd just brought for Granny. She might as well have a snack while she listened.

"William Cubbon's two girls were Katherine and Elizabeth. Katherine was nearly six and little Elizabeth, often called Bessie, was only around two. The journey was long and difficult and the two girls were apparently sick for most of the trip, but finally they made it to New York. William's brother, Fergus, had settled in Cleveland, Ohio, where a lot of Manx men and women ended up, and that's where William took his family." Granny paused for a sip of water and Carly tried again.

"Really, Granny, I can't possibly go to the Isle of Man this summer. I have too much to do."

"Just hear the story, that is all I'm asking you to do." Granny shook her head and muttered something that sounded like "blabbermouth" to Carly, which made her grin as she sat back to hear the rest of the story.

"Right, so William moved to Cleveland with his wife and two daughters. From what I understand, they did their best to settle in and make a new life for themselves and the girls. But, for whatever reason, it didn't suit them. William and his wife, Anne, tried it for something like fifteen years, but they finally decided to go back to the Isle of Man. It was a big decision, and an expensive one. Today you could just fly back and forth, but in those days it was a long and dangerous journey by sea. William knew when they went back that he wouldn't ever see his brother again, for one thing."

"It's almost impossible to imagine how much bigger the world must have felt," Carly remarked.

"Things have certainly changed," Granny agreed. "Anyway, William and Anne were determined to go and they started to make plans. The problem now was the girls. Katherine and Elizabeth both had suitors. Katherine was nineteen or twenty and she was in love with a young man from another transplanted Manx family. It was finally agreed that they would marry at once and then she would stay in America with her new husband."

Carly frowned. "But if she did that, she probably wouldn't see her parents ever again," she thought out loud.

"And she never did," Granny told her. "Katherine got married a month later and she and her husband, Peter Corlett, went on to have ten children. I was the youngest."

Carly smiled. "I can't believe you've never told me this story before."

"You always liked hearing about your mother when she was little. Anyway, it is an old story and not one that I think about very much. My mother didn't talk about her family often. I think she must have missed them so much that she didn't like to speak about them."

"How very sad." Carly felt sorry for her great-grandmother, separated from the family that she loved.

"Sad and romantic," her grandmother corrected her. "She gave up her mother, father, and sister to be with the man she loved."

Carly shook her head. "I can't imagine being that much in love with anyone," she told Granny Madison.

"That's because you haven't met the right man yet," Granny answered.

"Maybe." Carly didn't really want to start talking about her love life. She knew that Granny didn't like Tom and thought that her favorite granddaughter could do better.

"Anyway, with Katherine safely married off, William and Anne started getting ready to take Elizabeth back to the island with them. A few days before they were ready to go, however, Elizabeth announced that she wasn't going to go with them. She too had fallen in love and she wanted to stay in America to be with this man about whom they had known nothing."

Carly grinned. While she hadn't wanted to hear the story in the first place, it was certainly getting interesting now.

Granny continued. "His name was Matthew Saunders, and he was about ten years older than Elizabeth. He was from outside the Manx community. I don't think William and Anne would have minded his age or the fact that he wasn't Manx. The problem was that Elizabeth was only sixteen or seventeen and they felt that she was far too young to know her own mind."

"I don't know about that," Carly answered. "I've been with Tom since grade school and we're still happy together."

"And one day you'll realize how much better you can do than Tom," Granny told her, patting Carly's arm. "Just you wait and see."

Carly bit her tongue. There was no point in arguing with Granny about Tom. She'd tried often enough already.

"Right," Granny picked up the story again. "So Elizabeth dug in her heels and refused to go and her parents refused to listen. According to my mother, when the leaving day came, they practically had to carry her onto the boat where she immediately took to her bed and refused to speak or eat for the entire journey."

Carly shook her head. "How dramatic! What happened next? Did she fall in love with her next-door neighbor back on the island or rush back to America when she turned eighteen?"

"I told you this wasn't a happy story," Granny reminded her.

"Apparently Elizabeth was planning to do just that, return to America as soon as she was old enough to travel on her own, but then she got a letter. Matthew Saunders had decided to follow her to the island and bring her back to America himself. Elizabeth was thrilled and excited and, supposedly, even forgave her parents for forcing her to return to the island."

"Hurray for true love," Carly grinned and then sobered when she saw the look on Granny's face. "Okay, so what happened next?"

Granny shook her head. "No one is sure exactly what happened on Matthew's boat, but once any illness got onto a boat like that, pretty much everyone on board was at risk of getting infected. Apparently many of the passengers on the boat got sick and several died. Matthew himself passed away just before the boat docked in Liverpool."

Carly blinked back sudden tears as she felt a flood of sympathy for Matthew and Elizabeth. Sometimes life really wasn't fair. Granny wiped her own eyes and squeezed Carly's hand.

"Apparently, Elizabeth was inconsolable for months. She wrote long rambling letters to my mother, full of grief. My mother wanted her to come back to America to start again, but Elizabeth felt that she couldn't stand to be back where she had been so happy with Matthew. Matthew had written his will before he left America and he left all of his possessions to Elizabeth. It wasn't much, but it was enough money for Elizabeth to buy a small cottage where she could be away from her parents. She blamed them for the tragedy, you see."

"Please tell me there is a happy ending in this story somewhere?" Carly pleaded.

"Sorry, darling, but life doesn't always bring happy endings. Elizabeth lived out the rest of her life in that little cottage in Laxey on the Isle of Man. She never forgave her parents for Matthew's death and she never found love again. The women in my family are long-lived and she was somewhere near a hundred years old when she died last year. She left all of her possessions, including her cottage, to me. I kept in touch with her after my mother died, you see." Granny stopped there, seeming to consider carefully what she would say next.

"I have no idea what the cottage is like, whether it's habitable or whether she lived in total squalor. I've never met the woman. We started exchanging Christmas cards when my mother died twenty years ago, but she never put more than a seasonal greeting in hers. The lawyer on the island who's handling the estate thinks I should sell the cottage and all of its contents and be done with it. Apparently house prices are high over there and he thinks we can get a lot of money for the cottage and the land it sits on."

Carly thought carefully before she spoke. "He should know what's best, shouldn't he?" she said eventually.

Granny sighed deeply. "He said he would go through the house and send me any papers or anything of value and then sell all of the furniture and the house. All I have to do is sit back and wait for the big fat check."

Granny shook her head. "It just doesn't seem right," she told Carly, sounding tearful. "I know I never met her, but it doesn't seem right that some stranger should be going through her things and selling them off. I suppose I'm a stranger too, but at least I know her story and my mother loved her. She never had anyone else to love her, no husband, no children. Oh, maybe I'm just a sentimental old fool. If it wasn't for that fall, I would be heading there myself!" Granny wiped her eyes again, clearly unable to stop the tears that were flowing for a woman she'd never known.

Carly was crying now too, and feeling ridiculous. How could she feel so sorry for a woman who, before today, she hadn't even known existed? She shook her head and pulled herself together. It was a sad story and Granny was right, someone who was family should be going through the cottage, not some lawyer.

"I suppose I had better tell this Mr. Quayle to go ahead," Granny sighed, after she had regained her composure. "The faster this gets wrapped up, the sooner I can get him off my back about the whole matter."

Granny tilted her head and looked questioningly at Carly. "If you did want to do it, apparently Elizabeth set aside a special lump sum of money to pay for someone from the U.S. to come and go through everything. According to Mr. Quayle, if we don't use the money for the trip, he gets to keep it all for himself as part of his fees, since he'll have to do the clearing out of the house himself."

Carly snorted. "That doesn't seem right. I'll bet he's getting paid loads to sort out the estate. He shouldn't be allowed any extra."

"The money isn't really the issue," Granny told Carly. "I would just feel a whole lot better if it was you going through Bessie's things and handling the sale of the cottage, rather than some lawyer I don't know."

Carly sat back in her chair and sighed. Granny had talked her right into a corner and they both knew it. Granny had piqued her curiosity about Elizabeth Cubbon and Carly was dying to have a look around the cottage where she'd lived her entire adult life. Carly shook her head. There was no way she was going to give up this chance to see it and Granny had known that before she'd even started telling her the story.

"I suppose I can paint before or after the trip." Carly said slowly. "The trip won't take that long, will it?"

Granny smiled. "I think you should plan to go for a month. Legal stuff always takes longer than it should."

A month sounded like a long time, but if she promised Granny to spend all of August on the Isle of Man, she just might have her painting finished before she left. She would have most of June and all of July and that seemed like plenty of time for painting and decorating her small house. She'd been looking forward to painting slowly and carefully, but if she did it quickly there was no doubt she could manage it.

"I suppose I could go in August," she told Granny.

Granny looked disappointed. "I was hoping you could go as soon as school finished," Granny told her. "The lawyer is getting a bit pushy and making me feel pressured into making quick decisions."

Carly felt a flash of anger towards the lawyer involved. How dare he put any pressure on her granny? "All right, if we can sort out flights and things, I guess I can go as soon as the summer vacation starts," she agreed, suddenly eager to get across the ocean and sort out the aggressive attorney.

"Thank you so much, darling." Granny took her hand and squeezed it tightly. "I just know that we are doing the right thing for Elizabeth," she told Carly, one last tear trickling down her wrinkled cheek.

"I'm happy to help," Carly assured her, mentally rearranging her painting schedule as she hugged Granny goodbye. A month away would still give her around six weeks when she got back. That would be plenty of time. Anyway, she had never been to a different country before. This trip would be a great adventure for her.

2

Less than three weeks later, the adventure was about to begin as Carly headed for Pittsburgh and her first flight, bound for Newark. From Newark she would fly to London and then from there to Ronaldsway, the airport on the Isle of Man. After she'd agreed to make the journey, she'd spent some time on the Internet finding out all she could about the Isle of Man. She was surprised how interesting she found the place that her ancestors had called home a hundred years earlier.

The island wasn't part of the United Kingdom. It was an independent country, though it was dependent on the English Crown for protection and in some other official matters. It had its own laws, its own money, and its own stamps. She used a map of the island to locate Laxey on its eastern coast and Ronaldsway, where the airport was located, to the south.

Granny let her read some of the letters that Elizabeth had sent to her sister in America and Carly had found herself poring over them intently, trying to imagine what Elizabeth had been like. Elizabeth's earliest letters were full of her grief at Matthew's death and ran to several pages. Later ones were shorter and talked mostly about the weather and other bits of small town gossip about people that

Katherine most likely would never have met. Carly smiled as she read about Jane Christian's unexpected pregnancy while her husband had been away from the island for more than a year in the nineteen-forties. She laughed at the antics of neighborhood children who used to visit "Aunt Bessie," sure that they would be provided with cakes or cookies.

She felt sad when she read about the war years, which were difficult for everyone. From the letters she began to build up an impression of Elizabeth Cubbon that was somewhat different from the one her grandmother had painted. The Elizabeth Cubbon that sent regular letters to her sister in America seemed to have lived a rather full and interesting life, in spite of rarely leaving Laxey and, apparently, never leaving the Isle of Man after her return from the United States. The more she read, the more intrigued Carly became about her distant relative. By the time Tom picked her up to take her to the airport, she could barely wait to get started on finding out more.

"Try not to miss me too much," she teased her boyfriend of nearly twenty years as he drove down the highway.

"Aw, you know I'll miss you a little," Tom replied easily.

Carly fell silent. After all their years together, Carly thought it was about time for them to make a real commitment. While she'd finished college and immediately taken a job in her field, Tom had dropped out of Allegheny after only a year. He was still struggling to figure out exactly what he wanted to do with the rest of his life and still living in the apartment that he'd rented when he was a college freshman.

Carly had been patient over the last several years, waiting for him to be ready to settle down, but enough was enough. She had always pictured her perfect wedding in the small chapel near the house she had grown up in. She wanted to get married on Christmas Eve and let the celebrations spill over into Christmas and the New Year. One of her childhood friends worked at the chapel, and Carly had called her recently and asked her to make a note that she might need to use the space this coming Christmas.

"You think Tom's finally going to ask?" her friend had questioned.

"I think he'd better get around to it quickly," Carly laughed. "We're not getting any younger."

Her friend had laughed then. "You're what, twenty-five? I bet Tom isn't even thinking about marriage yet."

"He will be once I've talked to him." Carly had been quietly confident.

Now, in the car on the way to Pittsburgh, she decided it was as good a time as any to have a serious talk.

"I hope you're going to miss me more than a little," she began.

Tom cleared his throat and then sighed. "We've been together a really long time," he said.

"I know," Carly answered. "And maybe now would be a good time to think about where our relationship is headed."

"Yeah," Tom agreed. "Actually, I've sort of been thinking about that."

"Great." Carly felt relieved. She didn't want to have to actually tell him to propose, after all.

"The thing is," Tom continued. "Well, I've been thinking we need to try seeing other people."

Carly was speechless for a long time. When she spoke, she did so very carefully. "I'm sorry, did you say you want to start seeing other people?" she asked.

"Yeah, well, the thing is," Tom spoke quickly. "You're going away for a month. We've never been away from each other for that long. It just seemed like the perfect time for us both to try seeing other people, just to see what it's like."

Carly didn't answer. She just looked out her window for a long time, trying to stop her tears from falling. Half an hour later they arrived at the airport. Tom walked her to the check-in desk, carrying her suitcase for her. Wordlessly, he followed her to the security checkpoint and then took her arm.

"I'm sorry if I've upset you," he told her. "But I just thought that before we get married we should both try dating other people. It just seems weird to start thinking about marriage when you're the only woman I've ever kissed."

Carly shook her head, nodded and then shrugged. "If that's what you want," she said finally, unable to meet Tom's eyes. "By all means, date other women. Have fun while I'm gone. We can talk when I get back."

Tom held her arm for another minute and then dipped his head to try to catch her eyes. "Are you okay?" he asked.

"Sure," she lied, glancing into his green eyes and then looking away. Tom kissed the top of her head and then Carly pulled away and headed through security without a backwards glance.

Carly cried hard from Pittsburgh to Newark. She sobbed quietly all the way across the Atlantic. By the time she arrived in London after her overnight flight she was out of tears and exhausted. The last flight was a private charter and Carly was relieved when she finally sank into the seat on that final plane. She nodded off intermittently during the short journey. She was still feeling miserable about Tom, but she was also excited about the month ahead.

Her plane was finally cleared to land and then pulled up to one of the gates set aside for private charters.

"Watch your step," the pilot grinned at her as he helped her down onto the runway. "We can't have pretty women getting hurt on my planes."

Carly smiled vaguely at the man without really registering his words. She stopped at the bottom of the stairs and took a deep breath. The air smelled salty and different somehow from Meadville air. She shook her head at the silliness of the idea.

Finlo Quayle, the owner and pilot of the small private chartered plane that had brought her to the island, grinned at her. "Welcome to the Isle of Man. It's a little bit more beautiful than normal today, with you here," he told her, flirting.

Carly blushed, ignoring the words as she headed for the building. She made her way inside the terminal as quickly as she could, made nervous by the behavior of the gorgeous and sophisticated pilot.

A quick stop in the restroom revealed that she looked very tired, and as if she had been crying, something her transatlantic journey could only partially account for. Her long brown hair fell straight halfway down her back. Her eyes were red and puffy and her face looked pinched and drawn, her comfortable clothes hiding her slender figure.

She waited patiently at the baggage carousel, collecting her one small bag and then heading through the double doors into the main terminal building.

"Carly Munroe?" The question made her stop in her tracks.

Carly turned her head and looked at the man who had spoken to her. Whatever she had been expecting it, wasn't this. Granny Madison had complained so much about Mr. Quayle, the lawyer who was handling Elizabeth's estate, that Carly had built up a mental picture of an elderly ogre who was trying to cheat her beloved Granny.

The man standing in front of her was the definition of tall, dark, and handsome. He had to be well over six feet tall, with brown hair that fell in an obviously expensive and well-maintained cut. His eyes were brown as well, with a liquid warmth in them that made Carly blink when she met them. Carly looked down at his expensive and perfectly tailored suit and his shiny black shoes and decided that she was going to hate him.

"Mr. Quayle?" She thought that the dreaded lawyer might send an assistant or a secretary to meet her, but this man was far too polished to be anyone other than the lawyer himself.

"That's right, I'm Doncan Quayle," he smiled at her. "Welcome to the Isle of Man. Let me take your bag." He reached out and took the bag from Carly who either had to let go graciously or get into a tug-of-war in the middle of the airport. She hesitated for a moment and then released the bag.

"Thank you." Carly reluctantly smiled at Doncan. The smile lit Carly's face and made her eyes sparkle. The attractive woman suddenly became dazzling, even if she was completely unaware of it. Doncan shook his head slightly to clear it and then led Carly through the airport to his waiting car.

"I've booked you into a hotel in Douglas," he told her once they were both seated, with Carly's bag stowed in the trunk. "I thought you'd rather be centrally located and near the best shops and restaurants. If you would rather stay somewhere else, of course, that can be arranged."

"Can I not stay in Elizabeth's cottage, then?" Carly asked.

"Legally you can, of course, if you want to. The cottage is your grandmother's property and if she is happy for you to stay there then I can't stop you. But I suggest you leave that decision until you have seen the cottage. It isn't exactly up to modern standards and I thought you would be happier in a hotel."

"What does 'not exactly up to modern standards' mean?"

"Elizabeth lived there for all of her adult life. She made a lot of changes and modernized the cottage a great deal, but in the last twenty years or so she didn't bother as much. The cottage has running water, electricity and a gas supply, but it really needs a complete over-haul. The kitchen and bathrooms were installed in the fifties and haven't been updated, for instance. There isn't any central heating, so there's a problem with damp, and, as it's been empty for nearly a year, I would guess there are more than a few spiders and other creepy crawlies that have moved in, as well."

Carly shuddered and then shook her head. "I was hoping to stay in the cottage while I was here. I thought I could get it cleaned up and maybe paint it and then it would be easier to sell."

"You won't have any problem selling it," Doncan assured her. "Once you get it emptied, it will sell fast. The location is excellent, right on the water, and the plot of land is a fairly large one. You'll be able to get a great price for it, just the way it is."

"When can I see it?" Carly wondered.

"I would prefer to take you there myself, if that is okay?" Doncan told her. "Unfortunately, that means waiting until tomorrow. I've already spent more time than I had intended waiting for your flight to arrive and I have meetings all afternoon. I thought I would drop you off at your hotel and you could have a quiet afternoon and evening and then I could show you the cottage tomorrow morning?"

"I'm sorry that my plane was delayed," Carly began. "I was surprised to be picked up by a private charter, though. I hope that my visit isn't going to cost Granny a small fortune."

Doncan smiled. "I appreciate your eagerness to protect your grand-mother's interests. As it happens, we get a great price from Finlo. Not only is he a cousin on my father's side, but we put a lot of business his way," he assured Carly.

Carly shrugged, not yet convinced.

"I'm pretty sure your private charter cost less than a ticket on a commercial flight would have, but I'll have my secretary check and if there is a price difference, I will reimburse the estate out of my share," Doncan told her. "You really don't need to worry about expenses anyway. Elizabeth set aside some money especially for travel expenses for whoever came from the U.S. to deal with the estate. I'll warn you if that starts to run low, but it's a quite generous amount."

Carly nodded, pleased with herself for standing up to the man. She thought briefly about insisting on having a key to the cottage and the telephone number of a taxi company so that she could head straight there, but decided she was too tired to argue. "Great," she muttered, knowing she sounded annoyed, but not caring.

Doncan glanced at her, seemingly trying to gauge how annoyed she actually was, before he said anything else. After an awkward moment, he simply started the car and drove out of the airport parking lot, heading north. The silence in the car seemed to simmer between them, making Carly feel uncomfortable. The awkwardness was broken when Doncan spoke again.

"As we go over the white bridge, you must wave to the Little People," he told Carly.

Carly looked out the window and spotted the small white bridge, clearly labelled "Fairy Bridge". She watched, amazed, as Doncan lifted a hand from the wheel and waved. She confusedly waved at a tree on the roadside that appeared to be covered in tiny pieces of ribbon.

"What was all over that tree?" she asked, too curious now to stay silent.

"Notes and messages for the Little People," Doncan told her in a serious voice.

"What are you talking about?" Carly knew she was tired, but Doncan really wasn't making sense.

"The Little People live around the Fairy Bridge. When you pass over the bridge you have to wave or say hello, otherwise you might anger them. People leave notes and requests for the Little People on the tree there. Sometimes they even leave little gifts," Doncan explained.

"Right," Carly shook her head. "People here actually believe this sort of thing?" She turned to look out her window now, as if uninterested in Doncan's reply.

Doncan chuckled at her skepticism. "I went on a class trip to Castle Rushen when I was ten," he told Carly, smiling as she turned to look at him curiously. "Bob Henderson's family had just moved to the island from across and he didn't believe in the Little People. Everyone else on the bus waved, but Bob just laughed at us. A week later, just as the Christmas holidays were starting, Bob caught measles, even though he'd been immunized. He spent the whole of the Christmas break sick and just got better the same day we had to go back to school. He never laughed at the Little People again."

Carly stared at him. "You've just made that up," she accused Doncan.

"I can introduce you to Bob if you want me to," he told her, and then he sighed. "Look, I don't really believe in Little People or fairies or whatever, but it seems to me to be better safe than sorry about such things. It only takes a second to wave, after all!"

He shot Carly a devilish grin that made her whole body tingle. In spite of everything that had happened to her that day, she found herself grinning back. Maybe spending time with Doncan Quayle wasn't going to be so bad after all.

Douglas was a surprise to Carly. She knew that European hotels were very different from the standard American hotel chains that had provided her family with accommodation on their trips during her childhood, but the promenade in Douglas was amazing. It stretched for miles along the seafront in the island's capital city, with a wide walkway along the beach and the sea and then a wide road that provided both passage and parking for the hotels and guesthouses that were spread along the front.

The hotels appeared to be an almost continuous block of Victorian row houses, broken up by only an occasional narrow road that led behind the block. Each individual property, though joined on both sides to another property, was painted a different color, providing visitors with a stunningly colorful view. Brightly colored signs over the front doors advertised the names of the hotels and sandwich boards on the sidewalks out front advised guests as to the delights that could be found inside.

The Horizon Hotel offered "all en-suite rooms" and "colour televisions", while the Beachfront Hotel advised that you could get "hot food all day" and that there were "tea and coffee making facilities in every room."

Carly stared and gaped and felt like a stupid tourist as she tried to read every sign and guess what some of them meant. As she goggled at the hotels, Doncan suddenly called her attention to the other side of the car.

"The horse trams are running," he told her, gesturing towards the center of the road.

Carly was amazed to see a large horse pulling a bright red tramcar down a track that ran down the middle of the street. "Isn't that cruel to the horses?" she demanded as she watched the tram go by.

"Every year someone says it is and then someone else says it isn't," Doncan told her. "Apparently the cars take a bit of pulling to get started, but once they're rolling the horse hardly has to work at all. The animals are well looked after, and when they retire they go to live at the Home of Rest for Old Horses. We passed it on the way here, actually. The animals have big fields and the whole place is open to the public, who go and feed carrots to the horses and generally spoil them. The horses only work four months a year or so and they don't seem to mind. I think, if you were a horse, it wouldn't be such a bad life."

Carly found that her brain couldn't manage all of the information that she was trying to process and now it began to protest. She hadn't slept well in the weeks that followed her agreeing to make the trip to the island, having been both excited and worried about the trip. Saying goodbye to everyone had been difficult as well. The unexpected breakup with Tom had capped things off and now she'd been traveling for more than twenty-four hours and had missed a night's sleep. Her head was beginning to pound and all she really wanted to do was close her eyes.

Doncan found a parking space in front of the hotel where he'd arranged for her to stay. "Here we are." He grabbed her bag from the trunk and then helped Carly from the car. "Steady now. I think you need a long nap before you worry about anything else."

Carly wanted to argue with him, but she simply didn't have the energy. They made their way up a short flight of steps and into a large and elegant lobby. Carly knew that she would be impressed by the glamorous surroundings once she'd had some sleep. Doncan quickly handled the paperwork and took the keycard from the receptionist. He led Carly to a large elevator that whisked them up to the top floor. I must remember to call them "lifts" here, Carly thought to herself as they climbed.

Seeing her room dragged Carly out of her stupor for a moment. It was huge and expensively furnished, with a large bed along one wall and a small sitting area on the other side. There was even a small table with two chairs where Carly could eat or write letters home. The best part of the room, though, was the two enormous picture windows that showcased the sea below. Carly stood for a minute, watching the waves crash onto the shore. The view was spectacular and she felt like she could watch it forever.

"Carly, I'll just leave your bag here, if that is okay." Doncan's voice dragged her away from the window.

"Sorry, the view is just amazing, isn't it?" Carly shook her head to wake herself up and clear her thoughts.

"It's nearly the same view I have from my apartment, and I never get tired of looking at it." Doncan agreed. "Do you need anything else before I go?"

"I think I'm okay." Carly looked around the room, thinking fleetingly of food.

"The room service menu is on the desk." Doncan seemed to read her mind. "Make sure you eat something when you wake up. You need to try to get your body clock straightened out. It's noon now, so if you sleep until dinner time you should feel better."

Carly nodded at him. Doncan reached into his pocket and pulled out his business card. "My office number is on here. I'll add my mobile number as well so you can reach me any time if you need anything."

He scribbled a number on the card and handed it to Carly. "I'll collect you tomorrow morning about ten o'clock so we can go and have a look at the cottage, okay?"

Carly forced herself to shake off some of her tiredness. "Yes, ten o'clock is fine. Thank you for everything, I really appreciate it." She smiled at Doncan and hesitantly offered her hand.

He smiled back and took it, looking amused at the formal gesture. When their hands met, Carly felt a shock rush through her. She pulled her hand back quickly and found she was shaking her head again. She breathed in deeply and forced another smile onto her lips.

"Thanks, again," she muttered as she opened the door for Doncan.

He smiled at her as he walked towards the door. "I'll see you in the morning," he spoke softly, looking intently into Carly's eyes. "Sleep well."

Carly shut the door firmly behind him and tried to put him just as firmly out of her mind. She pulled the curtains on the enormous windows shut, taking only one more tiny peek at the spectacular view. She unpacked quickly and then washed her face and brushed her teeth. Then she changed into the T-shirt and shorts that she regularly slept in. She climbed into the large and incredibly comfortable bed, expecting another round of tears for Tom, but instead she fell asleep almost immediately. Her last waking thought was of intense brown eyes that seemed to excite her body all the way down to her toes.

The phone was ringing and Carly reached for it, but it wasn't where it was supposed to be. Confused, she sat up in bed, her hand fumbling around after a bedside lamp that wasn't there either. It took Carly a full minute to remember where she was and, while her brain struggled, the phone rang on endlessly. Carly finally found a light switch and then tracked down the phone that was on the bedside table on the opposite side of the bed.

"Hello?" she said tentatively.

Her voice sounded husky from sleep and she swallowed hard.

"Did I wake you?" Doncan's voice sent a rush of something through her.

"Yes." Carly was still too disoriented to tell the standard lie.

Doncan chuckled at the blunt honesty. "I'm sorry. I thought you might have woken up by now and be getting bored."

"What time is it?" Carly demanded, polite conversation seeming to have deserted her.

"Half seven." Doncan answered.

"Is that seven-thirty? And is it night or morning?" With the heavy curtains drawn, the hotel room was pitch-black.

Doncan laughed now. "Yes, half seven is the same as seven-thirty, and it's seven-thirty at night. I was just calling to check on you. I didn't mean to disturb you."

Carly struggled to snap out of her daze. "Sorry, I'm not really awake yet," she confessed the obvious. "The time change and everything has me all messed up."

"If you've been sleeping since I left you then you probably should get up for a while now," Doncan advised. "Have something to eat, if you haven't eaten, and then go to bed at eleven or twelve, whatever your normal bedtime is. Hopefully, you'll sleep well and wake up in the morning feeling like it should be morning."

Carly knew he was right. "I can't believe that I slept that long," she told him. "And now that I'm waking up, I am starving. I'll get something to eat and then follow your advice."

"Would you like me to come over and take you out for dinner?"

"Thanks," she replied, feeling surprised. "But I think room service is about all I'm capable of tonight." Her mind was racing. Had he just asked her out on a date or was he just being kind?

"I'll see you in the morning, then." Doncan told her. "Sleep well."

The connection was broken, and Carly sat for a moment staring at the phone. When it didn't provide any answers, she hung it up and grabbed the room service menu. A sandwich and a cold drink made her feel human again and a bit of television and a magazine made her feel tired once more. By ten she was ready for bed for the night. Flashy lawyers might go to bed at midnight, but elementary school teachers go to bed by ten, she thought to herself as she brushed her teeth again.

Back in the soft bed, Carly found herself tossing and turning in spite of her exhaustion. Her mind kept replaying the phone call and Doncan's casual invitation. The sexy tone in his voice when he said "sleep well" replayed again and again, as did the jolt that had raced through her when their hands had touched. Carly pulled a pillow over her head and burrowed under the covers.

She didn't want to think about Tom, either, although when she did she was surprised that the thoughts were already less painful than she expected. She pushed the covers back and fluffed her pillows for the tenth time. Just sleep, she ordered herself angrily. After what felt like hours, she finally drifted off, only to dream endlessly about handsome men with brown eyes holding her hand as she waved to dancing fairies.

3

Carly still felt tired and a little bit grumpy in the morning when the alarm clock on the bedside table beeped at seven. She was startled awake and glared at the unfamiliar clock. She'd set it the previous night just before she'd climbed back into bed and now she couldn't remember where the off button was located. By the time she'd figured out how to shut the stupid thing off, she felt fairly wide-awake.

The room had come with a small kettle that boiled water, as well as a selection of teas and instant coffees. Carly didn't drink either and had been delighted when she'd spotted the instant hot chocolate as well. Now she followed the instruction card next to the kettle, filling it with fresh water, plugging it in and turning it on. While she sorted out her clothes and selected an outfit for the day, the small kettle began to make a burbling noise. By the time Carly was ready for a shower, the kettle had boiled, and Carly mixed up a cup of hot chocolate to take into the bathroom with her.

I should do this at home, Carly thought to herself as she stepped out of the shower and wrapped a giant fluffy towel around herself. She took a sip of the now perfectly cooled chocolate and then padded back into the bedroom to get dressed. Her small suitcase had only held a handful of outfits, but during the summer she usually lived in jeans or shorts and simple T-shirts. She threw on her favorite jeans and a plain blue T-shirt for the day. If the cottage was dusty and full of bugs she would need something that she could wash easily.

She quickly brushed on a bit of makeup, wearing only her usual basic selection. After brushing and drying her hair, she pulled it back into a low ponytail. She wasn't going to wear it loose if there were spiders around. For a moment she studied her reflection in the mirror, frowning at what she saw as average good looks. Doncan must have just been being nice last night, she decided, not suggesting a date. She wasn't nearly pretty enough to attract a gorgeous and worldly guy like him. Heck, apparently she couldn't even hold on to Tom.

Carly had had many friends of both genders in high school, but she had never dated anyone other than Tom. They had agreed to "go steady" when she'd turned twelve and she had never regretted that decision. Occasionally guys had asked her out over the years, ones that didn't know about Tom, but Carly had never been tempted to stray. Of course, Carly had never met a man like Doncan Quayle before.

She was sure that he must have a string of beautiful women at his beck and call. He might even be married, Carly thought suddenly. He didn't wear a ring. Even in her exhausted and emotionally distressed state, she'd managed to look, but that didn't mean that he didn't have a wife or maybe a live-in girlfriend somewhere in the background.

Carly stared out the window at the waves lapping gently on the beach. She was on the island to sort out Granny's inheritance, and she wasn't about to allow an attractive lawyer to distract her. Dressed and ready to go more than an hour before Doncan was due to arrive, Carly grabbed her bag and her room key and headed out of the hotel. The sun was shining and the day was warming already and Carly intended to enjoy her vacation. She walked the length of the promenade from her hotel to the far end where a sign advertised the electric trains.

As she walked back she was amazed to see how far away the water had gone from where it had been when she started her walk. The tide was clearly going out and it seemed to have gone out a long distance in a fairly short space of time. The only real experience she'd had with bodies of water was summer vacations on Lake Erie, where the tide was barely noticeable.

She watched seagulls lazily circling and scavenging on the sand. Now families were emerging from the various hotels and making their way down to the beach with all the necessary equipment for perfect sand castles. She smiled as she watched children racing one another over the sand, mothers calling them back and fathers egging them on.

She walked past the tall war memorial that reminded her of the experiences that Elizabeth had lived through. Out in the middle of the water there seemed to be a very small castle that she wondered about. She would have to ask Doncan what it was.

A large boat glided through the water, sailing away from Douglas to somewhere else, blasting a loud signal as it left. Carly breathed in deeply, tasting the salty sea air. Granny's mother had been born here, she reminded herself, and had lived here until she was six. She watched the children playing on the beach again, her eyes searching for a little girl of about the right age. I wonder if Granny's mother and her sister ever played on Douglas Beach, she thought to herself.

When she got back to the hotel, she quickly ran a brush through her windblown and tangled hair and brushed a fresh layer of lip-gloss on her lips. Ready to go again, she waited in the sumptuous lobby for Doncan's arrival. Even though she knew what to expect, her stomach still skittered when the handsome man walked through the front door. He didn't see her for a moment and Carly studied his self-confident posture as he strolled into the hotel.

His suit today was a very dark navy with a subtle pinstripe. His tie was dark navy as well and looked perfect against a crisp white shirt. A different pair of expensive black shoes finished off the polished outfit. Carly watched him as he walked across the lobby towards the bank of elevators. For a brief moment some emotion flashed across his face as he waited for the car to arrive. Carly wondered what it was as she stood up from her seat in the corner of the room and called his name.

"Mr. Quayle." Her voice was too soft, almost a whisper, and Doncan spun around in surprise.

Carly jumped at his dramatic reaction. "Sorry, I didn't mean to startle you," she rushed out. "I just thought it would help if I waited down here for you." And I didn't feel comfortable with having you in the same room as my unmade bed, she added to herself.

"Good morning." Doncan spoke smoothly, sounding far more self-assured than she felt.

He took her arm and turned to lead her out of the hotel. All of her senses were humming as she immersed herself in his masculine presence. He smelled fantastic today, spicy and sexy with just a hint of soap, and Carly breathed in deeply to drag in as much of the scent as possible. As she moved beside him she could feel well-honed muscles under his expensive tailored suit. He walked slowly, matching his pace to hers in such a way that she didn't feel rushed. Carly drank in the experience, certain that he was just being friendly, but feeling as if it were much more.

Doncan helped Carly into his car and then quickly climbed in the driver's side. "All set to see your Granny's inheritance?" he asked with a smile.

"As ready as I'll ever be," was Carly's somewhat uncertain answer.

As Doncan started the car, he glanced over curiously at Carly. "That sounded a bit unsure," he said finally.

"Sorry." Carly forced a smile onto her face and then frowned. "The thing is, up until a few weeks ago I didn't even know that Elizabeth Cubbon existed, and now I'm here, halfway around the world, expected to sort through her things and sell her house. I'm feeling like I'm just not up to the job." Carly twisted her hands together in frustration.

Doncan reached over with one hand and took her hands in his. He gave them a gentle squeeze. "You're family, even if you didn't know about her before. You should be the one going through her things. If you want me to help, though, I'm happy to do so. I knew Aunt Bessie quite well and I would like to think that she would have been happy for me to help."

"I didn't realize you knew her!" Carly exclaimed, pulling her hands back in order to reengage her brain. "How did you meet her, how long did you know her and what was she like?"

Doncan laughed at the barrage of questions. "Slow down," he told Carly. "I knew her my entire life. My father was her advocate, that's the

Manx word for an attorney, as was his father before him. We didn't live far away from her in Laxey when I was a child. Aunt Bessie loved children and once we got to school age we always knew we could stop at her cottage and get a biscuit and a drink on our way home from school. She was a very intelligent woman and one who thrived on being independent. Everyone knew the story of her tragedy, of course, but I often thought, when I got older, that marriage wouldn't have agreed with Bessie. By the time I knew her she was already past middle age and very set in her ways. Perhaps things would have been different if she'd married in her teens."

Carly nodded slowly. "That makes sense. Granny told me the whole sad story, but the letters that Elizabeth sent to her sister don't sound like letters from someone who spent her whole life feeling sorry for herself."

Doncan laughed again. "Bessie never felt sorry for herself," he told Carly emphatically, and then sobered.

"Actually, she probably did in the early days, when she was still young, but I think she quickly got over Matthew Saunders. I believe she took a good look at her options and decided that she would rather be an independent single woman than get married and have children and a husband to answer to. She often talked about her sister living in America, with ten children and no time to call her own. I think she decided that that wasn't the life for her and, with Matthew's money, she was able to support herself and stay by herself."

While they had been talking, Doncan had been driving out of Douglas, and Carly noticed that they were now driving along the coast. She stared out her window at the amazing scenery, giving Doncan half of her attention and the view the rest. Perhaps noticing her preoccupation, Doncan seemed to concentrate on the drive, letting the conversation lapse.

A comfortable silence followed as the pair made their way through the village of Lonan and on into Laxey. Doncan turned right off the main road down a narrow single-lane road that descended steeply towards the coast. Carly found herself clinging to her door and peering out through half-closed eyes.

"What sort of road is this?" she hissed as another car approached and Doncan pulled over as far as he could into a small space on the side of the road.

"It's a single-track road with passing places," Doncan told her easily. "You just have to drive carefully and be ready for oncoming traffic. Remember that a lot of these roads were built a long time ago for horses, not cars. Short of tearing down several houses and starting again, we just have to make do with what we have."

He pulled in again to another "passing place" as a double-decker bus made its way up the steep road. Carly squealed in concern as the bus eased past them, barely missing the side mirror on Doncan's pricey luxury car. She sighed with relief as they reached the bottom of the road and turned. The new road they turned onto was unpaved and bumpy and they bounced along past a few small houses before the road seemed to just stop altogether.

"Here we are," Doncan announced, turning off the ignition. "This is 'Treoghe Bwaane.' It means something like 'Widow's Cottage' in Manx." Doncan gestured to the last house along the road.

Carly looked up and was instantly enchanted. "I thought it would be a tiny cottage. This is huge," she said to Doncan as she climbed eagerly out of the car.

The cottage was much bigger than Carly had been expecting. It was at least as big as her house back home. She could easily see what must have been the original cottage, a small section that was now at the middle of the larger structure. A central door and symmetric windows marked out the earliest part, what appeared to be a small two-story section. Later additions on either side of the earliest part were also two stories high, but they had more irregular windows. Carly looked up and down the building and then at the sea that was lapping up on shore far behind the cottage.

"You must get amazing views from inside," she remarked, turning delighted eyes towards Doncan.

"Want to have a look then?" he teased.

"Yes, please." She felt like she was flirting for some reason, which was silly. They were having a perfectly normal conversation, she told herself sternly. Besides she didn't even know how to flirt.

"Come on, then." Doncan held up an old-fashioned key and led her up the path to the front door. He unlocked the door smoothly and then held up a hand. "Hang on a minute while I shut off the alarm."

Carly was amused by the dichotomy of the old-fashioned key and the modern security alarm. "Do you need alarms like that on the island?" she asked, curious about crime rates in what felt like such a safe place.

"The cottage is fairly isolated and most of the neighbors are only here in the summer months. I persuaded Bessie to put the alarm on a few years ago, just for a little bit of extra protection. Now that the house is sitting empty, it's probably even more important. I'm not too worried about burglars, but I do worry about kids breaking in and using it for parties. Anyone that knew Aunt Bessie would never dream of doing any harm, but it would be easy for someone to cause serious damage without even meaning to do so."

Carly nodded and then, at his gesture, stepped inside and immediately sneezed. The cottage smelled musty and had clearly been sitting empty for some time. Carly stood in the doorway, letting her eyes become accustomed to the interior that felt dark after the dazzling sunshine outside. The door opened straight into the living room and Carly was suddenly homesick for her own tiny bit of independent living, feeling a sudden bond with her distant relative. The living room was small and dusty, but looked as if it had been tidy before it had been left. Comfortable looking furniture was dotted around and a small desk sat against one wall.

"No television?" Carly asked curiously.

"Bessie didn't care for television." Doncan told her. "She watched it occasionally when she visited other people, but she didn't see the point in having her own. She had a radio, tuned to the local station, that she used to listen to during the day. It might have some value, as I'm sure it is an antique. It is one of the things that I took out of the house when Bessie died. There are a number of things in storage in my offices in Douglas, because I felt they would be safer out of here and away from the damp."

Carly nodded her head and then walked slowly through the small room. The ceilings were low and she noticed that Doncan had to duck his head in order to move through the doorways. In spite of the additions on either side of the cottage, there was only one door out of the living room, neatly centered on its back wall.

"When Elizabeth had all the additions built and work done on the place she always insisted that the builders leave this room exactly the way it was when the house was first built. She did the same with her bedroom upstairs. It's directly over this room. I think it makes the room feel a bit claustrophobic, but she liked it this way."

Carly moved slowly now through the door and into the kitchen behind. It was a horrible nineteen-fifties style kitchen that badly needed replacing, but the placement and arrangement of the room had been well thought out. Carly imagined that, if she were to live there, she would arrange a modern kitchen in almost the exact same layout.

To the left a door led into a room that Elizabeth had furnished as a dining room. The room was as large as the living room and kitchen together and Carly wondered now, if she were redesigning the house, whether she might turn this room into a huge gourmet kitchen instead and then do something else with the old kitchen. Another door at the back of the dining room led to a large glass-walled sunroom that made the most of the fantastic and uninterrupted view to the sea.

Carly walked back through the kitchen to the door on the other side and walked into another equally large room that was the other new addition. Doncan had followed her from room to room and now he spoke.

"She used this as her bedroom once she began to have trouble with the stairs," he told her. Carly looked around the room. There was a double bed and a large wardrobe along one wall. Another door on the side of the room proved to be a small bathroom with a toilet, sink and shower cubicle. The back wall of the bedroom was almost entirely windows, again highlighting the sea views.

Tucked to one side of the kitchen was a small staircase that led to the second floor. The stairs led to a hallway that ran the length of the extended cottage with several doors opening off of it. Opening the first door revealed a large well-decorated bedroom, again with many windows on the rear wall. "This was Bessie's guest room." Doncan told Carly. "I suspect just about every teenager in Laxey spent at least one night in here, cursing their parents who just didn't understand them and wishing that their mum was more like Bessie."

Carly smiled at him. "Is that the voice of experience?" she teased.

Doncan looked sheepish for a moment. "I spent a few nights here in my teen years," he admitted reluctantly. "Children in Laxey never ran away from home, they just ran to Aunt Bessie's. She always listened to whatever horrible thing had happened and then gave you something to eat and tucked you up to bed in here. By morning everything always seemed so much better. I suppose at some point she must have called our respective parents and told them all about it, but even if she didn't, they would know where to look first if they were worried about missing offspring."

Carly smiled. "She sounds really wonderful," she told Doncan, growing even more intrigued about her relative. She walked through the room, touching various bits of furniture and then staring for a long time out the windows at the sea. When she was a teenager and her parents hadn't understood her, she'd always gone to stay with Granny Madison for a night. Like Bessie must have done, Granny would always listen and understand and make things better.

The next door revealed a garish 1950s-type bathroom that definitely needed to be replaced by anyone wanting to live in the cottage now. The third door led again into the original part of the house. There must have originally been two small bedrooms upstairs, one on top of each of the downstairs rooms, and Elizabeth hadn't altered the layout. Instead, she had used the smaller bedroom at the back of the house as a dressing room, and Carly moved past the wardrobes and chest of drawers, looking in amazement at all of the clothes that were tucked inside.

"I hope the damp hasn't caused any problems with anything," Doncan told her, frowning. "The surveyor said it wasn't too bad yet, just a minor problem with some of the older walls."

Carly walked through the door into the other part of the original cottage and stood still in amazement. The room had clearly been Elizabeth's bedroom, at least until she'd moved downstairs, and it was done in light and dark shades of pink in an incredibly girly fashion. The bed was still covered by a pile of pink blankets, and pillows were scattered across it. What looked to Carly like hundreds of stuffed animals jostled for space with one another. Pictures of cuddly animals were framed along every wall and Carly didn't know whether to laugh or doubt Elizabeth's sanity.

"She did love her cuddly toys." Doncan spoke from behind her, sounding suddenly aware of how bizarre the room might look to someone seeing it for the first time. "I would guess that every child in Laxey must have bought her something that's in this collection. My dad always made sure we brought back a new toy for Aunt Bessie every time we went on holiday and I'm sure lots of other kids would have done the same. She always remembered what every one was called and who had given it to her and why. I suppose it is a bit eccentric...." Doncan trailed off, looking from the bed to a long low shelf that was completely full of stuffed toys.

"Eccentric?" Carly smiled at him. "Maybe she actually hated the silly things but couldn't tell anyone?" she suggested with a wicked grin.

For a moment Doncan looked as if he felt annoyed that she would say something like that about Aunt Bessie, when she didn't even know her, but then he grinned at her. "I don't know whether she liked them or not, but they're all yours now," he told her.

Carly's smile fell away as she looked at the huge pile of toys. What on earth would she do with them all? She decided to ignore the problem for now and headed back through the dressing room to inspect whatever was behind the final door. Another very large room was fitted out as an office and Carly smiled at the professional-looking desk and chair that sat in front of a long row of bookshelves that were completely crammed full of books.

"What did she do in here?" she asked Doncan curiously.

"She wrote stories and articles for the local historical society, studied Manx history, and taught herself a great deal about everything," Doncan answered. "She didn't get a lot of formal education, but she loved learning and reading and she enjoyed picking a subject and finding out as much as she could about it."

Carly grinned, liking her long lost relative more and more. She glanced at a few books on the shelves and found everything from cookbooks to poetry to American history.

"I have her computer equipment back at the office as well," Doncan told Carly, grinning as her jaw dropped. "She used it for word processing and for managing her money. I couldn't persuade her to give the Internet a try."

Carly shook her head. Clearly Elizabeth had been a fascinating person, and she was suddenly disappointed that she'd never had a chance to meet her. She slowly followed Doncan back down the stairs into the living room.

"I had planned to help you sort things out for an hour or two and then head into the office later this afternoon, but unfortunately something has come up this morning that means that I have to be at the office by lunch time," Doncan told Carly. "Would you like to be left here or should I take you back to Douglas?"

"Left here for how long?" Carly wasn't sure she liked the sound of being left, but she was eager to explore the cottage on her own.

"I can come and collect you at half five after I finish for the day, if you want. Or you can walk up the main road and get a taxi at any time. Just ask Suzy in the shop on the road to ring one for you and bill it to my office." Doncan smiled at her. "If you can wait for me until half-five, I'll buy you dinner and we can figure out what you want to do next about selling the house."

Carly was sure this time that he was just being nice and doing his job, so she didn't hesitate to accept the dinner invitation. Undoubtedly, he wanted the estate sorted out and the cottage on the market as soon as possible so the whole matter could be finished and he could have his fee. After he left, Carly walked slowly through the cottage, sternly reminding herself that she couldn't possibly allow herself to fall in love with it.

❧ 4 ❧

arly walked slowly from room to room, stopping to inspect anything that caught her eye. The whole cottage had a musty smell from being empty for so long, but underneath it Carly could smell a hint of roses. She tracked the scent to Elizabeth's bedroom upstairs, where a box of dusting powder sat. When Carly opened the box the smell of roses filled the room.

She sat at the small dressing table and imagined Elizabeth covering herself in the powder. She must have worn it every day because the scent had permeated every room of the cottage. Carly shut her eyes and tried to imagine what Elizabeth's life had been like. After a few moments, she was forced to give up. Elizabeth had died only recently, but she had lived her early life in a world that was completely different from Carly's.

Carly moved on to Elizabeth's office and sat at her desk. There were three drawers on each side and one shallow one in the center. She started to open the bottom left drawer, but her hand froze. She felt like she was intruding. After a moment spent arguing with herself, Carly decided that it was her job more than anyone's. At least she was family. It was better that she clear out the cottage than leave it to strangers.

She closed her eyes and pulled out the drawer, and then she peeked inside carefully. The drawer was full of letters and Carly flipped through them slowly. They were all addressed to Elizabeth and, a quick check of the top one revealed that they had been sent from Granny's mother, Elizabeth's sister, Katherine. Carly had already read the letters that Elizabeth had sent to Katherine, but she felt reluctant to read these. I'll just have to call Granny later and check that she doesn't mind if I read them, Carly decided. She put the letters in a pile to take back to the hotel with her.

The drawer above it was full of bills and receipts and Carly raced through those. They had been carefully sorted into piles for electricity, gas, telephone, and the like and they all appeared to be at least three years old. That must have been when Elizabeth had stopped being able to climb the stairs easily, Carly surmised. More recent papers would either be downstairs or at Doncan's office.

❧ The top drawer on that side held copies of legal documents: the deed to the house, Elizabeth's will, and also copies of her parents' wills. The middle drawer of the desk housed dozens of pens in every possible color, a stapler and staples, paperclips and all the other office debris that clutters up center desk drawers around the world.

The bottom drawer on the right side was full of computer stuff. There were boxes from the software that Elizabeth must have used. Carly recognized both a word processing package and a home budgeting program that she'd heard of before. Neatly labelled disks were stacked in a corner and Carly flipped through them. "Antiquarian Society Lecture, April, 2000", "History Society Magazine Article, June, 2001", "Finances, 1999". Carly put the disks with the letters to take with her as well.

Again, everything was at least three years old. The drawer above was also full of letters and Carly pulled them out and studied them. They were old, with postmarks dating from the nineteen thirties and forties. The postmarks were Cleveland, Ohio, and Carly wondered who they might be from. She finally pulled one out of its envelope and read the flowing script slowly. The letter was dated January, 1941.

Dearest Daughter-in Law,

It was wonderful to receive your card at Christmas and I'm glad to hear that you are keeping well. You were often in our thoughts during the holidays. I hope that you were not too lonely in your little cottage by the sea.

We have been talking, Elizabeth darling, and, after much discussion we have decided to urge you to accept Peter's offer of marriage. We all know that you will never truly get over our Matthew's death, but we hate to think of you living all alone for the rest of your life. From your letter, it seems that Peter is a good man who will take care of you. If you write that you have married, we will not be unhappy.

You could ask your own parents for advice, of course. I have often suggested that you make amends with them.

With all very best wishes for the New Year.

All my love,

Eleanor Saunders"

Carly sat back in surprise. The letter was clearly from Matthew Saunders' mother. Carly supposed it wasn't surprising that they had stayed in touch after Matthew's death, but who on earth was Peter? Carly put the letters in another pile, unsure what to do with them.

It was one thing reading the letters from her own great-grandmother, but these seemed more personal. She would ask Granny about them as well. That left only one more drawer to check and Carly hesitated again. In her own office at home, she kept her most personal things in the top right hand drawer of her desk. There was no reason to suppose that Elizabeth had done the same, but Carly still hesitated. Finally she pulled the drawer open slowly.

A handful of old letters, cards and a faded ribbon were the only contents of the drawer. Carly studied them carefully, fairly certain of what she had found. These letters lacked envelopes, probably carelessly thrown away by a young girl who thought she would have forever with the writer. They were, of course, from Matthew, and the lack of envelopes made reading them feel less invasive. They were full of endearments and promises of undying love. In one he mentioned sending her a bit of ribbon "to tie up your beautiful hair, to keep it from your eyes as you watch for me to arrive." Carly wiped away a tear. This special collection would definitely have to go to Granny.

Having sorted out the desk, with all of its intensely personal contents, Carly decided that going through the rest of the cottage would be somewhat easier. The furniture was all well made and solidly built and Carly imagined that it could be sold for a fair amount of money, although some of it might be worth shipping to Granny. How on earth was she going to decide?

❧ Carly flipped through the racks of clothes in the dressing room, wondering if any of it was worth taking home to Granny. Perhaps some of it could be donated to a charity. She sighed. This wasn't going to be easy. After another trip around the house, she grabbed a piece of paper and a pencil and sat down at Elizabeth's desk. She gave up on packing and started to play with ideas of what she might do with the cottage, if she were given the opportunity. She was just remodeling her dream kitchen for the third time when Doncan returned.

"I should have told you to call me if you left," he told her as he came up the stairs looking for her. "I drove up here thinking I might arrive and find you gone."

"I would have called," Carly assured him. "But I found plenty to do."

"So what have you been up to?" Doncan asked.

"I've found lots of old letters to take home to Granny, some computer disks that probably need going through and I've peeked inside every closet and wardrobe at least twice." Carly smiled up at Doncan from her seat in the office. He looked stunningly handsome in his pristine suit and she was suddenly conscious of how filthy her hands, and probably her face, were.

"What are you working on now?" Doncan asked curiously, taking a step closer to Carly.

"Nothing really," Carly felt suddenly defensive. "Just rearranging the cottage in my own mind, seeing what I would do with it if it were mine."

Doncan smiled at her. "You're not having second thoughts about just selling the place, are you?" he asked.

"Just a little," Carly admitted.

"I'm sure that is only natural, to feel that way," Doncan told her. "It's a lovely cottage and it belonged to someone in your family for a long time. But surely it makes much more sense to sell it. No doubt your grandmother can use the money. Besides, it needs a lot of modernizing before it will be habitable, and you couldn't possibly live in it full-time, you know. You haven't any right to live on the island."

Carly shook her head. "I know keeping it is a silly idea. But it would be a lovely vacation home for the whole family and there are enough of us to keep it full most of the year, I would have thought!"

Doncan smiled tightly. "I suppose you need to talk to your Grand-mother about that," he told her, sounding as if he hoped the older woman would talk her out of keeping the cottage.

"How much is the cottage worth, anyway? If I know that, it might be easier to make a decision."

Doncan frowned. "Well, it is in reasonable shape and comes with some land, but it does need a great deal of modernizing or total rede-velopment."

Carly realized that he was trying to prepare her for a low figure. "Come on, out with it," she demanded.

"An estate agent valued it for me just after Elizabeth died. He reck-oned that if we put it on the market as it is, you should get about three-fifty for it from a developer."

"Three hundred and fifty pounds?" Carly was astonished. There was no way she was selling the cottage for that sort of money.

Doncan laughed. "Not three hundred and fifty pounds. Three hundred and fifty thousand pounds."

Carly was glad she was sitting down. "But that's...." her head spun. "Something like half a million dollars at the current exchange rate."

Doncan nodded. "Yes, that's about right," he agreed.

"Half a million dollars? For a tiny cottage that needs a lot of work to even make it habitable?" Carly couldn't believe him. "Do you have any idea what half a million dollars will buy in Meadville, Pennsylva-nia?" she asked him.

"Something much bigger and newer?" Doncan guessed. "House prices on the island have gone through the roof over the last fifteen years or so. Coastal properties have added value. A developer could do a lot with the property."

"If it's worth that sort of money, there is no way we could possibly keep it for vacations." She looked down at her kitchen plans and laughed. "That much money will totally change Granny's life. She'll be able to travel. She's always wanted to do that," she told Doncan.

Granny was the last of Katherine's ten children, but her brothers' and sisters' children and grandchildren were scattered around the United States. Granny had always talked of wanting to visit them all. The money would give her a chance to do so. Carly shook her head. Selling was the only sensible option.

"You need to talk to your grandmother and see what she thinks, I guess," Doncan told her. "I have a potential buyer who is interested in buying once you're sure you're selling. But he isn't going to wait around forever. Talk to your grandmother and then we can get the cottage cleared out and ready to sell."

Carly nodded. "I was hoping to spend a few days playing tourist before I got down to the hard work of clearing out the cottage," she protested.

Doncan sighed and then smiled tightly at her. "That's fine," he said seemingly reluctantly. "If my buyer decides to look elsewhere, I'm sure we can find another one."

Carly heard the doubt in his voice, but she didn't care. She was the client and she could do what she wanted. She stood up slowly, stretching and trying to relieve some of the tension she felt.

"Let's go and get something to eat," Doncan suggested. "You probably haven't eaten since breakfast, have you? I didn't even think about your getting any lunch. You must be starving."

Carly suddenly realized that she was, indeed, starving. "Food sounds good," she agreed. "I didn't think about lunch, either, and now I am hungry."

They made their way down the stairs slowly. Carly ducked into the bathroom to wash her hands and shrieked when she saw herself in the mirror.

"Why didn't you tell me I was covered in dust?" she demanded of Doncan when she joined him after scrubbing her hands and face. "My clothes are filthy, probably from brushing up against the furniture in every room. I can't go to a restaurant looking like this!"

"I think you look lovely," he countered. "But if you don't want to go out we can grab a pizza from around the corner and take it back to your room to eat, if you like."

Carly thought about it for only a second. "That sounds great," she told him.

Doncan dialed the restaurant on his mobile phone and ordered not just pizza, but garlic bread, salad and drinks. She followed him to his car where he drove a few blocks, rushed out and grabbed the food and then drove back to Douglas. The smells in the car had Carly's mouth watering by the time Doncan had parked in front of her hotel. She was out of the car and heading up the building's steps with the food before he'd even unfastened his seatbelt. He caught up with her at the elevator and they rode up silently to her room. Carly dropped the bags and boxes of food on the table in the sitting area of the room.

"If you want to sort it all out, I'll just change quickly," she told Doncan, grabbing a handful of clothes from the closet and locking herself in the bathroom just long enough to take off the dusty outfit and replace it with something clean. By the time she'd finished, Doncan had pulled out plates and cups and started opening up the food boxes and bags.

Carly grabbed a piece of pizza and took a bite, a low groan of delight slipping out involuntarily as she chewed. "This is fantastic," she told Doncan.

"I'm glad you like it," he answered, looking as if he was trying not to laugh at her unladylike approach as she devoured the first piece and grabbed a second.

A few moments later she finished the second piece. "Sorry," she said. "I was just so hungry by the time we got here that I couldn't help myself." She sat back self-consciously, aware that she must have looked greedy.

"Here, have some garlic bread." Doncan passed her another box and Carly eagerly took a piece, deciding that he must already think she was a greedy pig, so she should at least enjoy the food.

Half an hour later, both Doncan and Carly were stuffed and nearly everything had been eaten. A few lettuce leaves and half a slice of garlic bread were all that remained. Carly leaned back in her seat and smiled contentedly. Everything had been delicious.

"I hope you enjoyed that," Doncan teased, sinking back in his own chair contentedly.

"It was amazing," Carly murmured, her eyes half-closed.

For a long time they simply sat, Carly was watching the sea as it rolled gently onto the sand many stories below them. She could feel Doncan's eyes on her and she worked hard to keep hers focused on the water. She was surprised when he sat up quickly.

"Sorry, I was daydreaming the night away," he apologized, pulling out his appointment diary. "Tomorrow is Thursday and I have client meetings all day, unfortunately. Would you like to come into the office with me and have a look through Elizabeth's things that I have there in the morning? Then you can sightsee in the afternoon."

Carly smiled. "That sounds fine." She was feeling so full and content that she would probably have agreed to just about anything.

"I'll collect you here about nine, if that is okay?"

"That's fine." Carly smiled agreeably, thinking how incredibly gorgeous Doncan was.

"Oh, I forgot," Doncan added as he stood up slowly. "I have something else for you."

He reached into his pocket and pulled out a small mobile phone. "I had a SIM card put in this so that you can use it while you are here."

He pushed a few buttons on the phone and showed it to Carly. "There's a twenty-pound limit on the card, and you can track your usage on this screen. Let me know if you get down below five pounds and I'll top it up for you."

He spent a few minutes showing Carly the basics on the phone and then handed it to her. "All of my numbers are already programmed into the address book so you can reach me if you need me. I forgot the charger, so I'll get you that tomorrow, but it has a good battery in it, so it will last until then, no problem."

Carly took the phone reluctantly, uncertain what had prompted his kindness. "Thank you," she said hesitantly.

"I didn't like leaving you at the cottage on your own today." Doncan admitted. "At least this way you can reach someone if you need them. I've put in the number for the taxi company that my firm uses as well, so if you need a taxi you can ring them and have them bill it to us."

And that subtly reminds me that I'm just a client, Carly thought. She stuck the phone in her pocket and trailed after Doncan to the door. "Well, thanks for everything," she commented, wondering how much the pizza was going to add to her Granny's bill.

Doncan nodded. "Thank you," he answered, staring for a moment into her eyes. "I know you have a lot to think about right now," he told her after a while. "You need to figure out what you want to do with the cottage and everything. But here is one more thing I want you to think about."

Carly looked at him questioningly as he stopped talking. He took a step closer to her and then pulled her gently into his arms. For a long time he simply looked into her eyes. Carly felt her pulse racing and her heart hammering in her chest. Finally she shut her eyes in an effort to stop the intensity of what she was feeling. As her eyes shut, Doncan pulled her closer still and his lips met hers.

A sigh escaped from Carly and Doncan used it to deepen the kiss. Time and space stood still for an instant, as everything around her vanished and for Carly there was simply herself and Doncan and that kiss.

Doncan broke the connection and took a step back, holding Carly's arm as she felt the world spin suddenly back into place.

"Sleep well," he murmured as he opened the door. "I'll see you in the morning."

Carly leaned against the door after it shut, feeling drained. What was that about? She shook her head to try to clear it. Tom had been kissing her since she'd been ten and it had never felt like that. She straightened and pushed herself away from the door. Taking a deep breath, she forced herself to push all thoughts of Doncan from her mind. She needed to talk to Granny.

"Carly, darling, how is the Isle of Man?" Granny sounded so close that Carly suddenly felt homesick.

"It's fine, Granny. It has been lovely and sunny since I arrived and I spent the day at Elizabeth's cottage."

"What's it like? That lawyer said it needed a lot of work. Is it worth very much, do you think?"

Carly took a deep breath. "The lawyer figures it might be worth as much as three hundred and fifty thousand pounds if you sell it now."

Granny drew a sharp breath. "That sounds like a lot of money for an old cottage. Do you think he is right or is he just trying to justify a big fee?"

Carly hadn't considered doubting Doncan, but Granny was right. He could be inflating the figures for some reason. "I don't know, Granny, but I'm going to find out," Carly promised. She would find herself a realtor and get a proper quote herself.

"Did you find anything interesting in the cottage?" Granny continued.

"Lots of old letters," Carly told her. "I wasn't sure if I should read any of them or not, so I didn't, at least not yet."

Granny chuckled. "You go ahead and read whatever you like," she insisted. "You're family, after all. Maybe you could write a book about Elizabeth and use the letters. History has always been your thing, after all."

Carly smiled. She'd had a similar thought when she read the first set of letters from Elizabeth to Katherine. Now she had even more original source material and writing a book about her relative seemed possible.

"And what is this lawyer fellow like then?" Granny talked over Carly's thoughts. "He sounded slick on the phone and his letters are dreadfully professional. What's he like in person?"

Carly blushed and stammered for a moment, suddenly glad that Granny was over three thousand miles away. "He's been very nice," she answered after a moment.

Granny had raised three girls of her own, so she heard something in Carly's voice that caught her attention. "Nice? And?"

Carly hesitated, not sure what she wanted to say. "He kissed me," she finally blurted out.

"And why not?" Granny demanded. "Is he married, old, ugly, too short, too tall, too much of a lawyer?"

Carly had to laugh. "No, he isn't married, at least I don't think he's married. He isn't old or ugly, either. He's tall, with dark hair and beautiful eyes and...." she trailed off, remembering those eyes burning into hers.

"So why shouldn't he kiss you?" Granny asked.

"Granny, Tom broke up with me," Carly blurted out.

"Bah, Tom wasn't good enough for you when you were ten and he certainly isn't good enough for you now," Granny answered back. "Getting rid of him is the best thing that could have happened. A tall, dark, and handsome lawyer sounds perfect for you."

"I love Tom, remember?" Carly argued.

"You love the idea of still being with the first person you ever cared about," Granny told her bluntly. "I've seen you two together. He's like a brother to you, not a lover. If you're going to make a marriage work, you need passion, and you and Tom certainly don't have that."

Carly opened her mouth to argue, but there was little point. "I shouldn't be kissing other men," she replied feebly. "Tom just dumped me."

"Was it a good kiss?" Granny asked in a mischievous voice.

Carly sighed. "It was a scorcher," she admitted, as much to herself as to Granny.

"So go after him," Granny said encouragingly to her favorite granddaughter. "Life is too short to pass up hot men."

Carly laughed, feeling better. "Sorry, Granny, but I'm not looking for a short romance to fill my time while I'm here. I'm only here for a few weeks and then I have my life to get back to, remember? I would rather not fly back to the States with a broken heart."

Granny was quiet for a moment. "Do you think this lawyer is capable of breaking your heart?" she asked seriously.

Carly thought for a moment. "If I let him," she admitted. "He's totally different from Tom. He's mature and sophisticated and I think he's rich too. Totally not my type."

"If there is one thing that Elizabeth's story should teach you, it is that you should grab life's opportunities when they arise. He kissed you for some reason. Maybe next time you should kiss him."

"But he lives three thousand miles away from my home and my life," Carly argued.

"Stop putting up roadblocks." Granny told her. "And don't drag Tom back into the argument. We both know you didn't belong with Tom. At least this Mr. Quayle might be able to convince you of that."

Carly sighed. Granny was making it sound far too simple. There were a million things that made her getting involved with Doncan Quayle a bad idea.

"Carly," Granny spoke with quiet determination, "just relax and see what happens, okay? Stop worrying and planning your entire life out and just go with the flow for a little while."

"I'll try," Carly grudgingly replied.

Granny chuckled "I guess I will have to be happy with that. Has he put the house on the market yet?"

Carly blinked at the sudden change of subject. "Um, no," she stammered. "Sorry, Granny but I'm dragging my heels a bit. He seems to be in a hurry and that annoys me for some reason. I'll get it on the market soon. I just need to clear it out first."

"There is no great rush." Granny assured her. "The money would be nice, but I don't need it. I suppose when I get it all, I will have to go and visit everyone, won't I?"

Carly could hear the repressed excitement in Granny's voice. Granny had family in thirty-two of the fifty states and she'd often talked about buying a motor home, hiring a driver and traveling to see every one of them. Carly knew that she would have to put the house on the market soon so that Granny could have the chance to do just that.

"I'll sign the papers tomorrow," Carly told her.

"I'm sure they can wait for a little while," Granny told her. "Why don't you do some sight-seeing for a few days and worry about the cottage next week."

"Actually, I'm supposed to do just that," Carly told her. "I'm going to Doncan's office in the morning to look through some more papers and things and then I plan to see a few sights and have some fun."

"Good girl," Granny told her. "And I bet a certain handsome lawyer will be happy to show you around."

"Oh, no, he is far too busy with his law firm," Carly insisted. "I'll be on my own."

After the phone call, Carly got ready for bed. She snuggled down under the comfortable covers and tried to sleep. Sleep refused to come, however, as Carly's mind wouldn't shut down.

She thought endlessly about the cottage. It was a shame it was so valuable. She would have loved to buy it from Granny. Of course, she couldn't have lived in it, because she didn't have the right to live on the Isle of Man. Getting permission to live and work there was probably quite difficult, akin to getting a green card in the States.

Carly flopped back over the other way. Besides, she didn't want to live on a small island thousands of miles from her friends and family, no matter how much she loved the cottage. She had never lived outside of Meadville. It was home and she loved it there. It would be nice to have the cottage to visit once in a while, though.

She rolled over onto her back and stared in the darkness at the ceiling. "What about Doncan?" a little voice nagged at her. She told the little voice to shut up. Whatever she was feeling for Doncan was irrelevant. They had shared a single kiss, one that Doncan was probably already regretting. Besides, whatever Granny had said, she was in love with Tom and her heart had been totally broken by him. She was going to need months, if not years, to recover.

She sighed and tried to think about Tom, dredging up the happiest memories she could. Unfortunately her overtired brain just wouldn't cooperate, and she found herself thinking instead about their many arguments in the last year over money, Tom's drinking, and his inability to hold down steady employment. She was shocked to find that she wasn't really missing him, at least not as much as she missed her mother and grandmother. Sighing again, she buried her head under the pillows and fell into a restless sleep.

米   5   米

In the hotel room the next day, Carly paced anxiously. By three in the morning, she had already concluded that what had happened yesterday was a mistake. She wasn't going to mention the kiss to Doncan, ever. But that decision hadn't helped her to get to sleep. Now she was up and dressed, but she felt exhausted from her restless night. She checked the mirror again, glaring at the dark circles that had resisted being covered by her makeup.

She ran a hand through her hair, and then fluffed it up, hoping to draw attention away from her tired eyes. She thought about going down to meet Doncan in the lobby like she had before, but she was afraid she might look too eager. Carly sighed and sat down in one of the chairs that looked out at the sea. She watched the waves falling on the sand. In less than a month she would be back in America and Doncan would still be here. Their single shared kiss would have made no difference to her life in any way. She held on to that thought as she heard his knock on the door.

She wasn't in the mood for small talk, so she grabbed her bag and was out the door almost before Doncan had spoken. They were both silent in the elevator and during the short car ride to Doncan's office. Doncan had a very full schedule that morning, so he turned Carly over

49

to his secretary and went straight into a meeting. Carly was relieved and disappointed at the same time as she followed the secretary to the storage area where Elizabeth's things were being kept.

"Here you go." The woman smiled at Carly. She looked to be around forty and was soft and round without being fat. Carly imagined that she would be very comforting to people who needed the services of an attorney. "We've put nearly everything into these three boxes. The radio and a few other small electronics are in the storage room in the back and you're welcome to see them whenever you like. Take your time going through the boxes first and let me know if there is anything I can do to help."

&o "Thanks." Carly struggled to remember the woman's name. Doncan had raced through the introductions and Carly's mind had been elsewhere. "I don't think I'll be too long, Breesha." It was Breesha Quilliam, Carly remembered just in time.

"I'll pop back and see if you need anything in a little while, then." Breesha smiled and left Carly on her own.

Carly sat down at the long table where the boxes were piled and pulled the first one towards her. A quick flip through it revealed bills and receipts from the last several years. Carly didn't notice anything particularly interesting in them at first glance, so she put them aside and opened the second box. This box was full of letters and cards, and Carly pulled a few of them out of the box. There appeared to be several piles, each tied together with a piece of string, and Carly carefully untied the string on the top pile. This pile seemed to be cards and letters from Carly's Granny. There was little more than Christmas cards and odd notes, which was hardly surprising as Granny really didn't know Elizabeth.

There were other piles of miscellaneous correspondence, including many letters from men and women who had known Elizabeth when they were children. Carly read through some of them, touched by their stories. They all seemed to look on "Aunt Bessie" as a sort of maiden aunt who had been kind to them when they were young, and many wrote to thank her for her caring and understanding during difficult times. All of these letters would have to go to Granny, and maybe a few might be included in the book Carly was now certain that she wanted to write.

Carly was feeling very sorry that she'd never been able to meet Elizabeth during her lifetime. The third box was full of Elizabeth's computer equipment and Carly lifted everything out and set it up on the table. She looked around for a place to plug everything in, but couldn't see any. With a sigh she headed out into the reception area to ask Breesha for help.

"I'm really sorry to bother you," she began hesitantly as the older woman looked up from her desk. "But I'd like to plug in Elizabeth's computer and see what is on it, if that's okay?"

"Of course it is okay," the woman smiled. "But it is tea time, now. Come and have a cup of tea with me first and then I'll help you sort it all out."

Carly suddenly felt very thirsty and a cup of tea sounded wonderful. "Great," she answered, following Breesha down a short corridor to a small room that was set up as a mini kitchen. Breesha put a kettle on to boil and dropped two tea bags into a large teapot. As she bustled around, gathering mugs and milk and sugar, Carly, at Breesha's urging, sank into a comfortable chair.

"Have you worked here long?" Carly asked, trying to make conversation.

"I worked for the older Mr. Quayle from when I left school until he retired," Breesha answered with a grin. "By that time, young Mr. Quayle was ready to take over the firm and I just stayed on."

"I bet that was a big help for him." Carly answered.

"It sure was," the voice came from behind Carly and made her jump.

Doncan smiled at her from the doorway. "Everyone knows that Breesha has run this place since she left school."

He gave the older woman an affectionate smile. "I just finished talking to Bob Christian about the changes that he wants to make to his will," he told Breesha. "He's adamant that he is going to make them, and if I won't do it, he'll find another advocate who will."

"Silly old fool," Breesha snorted.

Doncan chuckled. "Be that as it may, I've told him that we'll make the changes and prepare a copy for him to sign at our earliest convenience. I suggest that our earliest convenience might well be in a few weeks' time. That might just give him time to get over his infatuation."

Breesha grinned at him conspiratorially. "If he rings, I'll make sure I tell him that you are working on it."

Doncan reached around Breesha and grabbed a box off the counter behind her. He pulled it open and pulled out a couple of chocolate-covered cookies. As he stuffed one in his mouth he held the box out to Carly and Breesha in turn. Carly carefully selected a cookie and tried a bite. It was delicious.

"For goodness' sake," Breesha said, as Doncan added a few more cookies to the carefully balanced pile he had made in front of himself.

Breesha pulled the box from his hand and shut it up tightly. "What will Carly think of your manners?" she scolded good-naturedly, quickly passing around plates for everyone.

Carly put the tiny bit that was left of her cookie on her plate and looked sheepishly at Doncan. He winked at her and then slipped one of his own cookies onto her plate. Carly blushed and looked to see what Breesha was making of the exchange. Breesha, however, was carefully pouring hot water into the teapot and apparently missed it.

Fortified by chocolate cookies and warm, milky tea, Carly was eager to get started on Elizabeth's computer. Doncan had taken his tea break quickly and, with little more than a smile at Carly, had returned to his office to make some more phone calls.

Breesha tidied the small kitchen and then followed Carly back to the storage room. She helped Carly set the computer up and found spaces for all the necessary plugs. Carly sat back and watched as the computer hummed to life. After a few moments, the whirring and clanking noises stopped and the computer flashed up a screen. Carly stared.

Blinking in front of her was the demand: "Enter Password." Carly frowned and dug through the disks and papers that she had found in the drawer that had been full of computer things. There was nothing written down anywhere that looked like it might be a password. Carly tried typing in "Elizabeth," and then "Laxey," and even "Katherine" but all were rejected as incorrect. Carly frowned and tried to think. What might Elizabeth have chosen? Finally Carly carefully typed "Matthew" into the box. She was surprised and then relieved when the password was accepted.

There was only the basic software that she had been expecting on the computer. Carly tried out a few of the disks and found each one contained exactly what was neatly written on the label and nothing more. Elizabeth had kept careful budgets in a simple budget program and Carly read though a few years' worth, noting that Elizabeth had been a frugal woman.

The word processing program was one that Carly had used herself, so she was quickly able to find her way around the documents that Elizabeth had saved on the various disks. They all appeared to be articles that she had written for various publications and Carly was eager to read them when she had the opportunity. Most appeared to be about various aspects of the history of the island and Carly wondered briefly about printing some of them out to read later in the hotel. The sheer quantity of the articles made her reconsider. She would have to take the disks home to Pennsylvania and read them there. It was just lucky that she still had an old computer at home that would be able to read the disks. Carly was just about to shut the computer down when she thought about the hard drive. There could be other documents and files stored there.

Carly found that she was correct. From the look of it, Elizabeth had saved draft copies of articles on the hard drive, only saving them to disk when they were complete. Also on the hard drive were odd bits of correspondence, letters to the bank requesting additional checks and acceptances or refusals for invitations to speak at local events. Elizabeth clearly had her own code for naming files. The file names were made up of the initials of the recipient and the date of the letter. Carly was just about to shut down again when she noticed one file that didn't follow the naming convention.

The file was called "mltb" and Carly clicked it curiously. The document opened and Carly was amazed to see the document headed "My Life – The Beginning". Carly read through it eagerly. It appeared that Elizabeth had been working on her life story. The document ran to several pages and Carly read them all, learning about Elizabeth's childhood as an immigrant in America.

Carly was hugely disappointed to find that the document ended with Elizabeth turning fifteen, before she'd even met Matthew Saunders. Searching through the list of files again, Carly hoped to find another file that might contain the next part of the story, but she couldn't find anything. She copied the document onto one of the other disks, making a note on it of the additional file.

She would have to check each and every disk to be absolutely sure, but it seemed that this was as far as Elizabeth had gone. That could be done from home, though. She didn't need to waste any more of her valuable time here on it. She was much more eager to do some sightseeing than she was to read through old letters to the telephone company and other similar correspondence.

She stretched. Her back was stiff and she was tired of looking at the computer screen, anyway. Besides, this was supposed to be at least partly a vacation, wasn't it? She had just about convinced herself to take the afternoon off when Doncan's face appeared in the doorway.

"How's it going?" he asked, concern flashing over his face.

No doubt she still looked exhausted, she thought. "I was just thinking about stopping for today," Carly admitted. "It looks like Elizabeth was thinking about writing her life story. I found a document that details her early years, but nothing after she turned fifteen."

"I remember her talking about writing an autobiography at one point, about five or six years ago." Doncan replied, frowning as he seemed to be trying to remember.

"I think the museum asked her to write it and they were going to publish it for her. She wouldn't have made any money from it, but it would have been a valuable resource for anyone interested in the thirties, forties and fifties, wouldn't it?"

Carly nodded. "I was thinking that I might have a go at writing her life story myself," she told Doncan. "My background is in history and she left so many wonderful documents that it would probably write itself. She seemed to have saved many of the letters she received, and my Granny has piles that came from her as well." Carly trailed off, worried about what Doncan might think of the idea.

"That's a great idea." His answer reassured her. "You should talk to Mark Blake at the Manx Museum. He's in charge of special projects, and it would have been him that Elizabeth talked to about writing the story herself."

"Maybe I should do that today." Carly wanted to go sight-seeing, but Elizabeth's life story was important as well.

"You should have some lunch now," Doncan told her. "You look tired. Lunch might get you some energy back. After lunch, I suggest you take yourself around the Manx Museum. It will give you a quick history of the island and there are lots of interesting displays. I'll ring Mark and see if he has time to meet with you around half-four, after you have finished touring the museum."

Carly smiled. She wasn't sure that she should be letting Doncan arrange her life for her, but his suggestions this time seemed both sensible and enjoyable. The museum was on her list of places to see and it was probably a good place to start learning about the history of the island. If she could finish it off by meeting with the man Elizabeth had worked with on her autobiography, all the better.

"That sounds great," she told Doncan.

"I'll just ring Mark now and then we can grab some lunch."

Doncan disappeared back down the corridor, leaving Carly staring at his back. He hadn't said anything about having lunch with her before, had he? She turned back to the computer and slowly shut it down.

As it happened, Mark was busy all afternoon, but he was free for lunch so Doncan and Carly quickly made their way to the museum instead. The building was huge and Carly was fascinated by its history.

"This was once Noble's Hospital, named for Henry Bloom Noble, who generously provided the building," Mark told her after they found a table in the small restaurant inside the museum.

"It opened in 1888 and was replaced by the new Noble's Hospital in 1912. That hospital was funded by Noble's estate. Eventually, it too was replaced, in 2003, by the new new Noble's Hospital."

Carly laughed. "Is it officially called the 'New New Noble's Hospital'?" she asked.

Mark laughed. "No," he admitted. "Though it probably should be."

Carly had been surprised when she met Mark. She had been expecting a wrinkled old historian, but Mark looked to be in his late thirties, with dark hair and surprisingly blue eyes. He was well built and attractive and Carly was shocked when the idea of flirting with him danced through her head. Tom seemed further and further away every hour.

After they'd ordered a light lunch, Carly quickly came to the point. "Doncan tells me that you talked with Elizabeth Cubbon, my grandmother's aunt, about writing her autobiography?"

Mark nodded as he sipped a cup of tea. "Doncan told me that you were going through her papers and found a first draft. We would love to have a copy of it and anything else that you find that might be interesting."

Carly was happy to agree to get him a copy of the document she had found. "Unfortunately, it starts when she's already in America and it only covers her life until she was fifteen," she told Mark. "From the look of it, she stopped there and never finished. Maybe she stopped when she was no longer able to climb the stairs?"

"I'm not sure." Mark looked to Doncan for a reaction.

"I'm not sure, either." Doncan told Carly. "I offered, many times, to move the computer downstairs so Elizabeth could work from it, but she always said she didn't want it. I suspect that she wrote as much as she felt comfortable writing and then stopped because she didn't want to do any more."

"Besides," Mark chimed in. "We talked about her doing the book quite a few years ago. She would have had plenty of time to write more than just one chapter before she stopped climbing the stairs, if she had wanted to."

Carly frowned. "So she was happy to remember the first fifteen years of her life, but nothing after that? That just seems really sad."

Doncan gave Carly's hand a small squeeze. "I don't think that means that she was unhappy forever after. I suspect she just couldn't bring herself to write about Matthew and couldn't figure out how to write what happened after his death without mentioning him."

Carly was still frowning. "Maybe I shouldn't write about her, then. Maybe she didn't want the story told."

Both men laughed then and Doncan answered. "One thing about Bessie that everyone knew was that story," he told Carly. "She was happy to talk about it with anyone and everyone. I think she really enjoyed casting herself as the devastated near widow whose life was ruined."

"Maybe she didn't want to write the story down because it didn't exactly happen in the wildly romantic and tragic way she'd always recounted," Mark suggested.

All three were silent as they considered the idea. Carly finally spoke slowly. "I suppose I can see where she might have enjoyed the attention that her story brought her. So much so that she might have exaggerated or stretched the truth over the years." Carly wondered again about the mysterious Peter, whom she had read about in the letter, but didn't mention him.

All three fell silent as the food was delivered. After they'd finished their lunch, the conversation turned to more general things as the three enjoyed slices of delicious cream cakes and more tea. Carly felt full and relaxed as the lunch finished.

Mark apologized profusely for rushing off straight after the meal. "I've got three meetings, back to back, this afternoon," he told Carly. "Officially, the museum would be delighted if you were to undertake to write Elizabeth's biography and unofficially, I would be too. I hope you enjoy your visit to the museum this afternoon. The staff is all very good so ask lots of questions." With a hasty smile, he dashed back to his office, leaving Carly and Doncan to finish their drinks.

Carly found the sudden silence awkward. "I suppose you have meetings all afternoon as well." She spoke only to fill the uncomfortable quiet.

"I wish I could join you for your tour," Doncan answered. "But yes, I have meetings all afternoon."

Carly blushed. She hadn't meant for her words to sound like an invitation. Before she could figure out what to say next, Doncan spoke again.

"I have a dinner meeting as well, unfortunately, so you are on your own tonight. The food at the hotel is excellent, though, and room service is very efficient." Doncan smiled at her. "Have an early night and catch up on your sleep," he suggested. "I think you are still suffering from some jet lag."

Carly stiffened. She knew she looked tired, but it upset her that he had noticed. "I probably will have an early night, thanks," she answered coolly.

Doncan grinned. "Then we can make an early start tomorrow," he told her.

"What are we doing tomorrow?" Carly couldn't remember them making any plans for the next day.

"I've taken the day off to take you sight-seeing," Doncan answered, with a grin. "I thought we would head south and visit Castle Rushen and Rushen Abbey. If we have time we can try to get to Peel Castle as well. Unless there was somewhere else you wanted to go instead?"

Carly thought carefully before answering. "I'm sure you have better things to do than dragging me around the sights," she protested, surprised that he had rearranged his work to suit her.

"I'm sure I do," Doncan agreed. "But I can't think of anything I would rather do than show you the sights."

Carly blushed again at Doncan's words. "If you're sure you can take the time away from work, I would love to see the two castles and Rushen Abbey," Carly told him, excitement at the prospect shining in her eyes.

His answering grin suggested that he found her excitement amusing. He walked her back to the front of the museum and left her at the entry doors.

"I'll see you in the morning, about nine," he called back to her over his shoulder as he headed back to the parking lot.

"See you then." Carly confirmed, pulling open the heavy glass door and making her way into the cool and dark interior of the museum.

Carly was just in time for a short film that encapsulated the entire history of the island into about twenty minutes. She watched, fascinated, as early settlers gave way to Viking invaders. Eventually the island moved on to independence as a Crown Dependency with its own stamps, currency and laws. The film ended with a quick peek at some of the other sights on the island and Carly was enthralled by her first glimpses of Peel Castle, Castle Rushen and Rushen Abbey. Tomorrow, she reminded herself excitedly, she would be able to see them for herself.

After the film she made her way slowly through the many galleries in the museum. An art gallery gave way to a study of the various rocks and minerals found on the island. Next, display cases showcased finds from the Stone Age, then the Bronze Age, and finally the Iron Age. Carly spent a long time in the Viking Gallery, fascinated by the coins and jewelry.

That gave way to more recent history and Carly found herself moving quickly through the centuries. She enjoyed learning about the island as a holiday destination, amazed at the footage of crowds all along the promenade and beaches, riding steam trains, electric trams and, of course, horse trams. She gasped at photos and accounts of the island as a prisoner of war camp during the Second World War. The museum had a large collection of beautiful objects that had been made by the men and women held in these camps.

She finally ended up in the gift shop, surrounded by a huge selection of things that she wanted to buy and take home with her. She finally settled on a few books about the history of the island and a pair of beautiful silk scarves with designs on them based on one of the stone crosses that had been found on the island. The crosses had been carved by early Christian settlers and the designs were both beautiful and complex. The scarves would be perfect gifts for Granny and her mother.

Carly carried her purchases back to her hotel room that was, thankfully, only a short walk downhill from the museum. It was nearly five o'clock and, after her light lunch, Carly was starving. She ordered a huge meal from room service and was glad she was alone as she ate every bite.

With her stomach full, she spent some time curled up in a comfortable chair, alternately watching the sea and reading from one of the books she had just bought. By eight o'clock her eyes refused to stay open any longer and she put herself to bed and fell asleep immediately.

6

Friday morning was overcast but dry, and as Carly watched the waves on the seashore through her windows while she waited for Doncan, she hoped it would stay that way. This was her first real opportunity to go sight-seeing and she didn't want to get caught in the rain.

She spotted Doncan's expensive car when it pulled up and thought about going down to meet him, but worried that they would end up missing each other in the pair of elevators. Since she was so excited about seeing the island, she was waiting at the door to her room as he got off the elevator on her floor, though.

"All ready to go?" he asked, as he gave her a smile.

"I can't wait to see everything," Carly beamed back at him, enthusiasm shining from her eyes.

"Let's get going, then," he suggested.

Once they were safely buckled into the car, Doncan pulled away from the promenade and headed south. "I thought we would start at Castle Rushen and work our way north from there," he told Carly. "Unless you have any objection?"

Carly hated that she seemed to be leaving Doncan to plan her entire life for her at the moment, but she couldn't possibly complain about his plans for today. "No, that sounds wonderful," she assured him. She would just have to work harder to assert herself from now on, she decided.

"Great." Doncan settled back in the comfortable driver's seat. He drove expertly, and they covered the short distance to Castletown quickly, only slowing to take time to wave to the Little People.

Carly marveled at the narrow roads and small roundabouts that were foreign to her driving experience. The parking lot for the castle was another revelation. She read the sign that was posted in the small lot in disbelief.

"The parking lot can flood at high tide?" she asked. "Seriously?"

Doncan chuckled. "It doesn't happen all that often," he told her. "I'm sure we'll be fine."

Carly stared at him for a minute and then shook her head. "Why would you put a parking lot where it might get flooded?"

"Because there simply isn't anywhere else to put it?" Doncan suggested. "Look, the castle wasn't built to accommodate visitors arriving by car. This is the space that's available," he shrugged. "Really, it's fine. Let's go see the castle."

Carly followed him across the small parking lot towards Castle Rushen. It was perched beside the water and it looked like a storybook castle from one of the books she read to her school children.

"That's the Old Grammar School," Doncan told Carly, pointing to a small white building not far from where they had parked. "It was built around 1200 as a chapel, but eventually became a school. Now it's a very small museum. If we have time we can stop there on our way out."

Carly looked at the tiny building and smiled. "I hope we have time," she told Doncan. "I'd love to see inside it."

Doncan grinned at her. "We can make time," he assured her, ushering her across the road towards the castle.

Carly couldn't help but "ooh" and "ah" at the drawbridge and the "murder holes" that marked the entrance to the castle.

"Anyone trying to invade could be trapped between the two sets of doors," the castle tour guide explained. "Then the defenders could drop hot oil or rocks or whatever they wanted on to the attackers through the holes in the floor above."

Carly shuddered as she looked up at the holes between the stonework of the floor above. The holes were now carefully covered with glass or plastic panels so that no one could accidentally drop anything on the guests below.

The first stop on the tour was a brief movie about the history of the castle. Carly settled on the hard wooden bench and Doncan slid down next to her. As the room filled with other tourists, the pair was pushed together. Carly found it next to impossible to focus on the movie with Doncan's arm resting casually around her shoulders.

She and Tom had clearly grown too comfortable together, she decided. There must have been similar sparks in their touches at the beginning of their relationship. She obviously just didn't remember them.

After the movie they were turned loose to explore the castle and Carly felt as though she could spend forever investigating every nook and cranny of the ancient building. The tour ended in the medieval kitchen.

"I can't imagine trying to cook over a fire like that," she told Doncan as they looked at the kitchen.

"Things have certainly changed," Doncan agreed.

They made their way down the stairs that led from the kitchen to the small courtyard below.

"I want to do it all again," Carly said eagerly, her eyes shining with excitement.

"Really?" Doncan was definitely less enthusiastic.

"Just once around, quickly?" Carly suggested.

Doncan smiled at her. "How about you go back around once more and I'll meet you in the gift shop when you're done?" he suggested.

Carly hesitated for a moment. "Are you sure you won't mind?" she asked.

"I'm positive. You go and have fun," Doncan smiled at her, chuckling softly as she charged away to have a quick second look at the building.

An hour later she was back in the courtyard, still brimming with excitement. "You should have come with me," she told Doncan as she reached his side. "It was wonderful."

"I've been going around this castle since I was in primary school," Doncan told her. "I'm pretty sure I've seen it all."

"Do you know the woman who works in the throne room?" she asked.

"What woman?"

"I don't know. It's just that she was wearing the most beautiful costume I've ever seen. It looked like it was really from the seventeenth century. I've never seen anything like it."

"They have lots of staff in period costumes scattered around," Doncan said, his voice thoughtful. "Didn't she introduce herself?"

"That's just it," Carly answered. "She didn't speak to me at all. I was in the throne room, just having a last quick look around and when I turned to leave she was just standing there, watching me."

"And she didn't say anything? Usually the tour guides are really helpful."

"She just smiled at me. Then I said something about how beautiful her dress was, but she just walked out of the room."

"She smiled at you?" Doncan said in a strangled tone.

"Yes," Carly looked at him curiously. "Why?"

"No reason," Doncan waved a hand at her. "Sorry," he coughed and cleared his throat. "I'm just glad she was polite, even if she didn't speak."

Doncan had her out of the castle and across the street for lunch before she could ask any more questions. Over lunch they compared notes on their childhoods, laughing when they found common ground in certain areas. Carly was fascinated by the things that Doncan had experienced on the island, and he was interested in what life in small-town America was like.

After lunch there was just time for a quick walk around the Old Grammar School before they headed for Rushen Abbey.

"What an amazing old building," Carly remarked as they climbed back into Doncan's car after their look at the Old Grammar School.

"If we had more time, we could check out the old House of Keys building and the Nautical Museum," Doncan told her. "But I want you to see Rushen Abbey. We are going to have to leave Peel Castle for another day."

Carly frowned. "That's a shame," she sighed.

"There's always tomorrow," Doncan told her with a smile.

"My boyfriend just dumped me the day I left to come here," Carly blurted the words out, suddenly concerned that she might be leading Doncan on in some way.

"I am sorry," Doncan told her after a moment of surprised silence. "Were you together for long?"

"Ever since grade school," Carly told him. "He's the only guy I've ever dated." And the only guy I ever kissed before you, she thought to herself.

"Wow, that's impressive," Doncan said.

Carly thought he might be mocking her, but she wasn't sure. "Sometimes you really do meet your soul mate when you're both just kids," she said defensively.

"And sometimes you meet your soul mate when you least expect it," Doncan smiled at her as he parked the car.

The parking lot for Rushen Abbey was as small as the one at Castle Rushen had been, but at least this far inland there were no warnings about high tide.

"Come and see the abbey," he told Carly. "While we go around you can tell me all about your former boyfriend."

Luckily for Carly there was plenty to see and talk about at the abbey, so she didn't have to talk about Tom. For some reason she felt uncomfortable discussing her former relationship with Doncan.

The ruins that were all that was left of the ancient abbey enthralled Carly. She admired the herb garden where the museum staff was working to grow the various plants that the abbey's residents would have grown centuries earlier. Archaeologists were hard at work in one corner of the site and Doncan and Carly learned more about what was being found there from the man in charge of the dig.

"You're both more than welcome to volunteer for a few hours a week and help us out," the man grinned at them as he wrapped up his short talk about the pottery finds from the previous month.

"Really?" Carly asked, amazed.

"Yes, really," the man chuckled. "We use a lot of volunteers on the site and are always happy to have more. We need a certain level of commitment, because it takes some time to train folks, but we'd love to have you."

Carly shook her head reluctantly. "I'm only here for a few weeks," she sighed. "Otherwise, I'd love to help out."

They were back in Doncan's car before the subject of Tom came back up.

"So, if you were with your boyfriend for that long, how come you weren't married yet?" Doncan asked.

"Tom wanted to wait until we were both totally sure that we were perfect for each other."

"And then he decided that you weren't?"

Carly sighed and looked at the car's side window. "I guess so," she said quietly.

They rode silently until they reached Fairy Bridge, when Doncan quietly reminded her to wave. The rest of the journey continued in silence until they were parked in front of Carly's hotel. As Carly got ready to jump out of the car, Doncan began to speak.

"I'm sorry about the kiss," he began. "If I had known about Tom, I would never have done that."

"I guess I should have told you about Tom earlier." Carly was willing to accept some of the blame for the kiss.

"It doesn't matter," Doncan waved her words away. "Now that I know that you're broken-hearted, I promise to behave like a perfect gentleman. You're only here for a short time, anyway, so it's probably best that we just stay friends. Anyway, you're a client, not potential girlfriend material."

"Great," Carly muttered, trying to convince herself that she wasn't disappointed.

"Great," Doncan smiled at her. "Now I'm afraid I have to run. I have plans for this evening and I need to get ready."

Carly forced out a smile and rushed out a garbled "thank you" as she left the car.

"I'll pick you up tomorrow around the same time," Doncan told her. "We can visit the House of Manannan and Peel Castle."

Carly opened her mouth to protest, but Doncan was already pulling away. She mentally shrugged her shoulders. If he wanted to spend the day showing her the sights, that was his problem. At least now he was just being friendly and she could stop worrying about him repeating that kiss.

Hours later, after a somewhat uninspired room service meal and some pointless television watching, Carly called her mother.

"Hey, Mom."

"Hey, yourself," her mother answered. "How are things in the Isle of Man?"

"Different and strange," Carly told her. "I got to do some sight-seeing today, though, and the history of the place is amazing."

"I talked to Granny this morning. She said that you and Tom broke up?"

"Actually, Tom dumped me on the way to the airport," Carly replied, expecting to feel tears as she tried to talk about it.

"Are you okay?" Her mother's voice was full of concern.

"I really am," Carly answered, surprised at the truth in her words. "Maybe Tom was right. Maybe we need some time apart."

"And what about the gorgeous lawyer?" Carly's mom had to ask.

"Granny has a big mouth," Carly laughed. She didn't keep secrets from her mother, but she felt uncomfortable talking about Doncan, and she might not have bothered to mention him if her mother hadn't.

"He's very handsome and we agreed to keep things strictly professional between us," she told her mother.

"I guess that's probably for the best," her mom agreed. "You are only there for a short time."

Carly found herself wanting to argue with her mother, which was just ridiculous. She sighed, and then told her mother all about Castle Rushen and Rushen Abbey. They both managed to avoid mentioning Doncan and Tom for the rest of the short conversation.

"I'll try to call again soon," Carly told her mother as they prepared to hang up. "But it's expensive, and the time difference makes it awkward, so I probably won't do it often."

Carly went back to watching television, but couldn't find anything to hold her interest. Her brain kept going back over every word that she and Doncan had said during their long day together. No matter how hard she tried, she couldn't stop the words "I have plans" from playing over and over in her head. No doubt his plans included a beautiful and sophisticated woman, one who would not only enjoy his kisses, but return them with enthusiasm.

Eventually she fell into an unsatisfactory sleep, visions of Tom and Doncan clouding her brain. The next morning, however, her most vivid recollection of the night's dreaming was of a beautiful woman in seventeenth-century dress smiling at her in Castle Rushen's throne room.

7

Saturday arrived in bright, sunny style and, as she ate her room service breakfast, Carly felt like she could watch the gentle waves splashing up towards the promenade all day. Doncan arrived promptly, however, and they were quickly on their way west towards Peel.

Doncan was an excellent tour guide again, pointing out the ruins of an ancient church as they drove past.

"And there's Tynwald Hill," he told Carly as they passed the historic site.

Carly studied it as for a brief moment as they were stuck behind turning traffic. "It's not as impressive as I thought it would be," she said eventually.

"It's just a hill, really, although it goes up in steps rather than gradually," Doncan shrugged.

"I think I was expecting it to be more grand, and not so close to the road," she said thoughtfully. "I mean, it's the meeting place for the government of the island. I thought it would be more elaborate or something."

"The whole point of it is accessibility," Doncan reminded her. "It's where the government meets and everyone can come and present their grievances. It's really only ceremonial now anyway. All the real work gets done in their building in Douglas."

"Tynwald Day is towards the end of my planned visit," Carly remembered. "I hope I can get out here to see the ceremony."

"We'll have to make sure that you get here," Doncan told her. "There's an all-day festival that goes along with it, with food and music and fireworks. It's well worth coming to see. I don't think there is another government in the world that functions quite like ours."

Carly nodded. The idea of a special "national day" where the entire government met at an outdoor venue was an unusual one. Carly especially loved the fact that the residents could present their complaints to that government on that day and the government would consider them.

"I can't imagine having a chance to complain directly to the President of the United States," she told Doncan. "It's a strange concept."

"It's a small island," Doncan replied. "It would be a lot harder to manage in a country the size of the United States."

Carly shrugged. "I wish they could figure out a way to do it," she told him. "I'd love a chance to tell our government a few things."

Doncan laughed as they began to wind their way through the streets of Peel. As they turned down a narrow road, a huge plate glass window caught Carly's attention. On the outside were several statues of Viking men, apparently pulling on the large ship that could be seen on the other side of the window. One of the Vikings was actually trapped in the glass, half inside the building and half outside.

"The House of Manannan," Doncan told her with a smile. "We can see the rest of the crew on the inside, along with their ship."

The museum was unlike any Carly had ever been to before. The first half of the tour consisted of several different rooms, each a recreation of an episode in Manx history. Carly was captivated as they moved from the earliest settlements, through the Viking era, to early Christianity. Short scenes were enacted by animatronic characters that told their stories and the history of the island.

In the center of the museum was the Viking ship that she had seen through the window when they arrived. Real water lapped around the ship's hull and on board were numerous crew members, each of whom could be identified by using the touch screen computers scattered throughout the space.

The next part of the museum was devoted to shipping and the kipper industry and Carly couldn't help but wrinkle her nose as the smell of smoking kippers hit her. Doncan laughed as they made their way past the display of women preparing the kippers for smoking, on their way to watch a video about Peel Castle. When the video finished, the windows in the room suddenly turned from cloudy to clear and Carly had a perfect view of the castle itself on the horizon.

"We're going there next, right?" she checked with Doncan anxiously.

"After lunch," Doncan told her. "I don't know about you, but I'm starving."

Carly hadn't realized how much time had passed, but it was after noon and she suddenly realized that she was hungry as well. "Lunch sounds good, but maybe not kippers," she grinned at him.

The small pub across the street did indeed serve kippers, but they had a large number of other options that satisfied both Doncan and Carly. Carly was eager to limit the conversation to safe topics, so they talked about television shows and movies, books and music. After lunch it was just a short drive from the museum to the castle.

Having spent a day exploring Castle Rushen previously, Carly was somewhat disappointed to discover that Peel Castle was primarily in ruins. Given an audio tour device, she eagerly followed the guide from spot to spot, soaking up the extensive history of the site. When she finished the tour, she realized that she hadn't seen Doncan for some time.

She carefully retraced her steps, wandering around the various ruined buildings and crumbled walls, looking for him. She caught up with him along one of the long walls that marked the outer boundary of the site.

"There you are," he greeted her with a smile. "I'm just watching the seals playing on the rocks."

Carly stood next to him and peered over the wall. In the sea just below them, where rocks were liberally sprinkled, a handful of seals were just visible, ducking under the water and then suddenly climbing out onto the rocks for a moment or two. Carly was transfixed by their antics.

She watched happily for several minutes as the seals bobbed around in the water below. As she leaned further forward to get a better look at one particular small one below them, Doncan put a steadying arm around her.

"I don't want you falling into the sea," he murmured as he pulled her close.

"I'm fine," she told him, trying to carefully twist away from him, all the while keeping one eye on the seals.

"I feel like you're safer if I'm holding on to you," he replied softly. "You're my client and I have to take good care of you."

Carly wasn't sure how to respond to that, so she remained quiet and stood still in his arms. For another minute she watched the splashing animals. Slowly, she became increasingly aware of the spicy scent of Doncan's cologne. She felt herself relaxing into his casual embrace and enjoying the feeling of his strong arms wrapped around her.

For a few moments she let herself enjoy the sensation before forcing herself to remember that they had a strictly professional relationship. She took a deep breath and then turned her back on the sea and took a big step away from the wall, out of Doncan's arms.

"Seen enough?" was all that Doncan asked.

"Yeah, I think I've seen enough," she muttered in reply, feeling uncomfortably saddened that the embrace had ended.

They walked slowly back through the castle grounds, Doncan taking care to point out a few things that Carly might have missed.

"You know a lot of the history of the island, then," Carly remarked as they reached his car.

"A distant cousin runs the Manx History Institute," he replied, shrugging. "He's always roping us into helping with research projects or to come and listen to lectures. I guess some of it has stuck over the years."

The drive back to Douglas passed quickly as the pair discussed everything that Carly had seen during the day.

"I think the House of Manannan was great," Carly finally summarized the day. "It was neat to see all of the recreations and learn all of the history. But Peel Castle was better. That was the real thing."

"So you enjoyed your trip to the west of the island?" Doncan asked.

"I loved it," Carly assured him. "But Castle Rushen is still my favorite out of all the places I've been so far."

"I'm not sure that we can top Castle Rushen," Doncan grinned at her. "For now, how about dinner?"

When Carly didn't immediately reply, he continued. "I have reservations at my favorite restaurant for tonight, and my friend had to cancel at the last minute. I hate eating alone, but I would hate to miss the chance to eat there. Please? You would be doing me a favor."

"Is it very fancy?" Carly asked, concerned that she didn't have anything appropriate to wear.

"Not really," Doncan grinned at her. "A sundress would be perfectly acceptable. They just have fabulous food and everyone on the island knows that, so it is always busy. You have to make reservations a couple of months ahead in the summer months if you want to eat there on a weekend night."

"I guess it would be a shame to miss your reservation, then," Carly spoke slowly, unsure as to whether accepting was a good idea or not.

"Consider it a business meeting, if that makes you feel better," Doncan told her with a smile. "We can even talk about Bessie's estate over the first course to make it official."

Carly grinned back at him. "That sounds like a plan."

Doncan dropped her off at her hotel, agreeing to pick her back up in an hour. That gave her just enough time to shower and change into her favorite dress. She added a jacket that made it a little bit dressier, figuring that she could take it off if she felt overdressed.

As she dried and styled her hair, she frowned at her mirror self. "This is a business dinner," she told herself sternly. "This is not a date." Mirror Carly took time to apply a little extra mascara and add some bright red lipstick before sensible Carly could stop her.

Ready with a few minutes to spare, Carly paced around the small hotel room. She grabbed a tissue, having decided to wipe off the red lipstick and replace it with something more sedate when she heard a knock on her door.

Carly nearly gasped out loud as she opened the door. Doncan looked gorgeous in a perfectly tailored dark gray suit with a lighter gray shirt and a slim black tie. For a moment she felt as shy and tongue-tied as if it were actually a date. She took a deep breath.

"Come in," she finally managed to speak. "I'll just grab my purse."

She turned away from the door. Her purse was on a small table near the windows and she deliberately walked slowly across to it, to give herself time to clear her head. Okay, the man was unbelievably good-looking. That didn't actually change anything. By the time she had her purse in her hands, she had just about convinced herself that this really was a business meeting.

Doncan had an amused smile on his lips. No doubt he'd noticed that she'd dressed and done her hair and makeup with care. No matter what either of them said, he had to realize that Carly was acting as if it were a date.

The restaurant was in Ramsey and Doncan drove slowly up the coast through Lonan and Laxey again.

"We can take the mountain road somewhere another day," he told her. "But for tonight I feel like driving up the coast."

Situated right on the waterfront, the restaurant had a wall of windows that provided all of its patrons with stunning views of the sea.

As they were shown to their table, Carly was relieved to note that most of the other women were dressed similarly to herself. For several minutes she simply drank in the incredible view, in no rush to open her menu. Finally, Doncan spoke.

"Yes, the view is amazing, but I'm hungry," he teased her.

"Oh, sorry." Carly opened the menu and quickly glanced at the options. The choice was extensive and she felt overwhelmed as she read the detailed descriptions of dish after dish. Finally she sighed and looked at her companion.

"It all sounds wonderful," she told him. "What would you recommend?"

Doncan grinned at her. "I can guarantee that everything is delicious," he told her. After a short discussion between themselves and the attentive waiter, the meal was ordered, along with a bottle of wine.

With the menus gone and a glass of wine in hand, Carly settled back into her chair with a happy sigh. "I could just sit here all night and watch the waves," she told Doncan.

"I don't know about all night," Doncan answered. "But we certainly aren't in any hurry."

"So tell me your life story," Carly suggested.

"Only if you'll do the same after I'm done," Doncan replied.

"That seems fair enough," Carly agreed.

"I'll try to skip over the most boring parts," Doncan grinned at her. "I was born and raised in Laxey. I went to the local schools until I finished my A levels and then went to the University of Liverpool to study law. After I got my degree, I came home and joined the family practice. That's about it, really."

Carly rolled her eyes. "That's just the boring parts," she told him. "I want to know the interesting stuff. What were you like in school? Did you enjoy studying in Liverpool? Why did you come back after you graduated? That sort of stuff."

"I studied hard in school," Doncan told her. "My father is an advocate and so was his father and they expected me to follow in their footsteps. I knew I needed to get good marks and work hard. I enjoyed math and science and I always thought that I'd have studied chemistry if I hadn't gone into law."

"Your parents made you study law? Weren't you given a choice?" Carly interrupted with even more questions.

"They didn't really 'make me' study law," Doncan shrugged. "But my father really wanted me to take over the practice that his father had started. My sister wasn't about to study law, so if I didn't do it, he would have had to shut it down or sell the practice. I think, if I'd really felt strongly about something else, he and my mother would have been supportive, but they both told me from my earliest memories that I was destined to be a lawyer and I never saw any need to argue."

"That seems sad for some reason," Carly told him with a frown.

"Well, I'm not sad about it," Doncan told her, refilling her wine glass. "I think your next question was about Liverpool?" He waited until she nodded before continuing.

"I liked Liverpool a lot. It's an interesting city and it was very different from what I was used to after growing up here. But after I finished my studies, I was also happy to leave. I didn't want to stay there forever or anything. My family has been Manx for many generations and I guess I just feel at home here."

Carly nodded. "I feel at home in my small town, too," she told him. "I even went to college there. This is the first time I've been away from it for more than a week."

Doncan raised an eyebrow. "Don't you worry that you might be missing out on things by staying in one place?" he asked gently.

"What sort of things?" she challenged. "I do travel and I love to visit big cities so that I can experience historical sites and museums and whatever. I just have no desire to live anywhere other than home."

Doncan nodded. "I'm exactly the same," he told her. "Even if the island does get a bit claustrophobic once in a while."

"In what way?" Carly was intrigued.

"When I was a kid, I played tennis against the same group of other kids at every single tournament," Doncan grinned. "There were four or five of us who were the same age and skill level and we played each other three or four times a year. We always finished in the same order as well."

Carly grinned. "That does sound like it would get a bit frustrating. At least in my small town I'm only a short drive from other towns."

"It got worse as I got older, too," Doncan told her. "I think I'd been out with just about every eligible girl in Laxey by the time I was sixteen."

Carly laughed. "So then you had to start dating girls from Douglas?" she asked.

"Which was hard, because I didn't have a car," he told her.

"So where do you find girls to date now?" she asked, knowing that the wine was behind the question.

Doncan laughed. "There are a lot more people moving to the island these days than there were when I was a kid," he told her with a smile. "With the growth of the banking sector, there has been a real influx of 'come-overs' to work with banks and insurance companies. And I have a car now, so I can actually take out women from anywhere on the island."

Carly felt herself blushing, although she wasn't sure why. "I'm sure handsome lawyers are in demand," she muttered as she drained her glass for the second time.

Doncan refilled it for her with a smile. "Does that mean that you think I'm handsome?" he asked as he leaned towards her to reach the glass. His face was far too close to hers for her comfort.

"Of course you are," she told him, staring into his eyes with all the artificial bravado she could muster.

Doncan only laughed softly. "Your turn," he told her after he had taken a sip from his own glass.

The waiter arrived with the first course, which gave Carly time to think. She was practically flirting with the man and that simply wouldn't do.

"My story is even more boring than yours," she told Doncan once the waiter left. "I was born and raised in Meadville, went to college there, and now I live and work there. Nothing exciting at all."

"What about your ex-boyfriend? How long did you say you two were together?"

"We met in third grade," Carly answered, feeling uncomfortable about the direction that the conversation was taking. "I was nine and his family had just moved from Ohio to Pennsylvania. Our teacher asked me to help him find the cafeteria on the first day of school and we were a couple from that day until last week."

"You never broke up for a short time, even?" Doncan was amazed.

"Not even a single day," Carly confirmed. "Tom went to Allegheny as well, although he decided after a year that college wasn't the best choice for him. He has an apartment downtown where he lives with a few of the same guys we've known since grade school. I just bought a little house in a more suburban area. I was supposed to be spending the summer painting and decorating, but now I'm here instead."

"You should have had Tom to do the painting and decorating for you while you were gone," Doncan suggested.

"Oh, goodness no," Carly was appalled at the idea.

"Why not?"

"It's my little house." She found she was struggling to explain how she felt. "I know exactly how I want it and I don't think Tom would get everything exactly right."

"But up until a few days ago, you were planning to marry him, right? So surely you expected him to live there one day?"

"Well, yes, I mean, I guess so." Carly frowned. She couldn't quite explain how she felt to Doncan, mainly because she wasn't sure herself. The little house was hers, and while she loved Tom, she really couldn't picture him living in it.

The waiter arrived with the main course just in time to save her from having to try to explain further. Doncan, perhaps sensing her unease, changed the subject to neutral topics. After an amazing chocolate dessert that left Carly stuffed almost to the point of being uncomfortable, the pair headed back to Douglas and Carly's hotel. Doncan insisted on seeing Carly safely to her room, where she had left the curtains open on the huge windows that overlooked the promenade.

"It is such a gorgeous view," she sighed once she'd opened the door. She didn't turn on any lights. Instead she walked to the nearest window and watched the people walking on the promenade and the waves washing onto shore. Doncan joined her at the window.

Carly took a deep breath, inhaling Doncan's spicy cologne. He smelled wonderful and expensive and Carly couldn't help but remember how good it had felt to be in his arms. She turned towards him, torn between wanting him to repeat the kiss and wanting him to leave.

Doncan studied her for a moment in the reflected illumination of the streetlights below. For several seconds Carly was convinced that he was going to kiss her again, but then he sighed and the spell was broken.

"I'd better let you get some sleep," he said quietly. "I hope you had fun today. I have plans for tomorrow, but I can arrange for a taxi if you wanted to go anywhere?"

Carly couldn't think. "No, that's okay," she finally muttered. "I'll just spend some time exploring Douglas."

"Do you want me to have a taxi here on Monday morning to take you back to Bessie's cottage, then?"

"Sure, that sounds good," Carly agreed. "I need to start sorting out the rest of the paperwork, her clothes, all the furniture...." she trailed off, feeling overwhelmed by the job at hand.

"I would suggest that the furniture should be your first priority," Doncan told her. "I know a local auction firm that would love to get their hands on all of it, assuming you don't want to ship some back to Pennsylvania."

"I'll have to talk to Granny," Carly said hesitantly. Shipping furniture would undoubtedly be expensive, but some of the pieces were gorgeous and Carly hated the thought of them all being sold to strangers.

"Great, I'll have someone here for you Monday morning at nine. You can meet them out front, if that's okay. If you can figure out the furniture by the end of the week, we can talk about getting the place sold."

"That sounds great." Carly was suddenly exhausted and just wanted Doncan to leave so she could get some rest.

Doncan hesitated for a second and Carly wondered again if he might kiss her, but he finally simply smiled at her and then turned and left. Carly stayed where she was at the window and watched. A few minutes later she saw Doncan walk out of the hotel and climb into his car.

She shut the curtains and got ready for bed slowly, thoughts of Doncan occupying far too much of her mind. "You did not want him to kiss you," she told herself in the mirror as she washed away her makeup. "You're still in love with Tom," she reminded herself as the brushed her hair. But it was Doncan who filled her dreams that evening, and she woke up on Sunday feeling mad at the world.

❧ 8 ❧

Carly spent her Sunday wandering around the small shops in downtown Douglas. She treated herself to some expensive but amazing looking chocolate truffles from a small chocolate shop and bought a few little gifts for the people back home. As she passed an estate agent's office, she gave in to impulse and went inside.

"Can I help you?" the woman behind the desk asked politely.

"I think I would like to get a property appraised," Carly said slowly, feeling as if she were sneaking around behind Doncan's back.

"Is this a property that you own?"

"Yes, it's a cottage really, in Laxey, and I don't think I need a formal appraisal, just an idea of what it's worth," Carly said, feeling again as if she were in over her head.

"This must be Bessie's cottage that you're talking about," the woman smiled.

"How did you know that?" Carly said in surprise.

"It's a small island. Bessie passed away last year and apparently left everything, including her cottage in Laxey, to her sister's family in America. You're clearly American. I just put two and two together."

Carly smiled. "You're absolutely right. It is Bessie's cottage I'm talking about."

"I thought Doncan Quayle was sorting out the sale on that property," the woman said in a questioning tone.

"He is," Carly answered, worried now about the whole conversation getting back to Doncan. "I just wanted to get a rough idea of the value of the place and I didn't want to bother him on a Sunday."

The woman didn't look convinced. "Well, I can't give you a formal appraisal without going through the property, but I can give you a very rough estimate based on location, if you think that would help."

"Oh yes, please," Carly answered.

"I've never been inside the cottage," the woman told her. "But I understand that it needs some modernization before anyone would be willing to live in it."

"Yes," Carly agreed. "It does need a new kitchen and new bathrooms at the very least."

The woman nodded. "In that case, I think the best thing you could do is find a developer who would be interested in the land rather than the cottage itself, especially if you're looking for a quick sale. Finding someone who wants to buy the cottage and redo it might take time, but a developer who would want to just tear it down and rebuild could move faster."

Carly nodded reluctantly. "I guess I feel badly about the idea of anyone tearing down the cottage," she told the woman.

The woman smiled sympathetically. "Well, emotions aside, I would suggest a developer might be willing to pay somewhere between three and four hundred thousand for the place. You would probably get closer to the lower end from someone who wanted to actually live in the cottage, because they would have to figure in the cost of renovations."

Carly nodded. "Thank you so much for your help," she told the woman.

The woman handed Carly her card. "If you decide to list the property, please consider giving me a call," she told her.

Carly promised to do that as she left the building. She headed back to her hotel to call Granny and tell her the news.

"It sounds like the quote from Doncan is just about right," she told Granny in summary, after telling her about the visit.

"Yes, it does," Granny agreed. "Especially if we sell to a developer."

Carly sighed and changed the subject, feeling reluctant to consider that someone might want to tear the cottage down. "We need to talk about the furniture, as well," she told her relative. "I hate to just sell everything to strangers. So much of it is really solid wood and a lot of things must be valuable antiques."

"I trust your judgement," Granny insisted. "If you really like some of it, get Mr. Quayle to arrange to have it shipped. It sounds as if the estate can afford it."

"I hate to be making all these decisions by myself," Carly told her grandmother.

"If you really aren't sure about something, see if Mr. Quayle can arrange to have some of it put into storage," Granny suggested. "Then, when I'm better I can go over there myself and check it all out."

Carly smiled at the phone. "What a great idea," she replied. "I think you'll love the island. It's just beautiful."

"Yes, well, you'll have to come with me when I go. Maybe we can plan it for your Christmas vacation."

Carly was silent for a moment. Christmas wasn't that far away and she'd love to have a chance to visit the island again. With a Christmas wedding off the cards, another trip to the island might be just what she needed.

"Let's not make any plans yet," she said slowly. "You need the okay from your doctor before you start planning to fly around the world."

Granny laughed. "The doctor says I'm healing really well for my age," she told Carly. "I reckon that by Christmas I'll be ready for a week in the Isle of Man. And then, once I get home, I expect I'll start on my travels around the states. I've got a lot of nieces and nephews and cousins and grandchildren to visit."

"That sounds wonderful, Granny," Carly told her. "You keep working on getting well and I'll put the best of the furniture into storage until you can see it."

"Great, now that's business out of the way," Granny replied. "Time for you to tell me about how you and Mr. Quayle are getting along."

"What do you mean?" Carly asked in an innocent tone.

"Well, the last time we talked he had just kissed you," Granny reminded her. "So has he kissed you again? Is he ready to marry you and keep you there forever?"

Carly forced out a laugh. "Honestly, Granny, what a crazy idea. He's a lawyer and I'm his client. That's all there is to it."

"So no more kissing?" Granny sounded disappointed.

"No more kissing," Carly said emphatically. "I've told him all about Tom, so he knows that I've just had my heart broken and I'm not looking for romance."

"Now why would you do something stupid like that?"

"Because I'm not available!" Carly insisted. "I still love Tom and I'm devastated that he dumped me."

"Are you really?" Granny asked, concern in her voice. "Because I don't think you are. I think you're just unwilling to accept just how ill-suited you and Tom really were."

"Even if Tom and I weren't a perfect match, Mr. Quayle and I aren't either," Carly argued. "I don't want to live here and he doesn't want to live in America. It would never work."

"So just have a fling with the man," Granny suggested with a wicked laugh. "Use him to get over Tom and then, when you get back, you can start working on finding the perfect man."

Carly sighed. "I don't think so, Granny," was all that she answered. The whole topic had worn her out, and she felt depressed and miserable.

With the phone call wrapped up, she ordered her dinner from room service and, after she had eaten it, ran a hot bath. Soaking in the tub, she ate her expensive truffles and let her mind wander. After several minutes, during which she fought to keep herself from thinking about Doncan, she gave up and pulled the plug on the tub.

She went to bed on Sunday night feeling even more fed up and frustrated with the world. Her dreams were a tangled mess of Doncan, her grandmother and the mysterious costumed woman from Castle Rushen who seemed to be trying to tell her something.

Monday morning she felt more tired than she had when she'd gone to bed. A long and hot shower helped only a little bit, but she got dressed and managed to throw on a bit of makeup and swallow a piece of toast in the hotel dining room by nine o'clock. She was sitting on the front steps of the hotel when Doncan pulled up.

She immediately felt flustered. "Oh, I wasn't expecting you," she said as a greeting when he reached her side.

Doncan smiled at her. "I forgot to arrange the taxi last night so it just seemed easier to stop by myself rather than try to sort it out this morning."

"So you've just stopped to tell me that you forgot?" Carly asked in confusion.

"No, I've stopped to take you to Laxey. I already called Breesha and told her that I'll be a little bit late this morning."

"Are you sure you have time?" Carly wasn't certain why she was arguing.

"I'm sure," Doncan took her arm and helped her into the car.

They were both silent as he pulled away from the curb into traffic.

"How much would it cost to ship some of the furniture to Granny in America?" Carly broke the silence with the question that had been nagging at her since she had spoken to Granny the previous day.

"That would depend on how many pieces you wanted to ship," Doncan answered. "It wouldn't be terribly cheap, but it would probably be worth it to send some of the more valuable pieces if you wanted to keep them in the family."

"That's just it," Carly exclaimed. "I want to keep some of Bessie's things and I think Granny would love to have them. But not if it is going to cost a fortune to get them to her."

"When I get to the office, I'll make a few phone calls," Doncan told her. "I have a friend who owns a shipping firm. I'll see if he can give me a rough idea of the costs involved."

"That would be great," Carly answered. "In the meantime, Granny suggests that we put the best things into storage. She wants to come and visit herself and make sure she gets what she wants."

Doncan laughed, sounding surprised. "I think I'm really looking forward to meeting her," he told Carly. "Storage isn't that expensive, but I may have a better solution. Let me make some calls from my office and I'll tell you more when I pick you up this afternoon."

"You're picking me up?" The words were out before Carly could stop them.

Doncan laughed again. "Yes, if you don't mind," he told her, grinning at her. "I figured I may as well, since I'm terrible at remembering to book taxis. I'll pick you up around five, if that suits you. We can grab a pizza or some Chinese takeaway on the way back to Douglas."

"That sounds great," Carly agreed, reminding herself sternly that this was all just business.

Doncan pulled up in front of the cottage and turned to face Carly. "I should have given you the key when you first arrived," he told her, handing her the front door key and a slip of paper with the alarm code written on it. "Did you think about lunch?"

"Lunch?" Carly asked.

"Lunch," Doncan grinned at her. "It's food that's usually eaten around midday, which is noon to you. It should keep you from being starving and grumpy when I get back at five."

"Oh, no, I didn't think about lunch," Carly admitted.

"Good thing I did," Doncan smiled at her and handed her an insulated bag. "It's just a couple of sandwiches and a cold drink," he told her. "Nothing exciting, but it should keep you from foraging through Bessie's kitchen. I guarantee you don't want to eat anything you find in there."

Carly shuddered as she thought about food that would have been sitting in cupboards for the last year. "I'd better clean out the kitchen first," she said, more to herself than to Doncan.

"I'm only teasing," Doncan assured her. "When Bessie passed away I had a crew come out and clear out the kitchen. There shouldn't be anything left in there, even if you're starving."

"Well, thank you very much for thinking about lunch for me," Carly said politely. "I guess I'll see you around five."

"See you later, then." Doncan waited as she climbed out of the car and unlocked the cottage door.

"You do have your phone for emergencies, right?" he called as she turned back to wave goodbye to him.

"Yes, thanks," Carly replied, pointing to her handbag with the hand that held the packed lunch.

Once inside the cottage, Carly shut the door and looked around. She suddenly felt overwhelmed and wasn't sure where to even start. With a sigh, she headed into the kitchen and set her lunch on the small table. She glanced in a few cupboards and was pleased to see that Doncan was correct. The cupboards were empty of food, but full of plates and glasses and whatnot.

She walked through each room, looking at the solidly built wooden furniture and wondering about its value. It would probably be best to just put it all in storage until Granny could look at it. Upstairs, she opened a huge wardrobe in one of the spare bedrooms and looked at rack after rack of Bessie's clothes. She pulled a top out at random and held it against herself. Clearly, Bessie had been on the thin side.

Carly flipped along the bar of clothes, surprised at all the bright colors and modern styles. Bessie might have been old, but she apparently didn't dress like an old lady. There were many items that Carly could imagine Granny or her mother wearing and even a couple that Carly herself might consider.

On the top of the wardrobe there were a few suitcases, and Carly pulled one down and opened it. She slowly began to pack up the newest and nicest items from the wardrobe. She had only brought one small case with her, so she should be able to take at least one extra one back when she returned home.

The case seemed to fill up very quickly and Carly pulled down a second case, amazed at how many of the clothes were in excellent condition. She had started a small pile of some of the more worn or less stylish pieces to donate somewhere, but the pile of things she was keeping was considerably larger.

She opened the second case and started to add the next dress when she noticed the small bag that was already in the bottom of the case.

The three small hardcover books that were in the bag had plain covers. Carly opened the first and gasped. She had found Bessie's diaries.

As soon as she read the first few lines, she stopped herself. Diaries were very personal. Maybe she shouldn't read them. Still, Granny had told her to read whatever she found at Bessie's house. And she really wanted to read the diaries. Arguing with herself, Carly carried the diaries down to the kitchen and put them with her lunch. Then she headed back upstairs to finish packing up the clothes.

By noon she was hungry and burning with curiosity in almost equal measure. She carried the two heavy suitcases downstairs and put them by the front door. She would take them back to Douglas tonight and figure out how to get them home later. It was time for a lunch break.

As she unpacked the sandwiches, drink, potato chips, cookies and candy that Doncan had packed, Carly suddenly wondered how the man had remembered to pack her a lunch, but forgotten to call her a taxi. It was an unanswerable question, so she simply dug into the miniature feast, one eye on the bag containing the diaries.

After she finished eating she washed her hands well, then she carefully opened the bag and took the books out. She glanced at the dates on the first page of each and put them into order. The first entry in the first one was dated the 15th of March 1939.

I saw mother in town yesterday. She didn't see me and I hid behind a counter until she left the store. Just looking at her makes me feel sad. I still blame her and father for Matthew's death. He's been gone for almost ten years and I sometimes still feel very alone. I do feel happy in my little house by the sea.

Carly felt tears springing into her eyes as she read the sad words. Poor Bessie had been so devastated by the death of her true love. She read through the next several pages. Each short entry was almost exactly the same. Bessie talked about her life on the island, telling what food she bought and prepared, the people she saw in the streets of the town, and what weather the day had brought. Some entries were happier than others.

10th October

I bought a new couch for my little house today. I moved it around the room about a dozen times, looking for the perfect spot to put it in. I finally settled on a spot near the window. I can sit and look out at the sea. My little house is just about perfect. I find that I don't miss America, even though I still miss Matthew. I wonder how he would have felt about us staying on the island after we'd married. Now that I'm feeling settled here, I can't imagine ever wanting to leave again.

Carly read a few more pages and then put the diaries to one side. She would read more later, back in her room. She glanced at her watch. It was nearly two o'clock. Doncan would be back in three hours and she had only just begun to sort through things.

She put the bag with the diaries on top of the suitcases in the hall and headed back upstairs, grabbing a handful of garbage bags from the kitchen as she went. In Bessie's room she filled three garbage bags with stuffed animals. Doncan would have some idea of what to do with them.

She then moved into the spare bedroom where she found another empty suitcase. She began to fill it with papers from the office, sorting them as she went along.

Bills, catalogues and receipts from grocery stores and similar papers all went into garbage bags. Receipts for things like furniture and remodeling the house went into a pile in the bottom of the suitcase. All of the letters and correspondence that she found went into the suitcase as well. It was hard for her to keep herself focused on sorting the paperwork. All she really wanted to do was sit down and read the diaries.

The afternoon passed quickly and Doncan was tapping on the cottage door as she was adding a couple of heavy sweaters to the top of the third case. She hoped that they would help hold all of the paperwork in place.

"Did you have a productive day?" Doncan asked as he took in her flushed and dusty face.

"I hope so," Carly answered, rubbing her nose, which felt dust clogged.

"What's in the bags and cases?" Doncan noticed the things that Carly had left by the door.

"The bags are filled with stuffed animals," Carly answered. "I was hoping you might have some idea of what we could do with them."

Doncan laughed. "Actually, the hospital will be happy to take them off your hands," he told her. "They can clean and sanitize them and then give them to small children who come in for treatment."

Carly smiled. "That's a great idea," she said.

"What about the suitcases?" Doncan questioned after he put the bags of toys into his car.

"Two cases are filled with clothes that are too nice to just give away," Carly answered. "The other one is full of papers that I want to go through back at the hotel. There are a few receipts for furniture and the various bits of work that Bessie had done on the house, but mostly there are lots and lots of letters."

"Bessie liked to write letters to people. Even in her later years, when everyone started emailing, she still enjoyed writing to people on her personal stationery."

"My grandmother still has a bunch of letters that Bessie sent to her sister. The stationery was something special. Maybe if I bought something like that I'd feel more like writing letters by hand, too."

Doncan laughed. "Email is too convenient," he told her. "Imagine having to wait for a letter to cross the Atlantic and then wait for the reply to make the return trip? Now you can email America and have an answer in minutes."

"And then the email is deleted and future generations will have no way of learning about us."

Doncan laughed again. "I'm not sure that's a bad thing."

Carly had to smile. "I still think we are missing out somehow," she told him. "I bet Bessie loved rereading the love letters she'd received from Matthew Saunders. No one has ever written me a love letter. Love emails just aren't the same thing." When she thought about it, no one had ever sent her a love email, either. Tom just wasn't the type of guy to express his emotions in print.

Doncan grinned at her. "I've never sent a love email or a love letter," he told her in a confiding tone. "I'm a lawyer. We never put anything in writing."

Carly laughed and then they loaded the three cases into Doncan's car with the stuffed animals. Carly carefully added the small bag with the diaries to the truck as well.

"What's in the little bag?" Doncan noticed and asked.

"Bessie's diaries," Carly said hesitantly. They were so very personal that she wasn't sure she wanted anyone else to know that they even existed.

"I have more of them at the office," Doncan replied. "I think there are probably half a dozen or more there, from the last twenty years or so."

"These are earlier," Carly told him. "Starting from about ten years after Matthew died. I only read a little bit, but they really just talk about her life on the island."

"I'll have to get the rest of them to you," Doncan told her. "They're from a later period, but you might find them interesting and they might help with your book."

Carly nodded and then climbed into the car, eager to get back to the hotel and do some reading.

"I thought since we did pizza last time, we should try Chinese tonight," Doncan told her. "Is that okay?"

"Sure." Carly didn't really care what they ate, now that she was done at the cottage. She wanted to get back to the diaries.

Doncan obviously noticed her distracted air. "Eager to read the diaries, are you?"

"Just a little," Carly grinned, feeling sheepish. "I'm fascinated by Bessie's life. It wasn't that long ago, but it feels so different from mine."

"What do you like to eat?" Doncan asked her.

"Oh, anything that isn't too spicy," Carly answered.

Doncan made a quick phone call, ordering several different dishes that all sounded like nothing Carly had ever eaten before. Then they made their way out of Laxey and back towards Douglas.

Doncan made a quick stop at the little Chinese restaurant a few blocks away from Carly's hotel, dashing in to grab a huge bag of food. The smell made Carly's mouth water as she held the bag on the trip to the hotel.

In her room, she quickly dug out the plates and plastic cutlery that the restaurant had provided, while Doncan took out and lined up the many boxes of different dishes. As he opened each one, he told Carly what it was, until Carly felt as if her head were spinning.

"You got way too much," she said as she studied the selection.

"I wanted to be sure to get something you would like," he countered.

"I'm sure it's all delicious," Carly said spooning up small portions of the least exotic looking choices.

Doncan quickly filled his dish with much larger helpings of his favorites. For a moment they were silent as they both ate.

"Everything is delicious," Carly said after a while. She quickly helped herself to a second helping of the dishes she had liked the best.

"I'm glad," Doncan grinned at her and she suddenly found herself inexplicably blushing under his gaze.

The food disappeared rapidly and Carly finally sat back with a sigh. "That was fabulous," she told Doncan, avoiding his eyes by looking out at the view.

"I'm really pleased that you enjoyed it," he answered. "And I know you're eager to get to those diaries, so I won't hang around."

Carly thought about protesting, but he was right. She did want to get back to reading the diaries. She was just as eager to get rid of him. There was something about being around him that made her feel unsettled.

"Do you want me to run you back out to the cottage again tomorrow?" Doncan asked as he headed for the door.

"I guess so," Carly answered. "There's so much more to go through."

"I'll make sure I bring you some boxes tomorrow," Doncan told her. "You can start packing up the smaller things. You need to make two piles, one for things you want to put into storage and a second for things you want to sell. Which reminds me, I have a house in Laxey that is currently sitting empty. If you want, you are more than welcome to move anything you think your grandmother will want to look at into that house. That way you don't have to pay for storage."

"Are you sure?" Carly asked hesitantly. "I mean, what if Granny can't get here for months and months?"

"I don't have any plans to use the house in the short term," Doncan assured her. "And I don't want to rent it out, either. I'm still working on remodeling a lot of it. If I do decide that I want to use it, I can always arrange to have your things put into storage at that point. In the meantime, you might as well save your Granny some money."

Carly nodded. "That would be great," she said, still turning the idea over in her head. Something about the plan worried her, but she wasn't sure what it was.

"I'll have a contract drawn up for you to sign," Doncan told her. "We can do an inventory of exactly what gets moved into the house and have it all valued as well. I'll add the contents to my property insurance and that way we are all covered if something goes wrong."

Carly nodded. Leave it to a lawyer to have it all figured out.

"I'll see if I can arrange for a moving company to start relocating things as soon as possible."

Carly gasped in surprise. "How soon would that be?"

"I'm not sure, but we might as well get some of the bigger furniture pieces moved sooner, rather than later," Doncan suggested reasonably. "Unless you would rather wait."

"No," Carly sighed. "If you can get me some boxes, I'll start packing tomorrow. I'm sure there will be a lot of things to sell, as well. I'm not planning on storing everything, just the things I think Granny might want."

"I suggest you store everything that you think she might even possibly want," Doncan told her. "We can always sell it later, but once it's gone we can't get it back."

Carly grinned at him. "You might just regret that advice," she sighed. "I hate the thought of getting rid of anything. Just how big is your house in Laxey?"

"Big enough," he told her with a smile.

He paused at the door to the room and looked back at her where she was still sitting at the small table. For a second she thought he might come back over and kiss her goodbye, but he simply stared at her for a moment and then smiled again.

"I'll see you tomorrow," he told her as he left.

Carly thought about the strange goodbye for a moment, but the lure of the diaries was stronger than her curiosity about Doncan's behavior, at least for the moment.

She cleared away the remnants of dinner and wiped the table carefully. Then she sat down and opened the first book again, quickly finding her place.

She read page after page of entries about Bessie's life, finding them somewhat interesting, but not exactly exciting. The Second World War had begun now, and many entries talked about how much had changed and yet how much had stayed the same on the island due to world events. Carly decided to finish the first book and then take a break. The last entry, however, changed her mind.

10th December

Doncan Quayle had a Christmas party tonight. Nothing very fancy, because of the war, but something to mark the season. He insisted that I come along. My parents were not invited. They don't do business with his firm. He did have an unexpected guest however. His brother, Mr. Peter Quayle, who now lives in Australia, came back to the island yesterday for an extended visit. He is a very handsome man, about two years older than myself. All of the ladies wanted to dance with him. He did ask me to dance, but I refused. Widowed ladies don't dance with strange men. We did talk for a short time, though. He was very pleasant.

Carly sat back and stared out the window. Could this be the Peter who was mentioned in the letter from Matthew's mother?

She opened up the suitcase of paperwork and dug through it, trying to find the letter in question. Rereading it did nothing to help her answer the question, however. She quickly opened the next diary, eager to find out more. The first few entries were the same repetitive account of daily life on the island. Carly scanned through them, looking for more about the mysterious Peter.

Christmas Day

It is hard not think about Matthew on Christmas. It was Christmas when he asked me to be his wife. I was so happy to say yes. This year I spent the day quietly. A few of the neighbour children stopped by with small presents for me and I gave them all little bits of sugar candy that I made from a recipe I learned in America.

I took a long walk in the afternoon and was surprised to bump into Mr. Peter Quayle. He said he'd needed a break from all of his brother's small children. I could sympathise. He walked with me for a short time, telling me all about life in Australia. He makes it sound very interesting.

Carly grinned. It seemed like a romance was beginning. She sobered when she remembered that Bessie had remained single. Clearly she and Peter weren't going to have a happily ever after. Frowning, she shut the diary and pushed it away. She needed a break from Bessie's life.

She looked out at the promenade below her. The day had been warm and it was dry. A walk along the seafront would clear her head, she decided. She grabbed a light jacket and headed out.

While she started the walk thinking almost obsessively about Bessie and the budding romance that was playing out in the diaries, her mind soon switched itself onto thoughts about Doncan Quayle. He had been a perfect gentleman all day, she reminded herself, strictly business without even a hint of flirting.

It disturbed her just how disappointed she was by that. She tried to turn her thoughts to Tom, but failed miserably. Her brain was uninterested in Tom. Instead, it wanted to ponder why Doncan had taken the time to drive her to Laxey himself instead of calling her a taxi. And why he'd brought her a packed lunch. And why he was picking her back up tomorrow, when he could have made other arrangements. And what he could possibly have been thinking when he stood in the doorway and stared at her.

Carly walked briskly the entire length of the seaside walkway. At the far end, she studied the memorial to the fifty people who died in the Summerland Disaster, a fire that had destroyed an entertainment complex on the site in 1973. Then she slowly made her way back to her hotel. She needed to stop thinking about Doncan Quayle as anything other than her lawyer, she reminded herself. She thought about how eager he was to help her get everything sorted out. And once everything was sorted, she would be leaving. He was probably eager for that to happen as well.

Carly sighed as, back in her hotel room, she got ready for bed. Her love life was turning into a big disaster. The man she was planning to marry had dumped her, and all she could think about was another man who was wrong for her in every possible way. Anyway, Doncan was probably completely and totally uninterested in her. She sighed. If she didn't want to think about how miserable her own love life was, she could think about Bessie's. The big difference was that she knew there wasn't going to be any happily ever after for Bessie. She could still hope that her own life would be different.

❧ 9 ❧

Tuesday turned out to be almost identical to Monday in many ways. Doncan drove her to the cottage in the morning, providing her with yet another carefully prepared lunch. She spent the day carefully going through the contents of the kitchen, packing box after box with plates, bowls, cutlery, and miscellaneous small appliances. Each box was carefully marked "for storage" or "for sale."

At five o'clock, Doncan picked her back up and drove her back to her hotel, this time stopping at one of the island's few fast-food chain restaurants to pick up some dinner. Carly was amazed as she ate the hamburger and french fries that were identical to the ones she could have had just down the street from her little house in Meadville.

Doncan joined her for the quick meal, but he excused himself politely as soon as the last fry was eaten. Carly sat by the huge windows and watched him walk to his car. Clearly he was determined to keep things strictly professional between them. Which was exactly what Carly kept insisting to herself that she wanted.

Wednesday morning Doncan was back at nine to pick her up again. She grinned at him as he handed her yet another packed lunch.

"You really have to stop being so nice to me," she said, teasingly.

"Why?" Doncan smiled back at her. "You're a client. Being nice to you is my job. Besides that, you're a good person and I like being nice to you."

Carly found herself blushing as she struggled to think of an appropriate reply. After an uncomfortable pause, Doncan changed the subject.

"Would you like to do something completely different tonight and have dinner with a real Manx family?"

Carly wasn't sure how to reply to the question.

Doncan smiled and then continued. "Breesha was talking to my father the other day and mentioned that you were here. My parents insisted that I must bring you to dinner at their house so that they can meet you. They were quite close to Bessie and they want to make sure that you're being well taken care of while you are here."

Carly smiled. "That's kind of them, but totally unnecessary."

"Okay, well, let me give you my mother's number and you can call and tell her that. I'm under strict orders to bring you to dinner tonight. I may be nearly forty, but I still follow orders from my mum."

Carly laughed at the thought of anyone giving the sophisticated man orders. "Really?" she giggled. "In that case I guess I better just go along."

Doncan gave her a relieved smile. "Thank you," he told her. "You have no idea how much easier you've just made my life."

Carly laughed again. "You're making your mother sound like an ogre," she told him.

Now Doncan laughed. "Please don't tell her that tonight," he pleaded with her, half seriously. "And please tell her that I'm taking very good care of you."

"Well, you are driving me back and forth every day and packing me a yummy lunch and buying me dinner. I don't think I could possibly find anything to complain about," Carly assured him, pushing all thoughts about their shared kiss out of her mind.

"Great," Doncan smiled. "I'll pick you up around five and take you back to the hotel so you can shower and change. You don't have to dress up or anything, but I expect you'll be dusty after packing all day."

Carly agreed easily, surprised that Doncan was taking the dinner so seriously. It was nice of his parents to want to meet her, as a mark of respect towards Bessie, but Doncan was almost acting as if he was bringing her home as a date.

As soon as the thought entered Carly's mind she firmly squashed it and quickly got out of Doncan's car. She welcomed the opportunity to talk to Doncan's family and find out more about Bessie, but that was all that this evening was about and she couldn't possibly read any more into it than that.

At any rate, Doncan was definitely right about the dust. Carly was pretty well covered in it when he returned to pick her up.

"What have you been doing?" he asked as he surveyed her filthy clothes.

"I thought I would see what was under the bed," she said, shrugging. "And right in the middle of the space was a piece of paper that had obviously fallen under there a long time ago."

"So you crawled under the bed to get it?" Doncan asked incredulously. Carly nodded.

"Why didn't you just wait until we move the furniture out of the room?"

"I guess I didn't think of that," she said sheepishly.

"Well, I hope it was worth it," Doncan told her with a grin. "What was it?"

Carly shook her head. "An electricity bill from 1993," she sighed. "I was so disappointed that I almost put it back!"

Doncan laughed, and after a second Carly joined in.

"Right, back to the hotel with you," Doncan told her. "I'll drop you off and you can get cleaned up and changed and then I'll pick you back up."

Carly chatted all the way back to Douglas about the various things she'd packed and sorted during the day. When she was nervous she had a tendency to talk too much and she found that she simply couldn't stop babbling as they drove along. Finally she ran out of things to discuss and took a deep breath. She forced herself to hold her breath until she felt herself calm down, at least a little bit. She needed to get herself under control before she met Doncan's parents or they would think she was an idiot.

Doncan, for his part, said very little on the drive. He dropped her off and promised to return in an hour.

Carly raced inside and tore off her grimy clothes. She took a quick shower and then, wrapped in just a towel, carefully styled her hair and applied fresh makeup.

"I want to look good for Doncan's parents," she told her mirror self sternly. "This has nothing to do with Doncan." Her mirror image didn't seem to believe her, but Carly ignored the skeptical look as she applied an extra coat of mascara.

She'd packed lightly for the trip to the island, only bringing what she absolutely had to bring. Now she was sorry that she hadn't brought more. She only had one dress left in her case that Doncan hadn't seen her wearing. She pulled the crumpled sundress from the bag and shook it out. The low-cut neckline seemed a bit too sexy for dinner with someone's parents.

She looked through her other choices, most of which had just been returned from the hotel's laundry department. The only other option was the dress she had just worn a few days earlier. She sighed and slipped on the dress that Doncan hadn't seen.

She did a slow turn in front of the mirror. "You look wonderful," her mirror self told her. "And very sexy."

Carly frowned at her reflected image. "I don't want to look sexy," she told herself. She glanced back at the clothes that had just been returned to her. A few items were being held onto their hangers with safety pins. That was just the thing she needed, she decided.

A few minutes later, with the neckline of the dress firmly pinned together, Carly decided that she was as ready as she would ever be. It's only dinner with some of Bessie's old friends, she reminded herself as she watched for Doncan's car to arrive. That didn't stop her heart from skipping a beat when she saw him pull up. Her pulse raced as she noted how wonderful he looked in the casual shirt and perfectly tailored pants he had changed into.

She quickly left her room and headed down to meet him in the lobby. Her room suddenly felt too intimate to be alone in with the handsome man.

The journey back to Laxey was an uncomfortable one. Carly felt inexplicably nervous about the dinner, and whatever Doncan was feeling, he kept silent during the drive. When he pulled into a long driveway that led to a huge house set among what looked like acres of trees, Carly's nerves got even worse.

Doncan smiled at her pale face as he parked the car. "It is a rather large house," he told her apologetically. "But they bought it a very long time ago when house prices were much lower."

"I wasn't expecting a mansion," Carly told him in a quiet voice.

Doncan laughed. "It isn't quite that," he assured her. "And my parents are perfectly normal people. Don't worry. They would love you just because you're Bessie's great-niece, even if you weren't wonderful."

Carly wondered exactly what Doncan meant by that comment. Did he think she was wonderful? Turning his words over and over in her head distracted her from worrying about the evening for a few moments anyway. Before she'd realized it, she was out of the car and walking into Doncan's parents' spacious foyer. She tried not to gawk at what looked like priceless antiques and original artwork as they made their way down a long corridor to a comfortable living room at the back of the house.

Carly relaxed slightly when she saw that she was appropriately dressed. The room was spacious, but not overwhelmingly so, and it was furnished with large and comfortable-looking couches and chairs that were all centered on a large wood-burning fireplace. Everyone in the room made their way to the door to greet the newcomers with a flurry of introductions.

"Ah, Carly." Doncan's father looked like an older and more distinguished version of Doncan himself. He was similarly dressed, but wearing slippers rather than shoes. His hair was gray but his eyes were bright and intelligent. "It is wonderful to meet you. Doncan and Breesha have both told me a little bit about you. It's unfortunate that Bessie never got to know you. I'm sure she would have liked to have known her family in America."

Carly felt herself blush, feeling suddenly as if she should have made more of an effort to find out about her family history. "I didn't know she existed until recently," she tried to explain.

"Oh no, of course you didn't," Doncan senior waved away Carly's explanations. "Bessie was such a private woman, and really quite shy. It would never have occurred to her to invite anyone whom she hadn't met to come to visit. I'm sure she used to invite her sister to come to see her, but once Katherine passed away, I'm sure she did little more than send an occasional Christmas card to Katherine's children."

"From what I understand from my Granny, that's exactly right," Carly told him.

"How do you do?" The woman was gray-haired as well, but her bright blue eyes seemed to miss nothing as she shook Carly's hand. Her outfit was casual, but looked expensive. "I'm Doncan's mother, Jane, and I'm ever so pleased to meet you."

Carly murmured an appropriate reply, hoping that she would remember everyone's name as the evening wore on.

"And I'm Elizabeth Christian." A younger woman extended her hand. "I'm Doncan's little sister and everyone calls me Beth." Carly smiled as she shook the woman's hand. She too looked casually but expensively dressed. She was very pretty, with light brown hair and her mother's blue eyes.

"This is my husband, Mark," Beth continued, gesturing towards the tall man who was standing behind her. He nodded at Carly and then shook her hand shyly.

Carly hid her surprise as she studied the couple. Mark was not at all the sort of man that she would have expected to be married to the stunning and vivacious Beth. While he wasn't unattractive, Mark was rather ordinary looking and seemed very shy.

"We're both doctors with the local family practice," Beth talked over Carly's thoughts. "I specialize in women's heath issues and Mark is our pediatric specialist."

"Wow, I'm not sure I would want to work with my husband," Carly blurted out without thinking.

Beth and Mark both laughed. "It has its moments," Mark told her in an almost whispery voice.

Now everyone laughed and Carly felt slightly more at ease with all of them. A second later she heard the thundering noise of a herd of elephants rumbling across the wooden floors above them. Suddenly a door in the back wall of the room flew open and three small children rushed in.

"Mummy, can we...?"

"Matthew said I was...."

"Is it time to eat yet?"

"But mummy, I need...."

The voices shouted over one another for a long chaotic moment and then:

"Enough."

Carly was surprised that the loud and firm command came from Mark Christian.

"Nothing like making a great first impression." Beth smiled ruefully at Carly as she tucked stray hair behind ears and straightened and tucked in rumpled shirts.

"I'm almost ashamed to admit that these little darlings are all ours," she told Carly with a proud smile. "Children, this is Carly Munroe. Carly, this is Heather."

Heather looked to be the oldest, certainly she was the tallest, with long blonde hair that tumbled around her shoulders, and her grand-mother's eyes.

"I'm six and I'm the oldest and that makes me the best," Heather said as she politely offered her hand to Carly.

"Does not," said the middle-sized child, who now pushed his sister away and stuck out his own hand.

"I'm Matthew and I'm four and three-quarters and I'm more hand-somer than Heather."

Carly struggled not to laugh as she shook hands with the small boy. His own tangled mop of hair was a slightly darker blonde than his sister's, but he shared the same beautiful eyes.

The smallest child had now been picked up by her father.

"And this is Maggie," Mark told Carly as the little girl hid her head on her father's shoulder. "Come on now, shake hands nicely," he coached his daughter.

Maggie peeked over at Carly and seemed to think it over. Carly gave her an encouraging smile, the same one she used on timid first graders on the first day of school. After a moment, Maggie grinned and stuck out a tiny hand.

"It's very nice to meet you, Maggie," Carly told the child. "How old are you?"

Maggie tilted her head and thought about it for a moment and then giggled and buried her face against her father's neck.

"Maggie is nearly three," Mark answered for her. "And once she is three, she'll have to be polite and answer questions for herself." He addressed the last sentence towards Maggie rather than Carly, and Maggie squealed as he followed his words with a quick tickle, before he put her back down on the floor.

"Don't I even get a 'hello'?" Doncan spoke from the doorway where he had been standing, evidently just out of sight of the children.

Three voices shrieked "Uncle Doncan," in delight, and then three small bodies hurled themselves at the man. Carly watched in amazement as all three children jumped on him at the same time. Doncan laughed as he staggered backwards and then gave up and collapsed onto the floor, covered in a pile of flailing arms and legs.

"Honestly, Doncan, I wish you wouldn't encourage them like this," Beth scolded as she waded in to try to separate the children before someone got hurt.

"What did I do?" Doncan asked innocently as he tried to sit up from under the pile.

Beth pulled Maggie out of the way as Matthew stood up and then jumped at Doncan again. Carly couldn't help but laugh as Doncan collapsed backwards, holding the four-year-old in the air as he did so. Now Mark stepped in and pulled Heather to her feet, leaving just Doncan and Matthew mock-wrestling on the floor. After another moment, Doncan and Matthew rolled apart, both panting for air.

"Did you bring us chocolate?" Matthew demanded once he caught his breath.

"Matthew, that's rude," Beth chided her son.

Doncan interrupted the scolding. "I brought pudding," he told Matthew with a conspiratorial look. "And it's definitely chocolate."

"Hurray for Uncle Doncan!" Heather shouted.

"Hurray!" Matthew agreed.

"'ray!" Maggie trilled from behind her fingers.

"I guess that means the kids are hungry," Jane smiled at her grand-children. "Go and get your hands washed and we'll have dinner."

The three children rushed off, back through the rear door, and Doncan slowly climbed to his feet.

"Really, Doncan, you shouldn't let them climb all over you like that." Beth tried again to talk to her brother about his behavior.

"And why not?" Doncan challenged. "No one got hurt and everyone had fun."

Beth looked as though a million different replies went through her head, before she simply shook it and sighed.

Doncan laughed. "You'd never guess that I'm the older brother, would you?" he asked Carly with a wink.

Carly shook her head, not sure how to respond to this relaxed and playful Doncan whom she'd never seen before.

"Maybe if you acted like the big brother, instead of like a big bother...." Beth gave her brother a gentle punch in the arm.

"Ouch," Doncan shouted and rubbed his arm. "Mum, she hit me."

Doncan's parents exchanged affectionate glances and Jane shook her head at Carly. "I can't imagine what you must think of us," she fussed as she took Carly's arm. "Please don't mind my son or my grand-children. They'll give you altogether the wrong idea about us."

Carly smiled at her. "I think your grandchildren are lovely. I teach first grade, so I'm pretty used to children. Those three were actually charming and very polite, right up until they jumped all over Doncan. But he was asking for it."

Jane laughed. "I see you understand the situation perfectly," she grinned. "I just hope you're hungry. I made enough to feed an army."

When she saw the house, Carly had been worried that the dinner might be more formal than she was used to, but the dining room was comfortable rather than grand. Dinner was served buffet-style and Carly helped herself to a bowl of salad and a huge portion of steamy, meaty beef stew. There were fresh rolls, hot from the oven, and Carly couldn't help but smother one in butter. Doncan poured red wine into her glass before she could protest and whatever kind it was, it was deli-cious with the meal.

Carly was happy to sit back and enjoy the show as the three children bounced in their seats eating, laughing and talking loudly over any attempt at conversation that the adults made. Doncan caught her eye at one point and shrugged as Heather shared a minute-by-minute summary of the animated television show she had watched earlier in the day.

After the last of the stew had been eaten and the rolls were passed around for the final time, Doncan brought in dessert. He opened the bakery box and pulled out an enormous chocolate cake, smothered in rich chocolate icing, and Carly decided that she had just enough room for a small piece.

"I've got jam-roly-poly as well, if you prefer," he told her as he pulled a second cake from the box.

Carly listened politely as he described the yellow cake with jam filling to her. She might have been more attentive if he had offered that first, but once she had seen the chocolate cake, nothing else was going to be a contender.

The children waited with ill-concealed impatience as Doncan insisted on serving Carly first. As soon as everyone had their dessert in front of them, Beth gave the children permission to begin and Carly fell on her cake with as much enthusiasm as Doncan's young relatives.

"Listen to the silence," Beth laughed as all three children busily stuffed themselves with chocolate cake.

A few minutes later, with dessert finished off, Carly helped Beth and Jane clear the table.

"Do you want me to wash the dishes?" Carly asked, looking around the gleaming and spotless kitchen.

"Oh, good heavens, no," Jane smiled at her guest. "I have a woman who comes around and cleans up for me twice a week. She'll be in tomorrow and she'll run everything through the dishwasher for us. Just stack everything on the counter and let's go and sit down and chat."

Carly smiled nervously at the thought as she stacked bowls and dishes neatly on the granite counter. Everyone had been welcoming and friendly so far, but she wasn't feeling much less nervous than she had been when she arrived.

Back in the comfortable living room, Jane pulled Carly onto an overstuffed couch and sighed. "I love my grandchildren," she told Carly. "But they are exhausting to be around."

Carly smiled at her. "Where have they gone, then?" she asked curiously. Only Doncan and his father were in the living room when she and Jane arrived.

"Oh, Beth and Mark have run them home," Jane explained. "I told them that I would say goodbye to you on their behalf. They're very strict about bedtimes, especially for the little one. I hope you didn't mind them taking over dinner, but I knew they would be out of the way as soon as pudding was finished."

"I didn't mind at all," Carly said honestly. The children's chatter had saved her from having to try to make conversation.

"Now, is there anything we can tell you about Bessie?" Doncan's father asked from the chair he had taken next to them.

"Oh, yes, please," Carly answered excitedly. "I'd love to hear anything and everything you can tell me about Bessie."

Doncan grinned and crossed the room from the bar area where he had been standing. He handed Carly a glass of wine and then dropped down next to her on the couch. Carly took the offered glass without thinking and then shifted in her seat to try to put a bit of space between her and the handsome lawyer.

Doncan smiled and slid backwards, relaxing into the comfortable furniture. Now his leg was pressed against the full length of Carly's and she struggled to ignore the tingles of electricity that she felt from the contact. She gulped her wine and then turned back to Doncan's father, who was watching the interplay with an amused look on his face.

"Seriously," Carly forced out, ignoring Doncan. "I'd love to know more about Bessie."

Doncan's father smiled. "She was quite a woman," he told Carly. "Back in the 1930s she was so unusual that everyone on the island must have been talking about her. Women didn't live on their own in those days, unless they were widowed. And widows usually found themselves a new husband pretty quickly. It was pretty much a given that women needed to be looked after."

Carly was embarrassed when she actually snorted out loud at the remark, but Doncan's parents just laughed.

"I know it's hard to believe that people felt that way, not even that many years ago," Jane told her. "But even when I was young, single women didn't live on their own."

"I'm so glad things have changed," Carly told her "So Aunt Bessie didn't care what people thought?" she asked.

"Remember that this is before my time," Doncan's father continued. "But I do recall my father and his brother, my Uncle Henry, talking about her. You should really talk to Henry."

"He's still alive?" Carly blurted out the question and then blushed at its rudeness. "I mean, that is...." She stuttered to a stop and sipped at her wine to fill the awkward pause.

Jane chuckled softly. "Yes, Uncle Henry is still alive," she told Carly. "He was a late-in-life baby for Doncan's parents. He's not even eighty now."

Carly's eyes widened. "I'd love to meet him. He must have known Bessie his whole life."

"That he did," Doncan's father agreed. "He would definitely be able to tell you more about her. He might even be able to tell you something about her and Peter."

"Peter?" Carly's heart skipped a beat. "Peter who?" she asked eagerly.

Doncan's father smiled. "Peter was my father's other brother. He emigrated to Australia as soon as he'd turned eighteen, but he came back to visit some years after Bessie returned to the island. There's always been family gossip that he and Bessie had something of a romance while he was here. Eventually he returned to Australia and Bessie stayed here, and she would never discuss it with anyone, so it's really just rumors. Maybe you'll find something about it in her diaries."

Carly bit her lip. She wasn't sure if she should tell them that she had already found something in the diaries or not. She was suddenly distracted as Doncan ran a hand up her arm. She tried to focus on Doncan's father, but Doncan's touch sent shivers through her entire body.

She gulped her wine and smiled at Doncan's parents. "I'd love to talk to him," she said, thinking that she was probably repeating herself, but she wasn't sure.

"You should come to the picnic on Saturday," Jane invited. "We're having the whole extended family for a big picnic lunch. Beth and Mark and the kids will be here and so will Uncle Henry and about fifty other people who would love to meet you."

Carly turned pale at the thought of meeting that many people. "Oh, I don't want to intrude on a big family event," she said in a strangled voice.

"It's no intrusion," Jane insisted. "Why, if Bessie had married Peter, we would all be family anyway."

Carly opened her mouth to refuse, but couldn't find the right words.

"I'll pick you up around eleven," Doncan said to her softly. "We can pick up Henry from his nursing home and bring him with us. That way you can have some time to talk to him privately before the party."

"But...." Carly turned to look at Doncan. Whatever she was going to say went out of her head as she felt herself getting lost in his eyes.

He smiled at her and then raised his hand and brushed a stray hair out of her eyes. The touch was electric and she held her breath as his hand dropped to her neck, caressing it gently.

"That's settled then," Jane sounded amused as her words dragged Carly back into the conversation. "You can ask Henry all about Bessie and Peter. Not that we aren't happy to answer more questions, but he probably knows a lot more than we do."

Carly nodded at her, feeling slightly dazed from Doncan's touch. The grandfather clock in the corner struck nine and Carly jumped up.

"Wow, is that the time? I probably should be going. I've got a lot more packing to do tomorrow." Carly rattled off the words quickly, suddenly eager to be away from what was feeling like an increasingly intimate situation.

"I'd better get you home, then," Doncan said easily, rising to his feet. "Thanks for dinner," he told his parents. "We'll see you Saturday around noon. I'll bring pudding again."

"You will insist on spoiling your nieces and nephews, won't you?" Jane mock-scolded her son.

"Chocolate cake is good for you," Doncan replied with a mischievous grin. "I'm sure Carly won't complain if I bring another one."

Carly just nodded, suddenly feeling completely out of her element. "Thank you for a lovely evening," she blurted out, trying to remember her manners.

"Thank you for coming. It was wonderful to meet you." Jane sounded completely sincere and Carly gave her a huge smile as she shook her hand. She shook hands with Doncan's father as well, murmuring polite words of thanks.

Moments later she was back in Doncan's car, feeling a little bit dizzy from everything that had happened. She was excited at the prospect of learning more about the mysterious Peter and she had enjoyed meeting Doncan's family, but she was thoroughly confused by Doncan's behavior during the evening.

"Your family is very nice," she said politely after her brain had given up on figuring anything out for the moment.

"They all liked you," he answered her. "Beth especially."

"She was very friendly and the kids were adorable."

"They are that. I can't believe how much I love those little monsters."

Carly looked at Doncan, surprised at the words and the intensity in his tone. He glanced over at her and then took her hand. "I'm glad you're coming to the picnic on Saturday. Big family gatherings are always really boring. I'm sure having you there will make it far more interesting."

Carly had no idea how to respond to that, so she remained silent as the sleek car glided into Douglas. Doncan kept a loose grip on her hand throughout the drive, which confused Carly even more. Back at the hotel, he walked her to her door and waited until she opened it. She flipped on the lights and he glanced inside, checking that every-thing was as it should be.

"I'll let you get some sleep," he told her in a soft voice. "I'll pick you up at nine and drop you off at Bessie's to do some more packing. I'm going to take the afternoon off on Friday and help you start sorting out the furniture, if that works for you?"

"That would be great," Carly answered without really thinking.

"I'll see if I can get a truck and a couple of good strong men to come with me. Maybe we can start moving some of the stuff you want to store from Bessie's cottage to my house."

"Great," Carly answered. She was distracted because all she could think about was whether or not he was going to kiss her good night.

"See you tomorrow," Doncan said, giving her a grin that suggested that he knew exactly where her thoughts were. He was gone before Carly could reply.

"I didn't want a kiss," she sternly told her mirror self as she washed her face. "I've got my little house and my perfect life and I certainly don't need some rich lawyer to mess it all up."

Her subconscious brain didn't seem to agree, however, and she spent a frustrating night dreaming about Doncan and waking frequently.

10

C arly hadn't read any more of Bessie's diaries for several days. Thinking about reading them made her feel sad, knowing how it was going to end. Now that she was going to meet one of Bessie's contemporaries in just a few days, she found herself eager to read more. Thursday was full of packing and sorting and Carly was actually pleased when Doncan couldn't stay for dinner after he'd dropped her off at the hotel. She quickly ordered a meal from room service and curled up with the second of Bessie's books.

She read through page after page about Bessie's daily life on the island. The details about life during the war were fascinating and, no doubt, exactly the sort of thing that the museum was interested in. Carly was too caught up in her fascination with Bessie's love life, however, to give them more than a glance now. She would come back and give them proper attention another time.

3rd April 1940

I saw Mr. Doncan Quayle in town today. He mentioned that his brother, Peter, has been in London for the last two months, but should be back on the island around the first of May. Apparently he is planning on staying here for some months after that, maybe even until early next year, but he does need to go back to Australia after that.

I've no idea why Mr. Quayle thought that I would be so interested in his brother's plans, but I showed polite interest throughout the conversation.

I had noticed Mr. Peter Quayle's absence, of course, especially after enjoying spending some time with him at Christmas, but his plans are no concern of mine.

Carly smiled at the words, certain that her relative had much more than a passing interest in the man's plans. She read through the next several pages quickly, hoping that early May might bring another mention of Peter Quayle. She was not disappointed.

🖎 *5ᵗʰ May*

I had an appointment with Mr. Doncan Quayle today to sign a few papers having to do with some investments that he recommended. I was surprised to find that his brother, Peter, was also visiting the office while I was there.

After we concluded our business, the older Mr. Quayle insisted that I join him and his brother for lunch at the little café across the road. The food was very good and it was just unfortunate that Mr. Quayle was called away almost immediately and had to miss the meal.

Mr. Peter Quayle did his best to make up for his brother's absence by being amusing and very entertaining. He told me more about Australia, where it seems the sun shines nearly all the time. As it is a rainy and cool day here, he made it seem quite appealing.

Carly grinned. Clearly Doncan Quayle had been doing his best to get his brother and Bessie together. She was torn between wanting to read more and feeling sad because she knew it was going to end badly.

She flipped through the next several pages. Nearly every entry now had a brief mention of "Mr. Peter Quayle." He now seemed to be popping up nearly everywhere that Bessie went, helping her carry her shopping home from the grocery store, nodding to her in the street as she passed, or sharing dinner with her at his older brother's home. The entries began to get longer as Bessie shared more and more about the man and about the stories he told about his adopted country of Australia.

The book ended in late September 1940 and Carly sighed as she closed its covers. Bessie appeared to be falling in love with the man she described as "almost handsome and incredibly kind," even though she never once mentioned her feelings in the book. Carly looked at the clock and was shocked to see that it was after midnight. While she was tempted to read the third diary, she needed to get some sleep. Friday was going to be a busy day and she couldn't sleepwalk through it.

The lateness of the hour helped Carly fall into a deep and dreamless sleep, but she was still tired and slightly bleary-eyed the next morning when Doncan picked her up. She sorted and packed the remainder of the spare bedroom at Bessie's house on autopilot. There was nothing in the drawers or wardrobes that she felt Granny would be interested in, so everything that wasn't obviously garbage went into boxes to either sell or give away.

As she ate the lunch that Doncan had once again packed for her, Carly wondered what time he might be back at the cottage. As soon as she finished eating, she took a few minutes to run a hand through her hair and refresh her lipstick. "I just want to look presentable," she grumbled at her disbelieving mirror image.

She was startled a short time later when the mobile phone Doncan had given her rang.

"Hello," she said tentatively, hoping she had pressed the right button to connect the call.

"Carly? This is Breesha at Mr. Quayle's office." The voice on the other end of the phone was all business. "He asked me to call you and let you know that he isn't going to be able to take the afternoon off after all. He still expects to be able to pick you up around five, though, unless you would rather get a taxi back into Douglas earlier?"

Carly swallowed a dozen questions that sprang into her mind. "Five would be great," she told the other woman after an awkward pause.

"I'll let him know," Breesha replied. "Someone will call you if his plans change further."

The call was disconnected before Carly could reply. She sat for a moment, feeling stunned by the sudden turn of events. Her mind raced through a dozen possible scenarios that might have caused the change. Finally, she sighed and stood up. There was no point in wasting her afternoon speculating on Doncan's change of plans. He would explain, or he wouldn't, when she next saw him.

She reluctantly went back to packing, but after another hour she decided that she had earned a break. The sun was shining and the beach looked incredibly inviting through the bedroom windows. She looked around the room. She had nearly finished it and the rest of the house was mostly done as well. Her original plan gave her another two weeks on the island and that was plenty of time to finish the packing and get the cottage cleaned before it went on the market.

Once that was done, she could sign all the necessary papers and Doncan could handle the actual sale. She looked around again. She really didn't feel like sorting one more drawer. The sun shone outside the window and tempted her.

A moment later she had stripped off her shoes and socks and was walking barefoot across the warm sand on Laxey Beach. She'd worn cropped trousers and a light T-shirt but they felt heavy in the warmth of the day.

Carly gasped in shock as the cold water from the Irish Sea washed over her toes. It was much colder than she'd expected it to be. She walked slowly along the water's edge, enjoying the feel of the sand between her toes and the cold splashes as the waves moved across her feet.

She wondered, as she made her way slowly down the beach, how often Bessie had made the same journey. Perhaps she had walked here with Peter Quayle, him telling her about the beaches of distant Australia, maybe. Carly smiled at small children and their parents as they dodged around her on their way in and out of the sea. She couldn't imagine submerging her entire body in the cold and salty seawater.

After a while, she reluctantly turned back towards Bessie's cottage, in no hurry to get back to the job she was meant to be doing. She was surprised to see just how far the tide had gone out while she had been walking. She found her path back was much further away from the cottage as she followed the water's edge.

A large rock was perfectly placed for her to sit down and have a rest. She settled on it, her back to the cottage and her eyes focused into the distance. Different thoughts crowded into her head. She wondered about Tom, how he was doing back home and if they were really finished or if he might change his mind. The distance seemed to have given her a new perspective on their relationship and for the first time in her life she was starting to feel that she and Tom weren't perfect together.

That made her feel sad and somehow older, as if she had just given up on a childhood dream that she wanted to hold onto. She sighed and turned her thoughts towards Bessie. Those thoughts, however, were sad ones as well. Her mind now turned towards the last thing she really wanted to think about, Doncan.

She sighed as she remembered their shared kiss. It felt like it had happened a very long time ago and yet she could still remember exactly how his lips had felt on hers. He had behaved strangely at his parents' house on Wednesday night, almost behaving as if they were a couple rather than business associates. But then today, he had not only cancelled their plans, but he had had his secretary to do the cancelling for him. She sighed again. Thinking about Doncan wasn't changing her mood for the better.

"Carly?" The voice, coming from behind her, surprised her and as she spun around she nearly fell off her rocky perch.

Doncan was standing at the water's edge, looking curiously at her. She glanced down and realized that the same tide that had been going out was obviously now coming back in. There were several inches of water surrounding her large rocky seat.

"Oh dear," she called as she looked back at Doncan. "I guess I didn't notice the tide."

"Do you need any help?" Doncan called, clearly amused by her predicament.

"Oh no," Carly called back, feeling a bubble of happiness as Doncan smiled at her. "Don't get your fancy clothes all wet."

Doncan was wearing an impeccably tailored dark suit and glossily shined black shoes and Carly hated the thought of them getting ruined.

She looked down again and then shrugged. She had little choice. With a laugh that became more of a shriek as her feet hit the cold water, she splashed down off the rock and waded back towards Doncan and the cottage. By the time she reached him she was shivering slightly. It wasn't just the tide she hadn't noticed. The air had turned cooler and the sun had disappeared behind a cloud.

Doncan noticed the shiver. "Here, put this on," he told her as he removed his suit jacket.

"Oh no, I couldn't," Carly protested. Doncan ignored her and put the jacket around her shoulders, drawing her arms though the sleeves as if she were one of his tiny nieces instead of a grown woman.

"I don't know what you were thinking about," Doncan told her as he led her back up the beach towards the cottage, "but you seemed to be miles away."

Carly snuggled into the jacket that was still warm from Doncan's body heat. The smell of his expensive cologne enveloped her and she nearly sighed with pleasure.

"I got tired of packing, so I went for a walk," she explained as they reached the cabin. "I thought I would sit on the rock and watch the sea for a little while, but I guess I lost track of time. What time is it?"

"It's not much past five," Doncan told her. "I got here around five and while I was looking for you in the house I spotted you on the beach."

"Wow," Carly shook her head. "I didn't realize that I was out there that long. I would have guessed that it was only two or three."

Doncan smiled. "The sea has a way of stealing time away from you when you start watching it," he told her.

"It really does," Carly agreed, suddenly remembering his abrupt change of plans earlier. "I hope you got all of the work done that you needed to do," she said politely, trying to sound unconcerned.

Doncan grinned at her. "Unfortunately, I didn't," he told her. "I've sneaked away to get you safely back to Douglas, but then I'm afraid I have to go back to the office."

Carly bit her tongue hard to keep herself from asking for more information. Doncan was her lawyer, not her boyfriend, and he didn't have to explain himself to her.

After a moment she spoke. "It was kind of you to sneak away," she said as she put her socks and shoes back on. "I could have grabbed a taxi."

"I wanted to see you," Doncan said simply, staring into her eyes for a moment and then blurting out words that surprised her. "I've had a terrible day and I needed a break. I couldn't think of anything I'd rather do than spend a few minutes with you."

Carly was speechless and she found herself simply staring at Doncan. After a moment he continued. "Okay, I lied," he said smoothly as he closed the gap between them. "I can think of lots of things that are nicer than just seeing you."

With that he pulled her close, and before she had time to think, he bent his head and kissed her gently. Carly felt a huge flood of emotions, but before long desire won out over the rest. Without thinking she wrapped her arms around Doncan and let herself fall mindlessly into the incredible kiss.

Within seconds, however, Doncan was pulling away. He took a step away from her and turned to look at the sea. She could just hear his ragged breathing over her own.

"Sorry," Doncan said after a minute. "One of my clients passed away this morning and his family is already in the middle of a huge and nasty fight over the estate. He had four children and they've each hired their own advocate so that they can fight every single sentence in the will that I wrote for him a few years back. I've spent the day arguing with one advocate after another and it looks as if it's going to get worse before it gets better. Three of the children are flying in tonight with their legal teams and the fourth should be here tomorrow morning. No one has even seen the will yet, but everyone is sure they aren't going to get exactly what they want, so they're all coming out fighting."

Carly wasn't sure how to respond to that. "How can families be so awful to each other?" she asked eventually.

"The worst part is that my client left most of his money to charity. His children never visited him, never even took any interest in his life, but now that he's gone, they are all dropping everything to get to the island and stake their claim." Doncan shook his head. "Sometimes I think I should have been a bus driver."

Carly couldn't help but laugh at the image of the perfectly pressed lawyer driving a bus. "I'm sure there isn't anything I can do to help," she told him softly. "But you know I would if I could."

Doncan smiled at her. "You've helped immensely," he told her. "Just spending a little bit of time with you has lifted my spirits. But I really need to get you home and get back to the office, I'm afraid."

Carly quickly made her way back to the house and grabbed her things. "I don't want to hold you up," she said, as she collected her purse and the insulated bag that had held her lunch.

They talked about the weather and other general topics on the short drive back to Douglas. Doncan walked her to her door.

"I wish I could stay and have some dinner with you," he said, tracing a finger down the side of her face.

"That would be nice," Carly said, her voice catching as she looked into his gorgeous eyes.

"I'm not sure what's going to happen tomorrow," Doncan said apologetically. "I'll definitely pick you up around eleven and take you and Uncle Henry to the picnic, but I might have to abandon you to my family for a while and head into the office."

Carly was sure that the sheer panic she felt at his words was visible on her face by the way he laughed. "Don't worry," he assured her. "They really liked you."

Carly could only nod silently, not trusting herself to speak.

Doncan looked at her for another moment and then sighed. "I've got to go," he said, "and I might need my jacket."

Carly flushed as she realized that she was still wrapped up in Doncan's expensive suit jacket. She rushed out an apology but Doncan put his finger to her lips to stop her.

"I would love to let you keep it," he told her. "I like the way it looks on you. But I might need to play 'big bad lawyer' tonight and the jacket helps."

Carly smiled at him as he pulled the jacket back on. He dropped a fleeting kiss on to the top of her head and then left quickly, clearly once again focused on the work he had to get done in the hours ahead.

Carly ordered room service yet again and settled down with Bessie's third diary. Maybe she would find out exactly what went wrong between her and Peter. And maybe that would keep her mind off of how wonderful it had felt to be in Doncan's arms.

The third diary surprised Carly. Whatever restraint Bessie had shown in the first two books vanished in the third. Page after page now described her growing feelings for Peter Quayle, now simply identified as Peter in nearly every entry.

3rd October

Peter and I had dinner at his brother's house tonight. After dinner we walked on the beach and talked. I once thought that I would never recover from losing Matthew, but Peter makes me forget my pain. He hasn't replaced Matthew in my heart, but it seems my heart has room for him as well.

I can't imagine leaving my little house and my island home, but Peter is determined to return to Australia in the New Year. I cannot be certain, but I suspect that he might ask me to marry him and accompany him.

I have written to Matthew's mother to ask for her advice, as I cannot consult my own parents. I do not want to betray Matthew's memory, but I cannot help having some feelings for Peter. He is so very kind and caring.

Carly read page after page of Bessie and Peter's courtship, smiling as Bessie described dinners with his family and long walks around the island. As Christmas approached, the entries revealed Bessie's certainty that a marriage proposal was imminent. Carly smiled as she turned to the last page in the book and saw the entry written across several lines in huge letters.

Christmas Day

HE ASKED ME TO MARRY HIM!!!!!!

I said I needed time to think. I don't know what I should do. I do care deeply for him and I think we could be very happy together. But I also love my life here and my little house. I can't imagine giving up everything in my life to move so far away especially with the war still going on.

What if we disagree or grow apart? I would be all alone among strangers with no place to go.

I have spent so much time and effort (and money) on making my little house perfect. I have shelves and shelves of books to read. I don't want to sell my home. But Peter talks of using the money from the sale to buy ourselves a little house in Australia. Somewhere to raise our little family.

I'm not sure I'm ready for a little family. I feel much older than my years, like the old widow woman I pretend to be. I should be the happiest woman in the world, but all I can do is think and cry.

Why does this have to be so difficult?

Carly frowned as she put the book down. Surely there had to be more books that she hadn't found yet. Bessie wouldn't have just stopped keeping her diaries, especially not at such an interesting point in her life. Her heart ached for Bessie, who would have been in her late twenties when Peter Quayle was wooing her. Carly couldn't imagine having to make such an important decision without her parents, or seemingly anyone, to turn to for advice.

Bessie had written to someone she trusted for help. Carly had seen the letter that came back from Matthew's mother. Carly wondered why Bessie had not listened to what Mrs. Saunders had said. She paced anxiously in front of the large windows that looked out at the seafront. She was frustrated with not knowing the next part of the story. She knew how it ended, of course, but that didn't really help.

Maybe Bessie was right to refuse Peter, she told herself sternly. She had her little house and her life seemed just about perfect to Carly. Maybe Bessie had lived her own happily ever after, and Peter was just a passing fancy. Carly wanted to believe that very much, but it was hard to do so having read page after page of the woman's most intimate thoughts. There was no doubt in Carly's mind that Bessie had been in love with Peter Quayle, however the story ended.

With a deep sigh, she got ready for bed. She tried hard to keep her thoughts focused on Bessie, because whenever they wandered she found herself thinking about Doncan. She briefly considered calling Tom, but she couldn't imagine what she could possibly say to him. She pulled the covers up over her head, hoping to block out the outside world. Her dreams seemed to recreate Bessie and Peter's romance, with cozy dinners and long walks. The difference was that Doncan

Quayle took Peter's place and every so often he pulled her close for a kiss that blew her away.

Carly dressed carefully for the picnic, wanting to make a good impression on the members of Doncan's family whom she hadn't yet met. She wore a lightweight pair of pants and a short-sleeved, cotton, button-down shirt that would be cool and comfortable as well as looking more sophisticated than a T-shirt and jeans would.

Doncan complimented her on the outfit when he picked her up, so she figured she must have chosen her clothes well. Beyond "hello" and the quick compliment, however, Doncan was quiet and seemed distracted as they drove from her hotel to the home where Uncle Henry lived.

"Is everything okay?" Carly asked tentatively as Doncan parked his car in the home's lot.

"No," Doncan answered sharply. He frowned and then ran a hand over his face, sighing deeply. "Sorry, it isn't your fault and I shouldn't snap at you."

He tried to smile at her but it was a miserable attempt. Finally he sighed again. "All four children managed to get here before the body got cold, even though they never visited when my client was alive. There's a trophy widow who is pretending to grieve while trying to figure out how to clear out the house before anyone else notices. Then there's the discarded first wife, who actually seems quite upset that her former husband has died. The dead man had a brother and a sister who have suddenly remembered how much they loved their brother and now they are both on their way to the island to stake their own claims. Monday I get to read out a will that isn't going to make any of them happy."

Carly impulsively took his hand and gave it a squeeze. "I wish there was something that I could do," she said softly.

"I was looking forward to spending the day with you and my family," Doncan told her. "But once I drop you and Henry off at the picnic, I need to go over to my client's house and go through the inventory. I suspect the widow has already taken a few important pieces and might need to be persuaded nicely to give them back."

Carly squeezed his hand again. "I promise not to have too much fun without you," she said with a grin, trying to lift his mood.

"Just save me a slice of chocolate cake," Doncan grinned back, seemingly feeling slightly better for her efforts. "This might help as well," he added as he slid an arm around her.

Carly realized what he was planning with just enough time to stop him. Except she didn't want to stop him. The kiss felt even better than the dream kisses had, and Carly felt herself falling deeply under Doncan's spell. When he pulled back, she very nearly pulled him back and kissed him again. Instead she closed her eyes and dragged up what little self-control she could muster.

Doncan smiled at her when she opened her eyes. "I was right," he told her. "That did help."

Before Carly could respond, he was out of the car. He quickly came around and opened her door for her, extending a hand to help her from the car. He used the gentlemanly gesture as an excuse to pull her close for a very brief moment before they turned to enter the retirement home.

Doncan's Uncle Henry was waiting in the lobby of the home.

"It's a real pleasure to make your acquaintance," he told Carly, taking her hand and then bowing as he shook it. "I understand that you're related to Bessie." The man studied her for a moment. "Yes, I can see a resemblance," he said eventually. "Bessie was a real beauty, and so are you, but there's also a family resemblance around the eyes."

Carly smiled at him and his eyes widened.

"Well now," he said with a grin. "You have Bessie's smile for sure. She had the most beautiful smile. Peter always said it was her smile that won his heart."

Carly's heart beat faster at the comment. "Your brother, Peter?" she asked.

"Yes," Henry shook his head. "Bessie was the love of his life, but he ended up going back to Australia without her. He wouldn't ever talk about it, especially with me. I was his baby brother, after all. I was a good many years younger than Peter, barely knew him as a child, really. I don't know what happened between him and Bessie. All I know is that he went back to Australia and eventually married someone else, but he never really stopped loving Bessie."

"I hate to interrupt," Doncan interrupted, "but I have to get to the office. Maybe you can talk in the car?"

Carly was instantly apologetic. She had been so excited to learn more about Bessie that she had forgotten that Doncan had to get to work. Henry took Carly's arm and the pair walked out of the home together, already chatting like old friends. Doncan followed.

Carly felt reluctant to share what she'd read in Bessie's diaries with Henry. Luckily, she barely got a word in edgewise as they made their way to the park in Laxey where the picnic was being held. Henry kept up a steady stream of reminiscences about Bessie that fascinated Carly.

"Ah, she was so beautiful and so independent," he told Carly. "Women didn't live on their own in those days, but she had enough of her own money that she could do what she liked. That Matthew of hers left her well looked after. And she loved her little house and her books and her life on the island."

Carly smiled. "I love her house, too, but I can't imagine living in it."

Henry grinned. "Bessie wasn't too bothered about modern conveniences. I kept trying to get her to move to the home where I am, but she wouldn't hear of it. I was just Peter's baby brother. She never did take me seriously."

Carly laughed, amused at the idea that the elderly man was someone's "baby" brother. "So Peter ended up marrying someone else?" she asked.

"Yep, a few years after he went back. And he never visited the island again. I went out to see him a few times, once airplanes made the trip easier, but I could never persuade him to come back here. I asked him once why he didn't want to visit and he told me that he couldn't bear the thought of seeing Bessie. He and his wife had a good marriage and three sons, but he never got over his love for Bessie."

Carly frowned. "That's really sad," she told Henry.

"And I guess Bessie never got over young Matthew," Henry shrugged. "I got lucky, because I fell in love with the first woman I dated and we had fifty-three good years together and five healthy children before she passed on. Can't say for sure how I would have felt if she'd thrown me over for someone else."

"I had been with the same man from the time I was little until recently," Carly told him. "I always thought we would get married some day." She kept her voice quiet, talking to the man whom she had joined in the backseat of the car, hoping that Doncan couldn't hear her.

Henry surprised her by laughing. "If you'd been together that long and you aren't married yet, something was wrong," he told her. "Oh, I know young couples these days live together and sleep together long before they get hitched, but it seems to me that if you really love someone you want to be linked up in front of God and everyone. What's that Beyondy say? 'Put a ring on it', that's what smart men do."

While Carly didn't necessarily agree with his words, they made her smile. "Are you a fan of Beyoncé?" she asked.

"Don't have much choice," Henry told her. "The staff puts music on for a 'disco night' every Friday night. We used to have old stuff like from the thirties and forties, but a bunch of us complained. Now they play modern stuff like Beyondy and that Lady Gaggle. It's much better than listening to the oldies anyway."

Doncan pulled up and parked in the lot outside the park in Laxey. Carly was out of the car quickly, eager to help Henry as he climbed out. The elderly man, however, was far more spry than she gave him credit for. He was out of the car and headed through the small gates that marked the park entrance before Carly made it to his side.

Doncan grabbed her arm and turned her back towards him. "I really have to get to work," he told her with a frown. "Can you give me a hand with the desserts so that I don't have to make two trips?"

"Sure," Carly agreed easily. She could see that several people had already rushed up to greet Henry. There was no way he was going to need her assistance.

Doncan popped open the trunk of his car and disappeared behind it. Carly quickly joined him, grinning when she saw the number of bakery boxes inside it.

"How many people are going to be here?" she asked, suddenly nervous about being at the picnic without Doncan.

"Probably about fifty," Doncan smiled at her. "And they'll all love you, so don't worry."

Carly smiled back tentatively, still worried. She reached into the trunk and began to gather up boxes.

"Hang on a second," Doncan told her. He looked around the parking lot, which was empty, and then in the direction of the picnic. The trunk lid completely hid the pair from the other guests. Again, Carly had an idea where his thoughts were going, and again she didn't feel like resisting. The kiss was fleeting, but it helped calmed Carly's nerves and brought a smile to Doncan's face.

"Okay, let's get these cakes delivered," Doncan said after adding a quick and tight hug.

They made their way through the park as quickly as they could, both laden down with several boxes. Several people shouted "hello" at Doncan as he passed, and one or two even offered to help, but it was really only a few steps from the gate to the large shelter where the food was being collected.

"Honestly, Doncan, how many cakes did you buy?" Jane Quayle was in charge of the shelter and she laughingly scolded her son as he and Carly spread their boxes across the large dessert table.

"Just about the perfect number," Doncan answered, giving his mother a hug and a kiss on the top of the head. "Now I'm afraid I have to go to work, but I'll be back by five at the latest. Look after Carly for me, please?"

"I'm sure Carly will be just fine on her own," Jane answered with a grin. "I'll probably just put her to work."

Carly smiled at that. "I'm happy to help," she offered eagerly. The busier she was kept, the fewer strangers she would have to meet and try to keep straight.

"Right, if you get bored and want to leave early, call me, otherwise I'll be back around five," Doncan told Carly as he turned to leave. "And somebody better save me something to eat," he added as he walked off.

Carly grinned at him and then smiled at Jane. "It's nice to see you again," she said politely, suddenly feeling quite tongue-tied.

"It's nice to see you again, too," Jane gave her a huge smile. "I hope you don't mind giving me a hand with the food, at least for a little while. We're planning to eat in about an hour and nearly all the other youngsters have children that they're busy chasing around the park."

Carly smiled at her, amused at being a "youngster" in Jane's eyes. "I don't mind a bit," she told her. "I'm nervous about meeting everyone anyway," she confided. "I'd rather stay out of the way."

"Well, you can't hide all day," Jane told her. "Everyone is eager to meet you. Bessie was like family to us. In fact, if she were still with us, she would have been here today. That makes you like family as well and we're all thrilled to have you here."

Carly felt her heart warm at the kind words. She was pleased that her elderly relative had had such great friends in her life. As she helped put out plate after plate of food, she watched the kids chasing each other around the large grassy field. She spotted Maggie on the swings, being pushed gently by her father. Henry had joined a large group of men that included Doncan's dad and the snatches of their conversation that Carly occasionally caught all seemed to be about cricket, a subject she knew nothing about.

After a while, Beth came in to help as well and the three women worked quickly and efficiently together, laying out food, making sure that there were enough serving spoons and filling bowls with chips and popcorn. Beth used the time to talk to her mother about her children's latest accomplishments, and Carly found that she enjoyed learning about their various activities and achievements.

When it was time to eat, the shelter was quickly filled to over-flowing with a crowd that seemed much larger to Carly than the fifty she had been told to expect. Before the first spoonful of food hit the first plate, Doncan's mom said a few words.

"Okay, everyone, this is Carly," she told the group, gesturing towards Carly who was stationed behind the hot foods to help make sure the children didn't get burned. "She's Bessie's great-grandniece visiting from America and that makes her part of the family. Everyone can tell her after lunch how wonderful Bessie was. I'm sure she'd love to hear stories about her."

Carly nodded eagerly at the sea of faces. She couldn't imagine anything better.

"Let's eat, then." Jane barely got the words out of her mouth before everyone descended eagerly on the food. The next half hour or so was a blur as Carly rushed about supervising the hot dishes. When the last plate had been filled to capacity, it was time for her, Jane and Beth to get something to eat and Carly eagerly tried a little bit of everything.

The rest of the afternoon went past quickly as it seemed that everybody at the picnic wanted to meet her and share at least one story about "Aunt Bessie" with her. Most of the stories were funny and Carly felt that she laughed more in that afternoon than she had in years. She just hoped she could remember at least some of the stories for Granny.

She was happily pushing Matthew on the swings when Doncan got back to the picnic. He hadn't yet spotted her, so she took a minute to study him. He had changed out of his suit and into casual clothes, and she noted that he had athletic legs peeking out under knee-length shorts. The clothes, like his suits, appeared to have been custom-tailored for him. Carly admired his broad chest and strong arms as he picked up Maggie, who had thrown herself at him as soon as she saw him.

When he spotted Carly, she felt herself blushing under his gaze. He quickly crossed to the swings, where he sat little Maggie in the swing next to Matthew's.

"Having fun?" he asked Carly casually.

"It's been wonderful," she answered enthusiastically. "Everyone shared stories about Bessie and the food was amazing and I managed to sneak in two slices of chocolate cake without anyone noticing."

Doncan smiled at her obvious pleasure. "I hope you saved me a piece," he told her as Maggie shrieked with delight.

"I did," Carly assured him. "And some proper food as well, so you don't make yourself sick filling up on junk."

"Chocolate cake isn't junk," Doncan argued with a smile. "It's practically its own very important food group."

Carly could only laugh. The pair turned Maggie and Matthew over to their parents and made their way to the shelter, where Carly had left a huge plate of food wrapped up for Doncan. While he ate, he told her about his day.

"Well, three out of the four lawyers representing the children have agreed to simply sit tight until Monday, which is really all they can do. The fourth had to fly home for some other urgent client and hasn't agreed to anything, but also isn't here to drive me crazy, so I guess it doesn't matter. The widow is safely tucked away in a hotel until the will is read and we can determine exactly who gets what. Otherwise, I've told Breesha to put on the answering machine and just ignore everyone for the rest of the weekend."

"That's good," Carly told him. "You need a break."

"I do at that," Doncan admitted, still steadily working his way through the plate of food she had provided.

Beth joined them a moment later. "Hey, you guys," she greeted them. "You missed all the good stuff," she told her brother. "And I know you are really disappointed that you didn't get to spend the day with your nieces and nephew."

Doncan raised his eyebrows at his sister. "Um, yeah, really disappointed," he agreed, if reluctantly.

"So here's what I was thinking," Beth continued with a mischievous grin. "Mark and I haven't had a day off from the kids in ages. We thought maybe you'd like to make up for missing them today by taking them to the Wildlife Park tomorrow."

Doncan frowned.

"Oh, that sounds like such fun," Carly said before Doncan could reply. "Can I come, too?"

Doncan's frown deepened. "I was really looking forward to a relaxing day tomorrow," he began, looking from Carly to Beth and then back again. "Chasing three small children around the Wildlife Park isn't exactly what I had in mind."

Carly immediately picked up on Doncan's mood. "You're right," she agreed with him. "You need a nice relaxing day tomorrow. Monday's going to be hard work."

"Nonsense," Beth interjected. "If you stay home and 'relax' all day, you'll just sit around thinking about all your problems and getting even more stressed. I guarantee that spending the day with my kids will completely keep your mind off your problems."

Carly and Doncan both laughed at that. "Besides," Beth continued. "I'm getting a bit desperate and I'm not too proud to beg. Mark and I haven't had ten minutes alone together in I don't know how long and we really need to recharge. You can pick the kids up at nine-thirty, take them to the Park, grab lunch there or at a convenient pub and drop them back off to us any time after one. Then you have the rest of the day to relax and I get something like three blissful hours of peace and quiet. Please?"

"Can't Mum and Dad have them?" Doncan sounded as if he knew he was going to give in, but that he was determined to make his sister work for her result.

"Mum and Dad have them during the week, while I'm at work. They need time to rest, especially after today. Mum hasn't sat down once."

Doncan looked at Carly, who was looking hopeful. "Okay, I'll do it," he began. "Or rather, we'll do it. I'm not having all three of them without Carly to help."

"I'm happy to help," Carly told them both. "I can't wait to see the Wildlife Park. I saw a brochure about it at the hotel and I've been wanting to get there."

"I just hope you manage to see a few animals, other than the three we're going to be trying to keep track of," Doncan told her with a pretend grimace.

"It'll be great fun," Carly insisted to him.

❧ 11 ❧

Sunday was warm and sunny again, and Carly was grateful. She didn't imagine that the wildlife park would be much fun in the rain. She ate breakfast in the hotel dining room and then sat down on the steps at the front of the hotel, enjoying the sunshine.

She'd chosen a pair of shorts that were cut to fall just above her knees and a light T-shirt for the day, and then added a pair of sunglasses and an old pair of sneakers that she'd tossed in the bottom of her suitcase for one reason or another. She'd been living in a couple of different pairs of sandals since she had arrived on the island, but today seemed more of a sneaker kind of day.

Doncan was similarly casually dressed, but he looked anything but relaxed when he arrived.

"What's wrong?" Carly asked, concern in her voice as she studied his face.

"Is it that obvious?" Doncan shook his head. "Just more advocates trying to make more trouble," he told her. "I spent an hour on the phone this morning with one who keeps insisting that his client deserves to know what's in the will right now. I finally told him that we would have to agree to disagree and that I'd see him tomorrow at nine in my office, with the rest of the beneficiaries and their attorneys. I just hope we can find a meeting room big enough for everyone who's planning to turn up."

Carly sighed and impulsively squeezed his hand. "I wish I could do something to help," she told him again.

"Just help me keep my mind off it all," Doncan suggested. "I hate to admit it, but my sister just might have been right about how I should spend today."

"Her kids are much more fun than any lawyers," Carly told him with a grin.

Doncan smiled back, seemingly feeling at least a little better. The pair made their way up the coast, chatting easily about the weather, the people Carly had met the previous day, and what she should expect at the wildlife park.

"It said in the brochure that some animals are 'free-roaming.' What does that mean?" she asked a bit nervously.

"Don't worry." Doncan gave her hand a comforting squeeze. "It isn't the dangerous animals or anything. But the wallabies and some odd deer and probably a bunch of others that I can't think of are free to roam around their entire enclosures. We get to walk inside the cages, as such."

"That sounds, well, interesting," Carly said hesitantly.

"It's great," Doncan assured her. "Better for the animals and more fun for us. You just have to watch where you step."

Carly gave an involuntary shudder, suddenly really pleased that she had worn her sneakers rather than open-toed sandals.

Carly glanced into the backseat at the child seats already strapped into place. "Did you pick the seats up from Beth early, or do you have your own set?" she asked curiously.

"I have my own set," Doncan told her. "When she had Heather I bought a car seat right away so that she didn't have any excuse not to let me take her for a few hours now and then. I've spent a fortune on seats now, as the children keep coming and then they insist on growing as well!"

Carly laughed. "So you've been the doting uncle all along?"

"I was surprised, when Heather arrived, just how doting I quickly became. All three of them can get just about anything they want from me and they know it. But they're terrific kids and I love them a lot."

"They really do seem like great kids," Carly agreed. "I hope they don't wear us out too much today."

"Oh, they'll wear us out, but it will be worth it," Doncan smiled at her briefly. "We're here."

He stopped the car on the driveway of a large family home. The front door was open as soon as the engine stopped and three small children charged out the front door to swarm their beloved uncle.

"Can we see the...."

"I want to get ice cream...."

"Ducks, ducks, ducks...."

"What about...."

Doncan laughed and then shouted over the excited voices. "Okay, enough! We can see every animal at the park. We can have lunch at the café there and if you eat everything on your plates you can have ice cream for dessert. And yes, there will be lots of ducks." The last comment was aimed at Maggie. Doncan now swung her up in the air and then pulled her close and kissed her flushed face.

"Everyone ready to go?" he asked the little gang.

"YES!" The reply was shouted by all three of them.

"Into the car, then," Doncan instructed. The three kids nearly fell over each other in their eagerness to get into Doncan's car. Beth had now made her way out of the house and she watched with an amused smile as her brood tumbled over one another in their excitement.

"Everyone be good for Uncle Doncan and Aunt Carly. I don't want them bringing you back early because you didn't behave," she told the kids as she leaned into the car to check that car seat straps were hooked nice and tightly. Then she turned to her brother. "For goodness' sake, don't spoil them too much," she said, giving him the same indulgent smile she had given Matthew at dinner when he had asked for a second piece of cake.

Doncan grinned at her. "It's my job to spoil them rotten. You get to do the same to my kids if I ever have any."

Beth looked slightly surprised by the words, but didn't reply. Instead she turned to Carly. "Please make sure that they eat something with some nutritive value before they eat their own body weight in ice cream," she said with a grin. "If they don't behave, bring them back early and I'll make them spend the rest of the day on the naughty step."

Carly smiled at the other woman. "I'm sure they'll be wonderful," she said. "I'm really looking forward to it."

Beth grinned. "I just hope you're still smiling when you get back."

The drive to the wildlife park took them across the mountains and Doncan pointed out that they were driving on the TT course. "It's one of motorcycling's great road racing challenges," he told Carly. "The course is nearly thirty-eight miles of tight turns, hills and valleys and a long climb over these mountains."

Carly nodded. When she had read up on the island, she had learned a little bit about the Tourist Trophy (TT) races. "It's also very danger-ous, isn't it?" she asked quietly, not wanting the children to hear the conversation.

"The riders are moving at very high speed along closed public roads. There are a lot of dangers, but the people who do it swear it's worth the risks. If you look at the curb, you can tell that this is part of the course."

Carly looked over at the curb that ran along the side of the road. It was painted in alternating sections of black and white paint. "Wow, they paint the curbs for the whole thirty-eight miles?" she asked in amazement.

"There might be some sections that don't have curbs," Doncan shrugged. "But every section that does is painted."

Carly shook her head. The island was an interesting and, in some ways, very foreign place.

"There's Snaefell," Doncan told her, pointing to the top of one of the mountains they were passing. "The top of that is the highest point on the island."

Carly looked at the mountain. It didn't look much taller than its neighbors. Before she could comment, however, Doncan continued.

"There's the mountain railway," he told her. She looked to see a bright red train car making its way up the side of the mountain. "Oh, how fun," she exclaimed. "I'd love to ride the train up the mountain."

"We'll have to see if we can fit it in during your stay," Doncan told her.

"What's at the top?" she asked eagerly.

"A small café and a rock that marks the highest point," Doncan shrugged. "It isn't very exciting, really, but if you want to go, we can try to find time."

Carly smiled at him. "I know you're really busy right now," she answered. "Maybe it will have to wait for my next visit, when I bring Granny."

"They shut the train during the winter months," Doncan told her. "I guess you'll have to visit again another time." Before Carly could answer, he was pointing in the opposite direction from the mountain that was disappearing behind them.

"You can just begin to see Ramsey, where we had dinner the other night," Doncan pointed ahead of them at the valley that Carly could just see below them. He slowed down as they began their descent into the town. Carly watched as the houses and buildings got larger as they got nearer.

She was shocked by the incredibly tight turns that marked the entrance into Ramsey. "It's called the Ramsey Hairpin," Doncan told her as he noted the surprised look on her face. "The TT course goes in the opposite direction, but imagine racing up this turn."

Carly shook her head. She wasn't all that happy riding in a car around the tight bends. She didn't want to think what it might feel like on a motorcycle at high speed. Ramsey was a small town, and they passed through it quickly, back into the stunning beauty of the countryside.

"You guys are awfully quiet back there," Doncan said to his nieces and nephew as they drove. "I hope you aren't plotting something."

The children giggled and then Heather spoke. "Mum said we were to be good and quiet and not be hard work for you guys. She said Carly is too nice to scare away."

Doncan raised an eyebrow and Carly blushed. "What did she mean by that?" Doncan asked.

"She said Carly was perfect for you and we weren't to make her think children were impossible," was Heather's reply, innocently repeating exactly what her mother had said.

Doncan laughed loudly and Carly blushed and stammered, trying to think of how to explain to the kids that she and Doncan were business associates and nothing more. After a moment, Doncan shook his head at Carly. "Not worth trying to explain," he murmured to her. "Heather's six, adult relationships are a mystery to her."

Carly nodded, willing to let things go with Heather, but determined to have a serious talk with Beth when they took the children back in the afternoon.

Doncan had a season ticket to the Park that included his nieces and nephew and an occasional guest. Carly grinned. He really was a doting uncle.

"Where do we start?" he asked the three excited children as soon as they were inside the gates.

Heather laughed. "We always start with the mongooses," she reminded him. "That way the penguins are last, because they're the best."

"They are not," Matthew insisted. "The wallabies are the best, but since they are in the middle we can't stop or start with them."

"Duck," Maggie shouted, pointing to a chicken that was wandering around the entrance area.

Doncan laughed. "Okay, mongooses first, wallabies in the middle and penguins last. I suspect we'll have ducks pretty much all the way through." He opened the first set of gates and held them for everyone to pass through.

"Ducks aren't on exhibit," he explained to Carly. "They just stop by to visit. Maggie pretty much thinks all birds are ducks anyway."

Inside the gates, everyone stopped to look at the single mongoose that was sunning himself in his enclosure.

"Okay, then," Doncan said once the children had watched the sleeping animal for a few moments. "What are the rules?"

Heather grinned. "Everyone holds hands, stays together and no one shouts."

"Good girl," Doncan rewarded her with a kiss on the top of the head and then he grabbed her hand. She took Matthew's hand and Matthew took Maggie's.

"Come on, Aunt Carly," Heather instructed Carly. "You have to take Uncle Doncan's hand before we can go any further."

"Maybe I should hold Maggie's?" Carly suggested nervously.

"She needs one free to point out ducks," Doncan said to her quietly. "Everyone has to follow the rules," he added, giving her a playful grin.

Carly gave him a determined smile and took the offered hand. There was no way she was going to make a scene in front of the children. The electric charge that ran through her when their hands touched subsided to a warm glow as they walked from enclosure to enclosure.

Each section had a double set of gates and at every set Doncan carefully swapped Heather's hand into Carly's while he held open the gates. Once through, he reinserted himself between them once again.

Carly was almost as excited as the children as they made their way past pelicans, cranes, different types of deer and then, finally, the wallabies.

"I think these are my favorites," Carly told the kids as they watched the marsupials bounce around them. "At least so far."

"Ducks," Maggie announced solemnly, pointing to a large aviary that was the next section they would be walking through.

After the aviary came the "North American Trail" and Carly laughed when they came to the raccoon enclosure. "They're not zoo animals where I live," she told the others.

As they emerged from the trees surrounding the trail, they came to a large café. "Who's hungry?" Doncan asked. The excited chorus of "me" meant that it was time to stop for lunch.

Carly took the girls into the ladies' room so everyone could wash their hands. Doncan took Matthew to do the same.

"This is much better than when we come with just Uncle Doncan," Heather said confidingly. "He makes us all go in the boys' room with him."

Carly grinned at her. "I'm having a wonderful time," she told the little girl. "I'm really glad that I got to come with you."

"You should marry Uncle Doncan and stay here," Heather told her. "Then you could come with us every time."

Carly flushed and then shook her head. "I've got to go back to my home," she told the child. "But I hope I might come and visit again someday."

Lots of french fries, a few chicken nuggets and an incredible amount of ice cream were consumed over the next hour or so. Carly and Doncan had sandwiches rather than chicken nuggets, but the children managed, with very little effort, to persuade Carly to indulge in some ice cream.

After lunch the happy little group finished going around the park, seeing capybaras swimming in a small pond, scarily large and free-ranging rhea (similar to an ostrich) and adorable monkeys. The penguins did come last and everyone enjoyed watching them swim in their pool and waddle around their enclosure.

Maggie's feet had given up shortly after lunch and Doncan and Carly took turns carrying her through the enclosures. By the time they reached the penguins, Matthew's feet were dragging, and Doncan handed Maggie to Carly so that he could carry Matthew back to the car. The little group, tired, happy and stuffed full of ice cream, made their way out of the last exhibit.

"I'm sorry to bother you," said a voice from behind Carly. She turned around and smiled instinctively at the elderly woman who had tapped her shoulder.

"I just wanted to tell you how lovely your children are," the woman continued. "I've been following you around all afternoon and I must confess I've been watching your children as much as I've been watching the animals."

Carly smiled as she tried to think what to say in reply. The woman continued before Carly could explain.

"You and your husband do such a great job with them," she said patting Carly's arm. "Taking turns carrying the baby and answering all of their questions. He's a handsome one," the woman grinned at Doncan. "And you can tell that you two are very much in love. It just shows in everything that you do."

Now Carly opened her mouth to explain, but Doncan interrupted smoothly. "Thank you so much," he told the woman. "The kids actually belong to my sister. We've just borrowed them as an excuse for a day out."

The elderly woman smiled at his words. "I hope you're going to have a few of your own," she told them both. "You're both wonderful with little ones."

Again, Doncan spoke before Carly could explain. "That would be the plan," he assured the woman with a smile. "Thank you again for your kind words. I'll make sure I tell my sister how impressed you were with her children."

The woman walked off after that, before Carly could say anything. "You should have explained the truth," she hissed at Doncan.

"I told her they weren't our kids," Doncan said easily.

"Yeah, but you let her think we're a couple."

"No harm done," Doncan assured her. "It was hardly worth making long explanations to a total stranger."

Carly shrugged. Doncan was probably right. What difference did it make what a stranger thought? The woman's words kept playing through her head on the drive back to Laxey, though. As Maggie slept and the other children sat quietly resting from their active morning, all Carly could hear in her head was "you can tell you two are very much in love...." over and over again.

❧ 12 ❧

↓

Carly didn't get a chance to talk to Beth when they dropped the children back off at their home. By the time little Maggie was carried off to her bed for a nap and the older two kids started telling their parents all about their day, Doncan was eager to get back to Douglas.

"I'm really sorry," he told Beth and Mark as well as Carly. "But I have about three days' worth of work to get through this afternoon."

The drive back to Douglas was a silent one. Carly found that she was tired after the day spent in the sun and she was happy to just relax back in her seat and let Doncan focus on the things on his mind.

"I wish I could take you to dinner later," he told her as he walked her to her door. "But I really don't think I'll get a break."

"It's fine," Carly insisted to him. "It isn't your job to keep me entertained. I'll probably grab room service again. That isn't a luxury I get at home, so I really should use it as much as possible."

"I'm going to have to get you a taxi to Laxey tomorrow morning," he told her with a frown. "I'll need to be in the office really early."

"That's fine," Carly assured him. "I've just about finished the packing up. I expect to be finished by Wednesday at the latest."

"Terrific," Doncan smiled. "Maybe you can go sight-seeing on Thursday. I'm planning on taking Friday afternoon off to get Bessie's things moved to my house, assuming this estate is settled by then. I was hoping to get everything done much sooner, but maybe we can get all of the paperwork sorted out and signed for the cottage on Friday as well."

"That sounds good," Carly answered. She studied his face and found herself frowning. He looked tired and stressed now. At least while they had been out with the children he had managed to look relaxed and happy.

"I hope I'll be able to pick you up around five tomorrow night at Bessie's," Doncan told her. "I'll call you if I can't make it."

Carly nodded and Doncan kissed the top of her head in a distracted gesture and then disappeared back towards the elevators.

Carly was waiting on the hotel's steps the next morning, watching for a taxi, when a small car pulled up. The driver beeped the horn twice and then waved. Carly was surprised to see Beth driving the little vehicle.

"I have a half-day today at work and Mum has the kids, so I told Doncan I would pick you up," she explained to Carly as Carly climbed into the car.

"That's very kind of you," Carly said, smiling at the other woman.

"Please, it's the least I can do after you took the kids for most of yesterday for me."

"We had a great time," Carly laughed. "They are terrific kids and the Wildlife Park was wonderful."

"I'm glad you had fun," Beth told her. "They are great kids, but they can be a handful."

"Doncan has strict rules for them and they followed them perfectly," Carly told her. "They held hands and stayed together and no one shouted, well, not too much."

Beth laughed. "I bet Maggie yelled 'duck' every five minutes."

"Pretty much," Carly agreed.

The two chatted like old friends as Beth drove Carly to Bessie's cottage, both carefully avoiding any mention of Doncan. Carly wasn't sure why Beth didn't bring him up, but she was more than happy to stay well away from the sensitive subject. At the cottage, Beth smiled at her.

"I remember spending a few nights here when I was younger," she confided to Carly. "Sometimes no one seems to understand you when you're a teenager. Bessie always seemed, if not to understand, then at least not to judge."

"I wish I could have met her," Carly said sadly.

"At least you're getting to see her cottage and meet all of us," Beth answered. "We've all come to think of you as part of the family."

Carly blushed. "That's very kind of you," she muttered, at something of a loss for words.

"Doncan's going to ring me if he can't get back for you. I've told him I'm happy to run over and grab you around five. I have to take Matthew to his Tae Kwon Do class in Douglas anyway, so it's no problem."

As Carly rushed out many thanks, Beth spoke over her. "And here's your lunch. Doncan was quite specific about what I was to pack for you." Now Beth looked at Carly with open curiosity as she handed her the bag of food. "It isn't like my brother to worry about other people," she said in a questioning tone.

"I guess he needs to look after his clients," Carly blushed and moved to get out of the car.

"I suppose so," Beth replied softly, still giving Carly a considering look. "I may well see you later."

"Great." Carly rushed away into the cottage, suddenly needing to put space between herself and Doncan's inquiring sister.

The day passed slowly. The highlight was the lunch that Beth had packed, which was delicious. Carly felt like she was winding down now, packing up the last few rooms, and she felt sad about that. Somehow it made Bessie's death feel more real. Now that she had met so many people who had known Bessie, she felt close to the relative she had never met and she was reluctant to sell the house and break her ties with her great-aunt.

It was Beth who reappeared at five to take her back to Douglas.

"Doncan asked me to apologize for not ringing you," she told Carly.

"He only had time for one conversation, so he rang me to ask me to pick you up."

"That's fine," Carly said in a determinedly cheerful voice. "I'm sure he's really busy."

"Apparently things have become really ugly," Beth said. "No one was happy with the will and all of the lawyers are threatening to sue. It's just a big mess."

"Wanna come and watch me kick stuff?"

The voice from the back of the car had Carly turning around to look at Matthew. "What are you going to kick?" she asked curiously, happy for the change in subject.

"Mostly we kick big pads," Matthew shrugged. "Once in a while we get to kick each other."

Carly swallowed a laugh as Beth spoke. "Only when you're in full safety gear, right?"

"Yeah," Matthew smiled. "It's really neat. We have all this padded gear and then we can kick each other and not get too hurt. That's the best part."

Carly smiled at him. "It does sound like fun."

"So you'll come and watch?" Matthew said hopefully.

"Oh, well, I mean...." Carly wasn't sure how to respond.

"Carly might be busy tonight," Beth said smoothly. She turned to Carly and spoke softly. "You're more than welcome to come and sit with me at the sports center. We can grab a cold drink from the café and watch the kids through the windows and chat. Or you can just tell Matt that you're busy. It isn't really a big deal, whatever he says."

Carly turned around to tell Matthew "no", but he gave her a huge, heart-melting grin.

"Please, Aunt Carly?" he begged.

"Oh, all right, if your mother doesn't really mind," Carly couldn't help but laugh. It wasn't like she had any exciting plans for the night anyway.

The sports center was large and well-equipped with several pools and a number of different sized gym spaces. Matthew's class took place in a large space that had windows overlooking it, so Carly and Beth got drinks and sat and watched the kids.

They were quiet for a few minutes, just watching. Carly winced as Matthew moved to kick a large pad and missed, falling over instead.

"Ouch, that had to hurt," she remarked.

"Matthew won't notice," Beth said calmly. "He's a pretty tough little guy."

"I can't imagine watching my kids getting kicked," Carly told the other woman.

"It isn't always easy," Beth admitted. "Especially when I watch him work with the older ones who actually manage to connect now and then. But he absolutely loves it, so, for now at least, I go along."

Carly winced again as Matthew's next kick connected and he fell over backwards from the impact. "Being a parent is harder work than I realized," she laughed as Beth gave her son a "thumbs up" when he jumped back to his feet and waved to them through the glass.

"There's a lot more to it than you realize when you start," Beth agreed. "But if you knew what you were getting into, you wouldn't have kids in the first place. And then you would miss out on so much joy and love. It really is worth every impossibly hard and amazingly wonderful moment."

Carly smiled. "I hope to find out some day."

"Doncan surprised me the other day when he mentioned having kids some day," Beth confided. "He's always sworn up and down that he would never have kids. That's one reason he dotes on mine so much."

"Maybe yours have finally convinced him that he wants some of his own," Carly suggested, feeling uncomfortable with the topic.

"I think it's more likely that he's finally met someone he can imagine having children with," Beth said, looking at Carly steadily.

Carly instantly shook her head. "I'm sorry, but I just got dumped by my boyfriend and I have a life I love in Pennsylvania. There's no way I'm giving up everything and moving over here for a man I barely know."

To Carly's surprise, Beth just laughed. "We all think we know what we want, don't we?" she asked.

"What do you mean?" Carly was confused.

"I was engaged before, wait, here, look." Beth scrabbled in her purse and dug out her wallet. From a pocket, she dug out an old photograph. It showed Beth and an absolutely gorgeous man smiling together. Beth was wearing an engagement ring, with her hand resting on the man's chest.

"Wow, he's gorgeous," Carly said, almost without thinking.

"Yeah, he is," Beth agreed. "And he's rich. I thought he was just about perfect many years ago."

"So what happened?" Carly asked.

Beth grinned and slid the picture back into its pocket. "He dumped me. It's kind of a long story. Are you sure you want to hear it?"

Carly could tell by the smile Beth gave her that she was just teasing. "Of course I want to hear it," Carly told her, stating the obvious.

"His name is Paul, and we met when I was just finishing up my studies at medical school. His father was actually a private patient at the hospital where I was working and Paul asked me out for coffee one night during his father's stay. Things progressed from there, really. I had a couple more years of training to go, focusing on obstetrics, but Paul wanted me to quit school and travel the world with him."

"Sounds dreamy," Carly told her as Beth stopped, lost in thought for a moment.

"Yeah, 'dreamy' is a good word for it. But do you really want to live in a dream long term? That was the question that Mark asked me when I told him I was marrying Paul. What he meant was that he could see me getting bored with doing nothing with my life very quickly. Paul was about as arrogant and self-centered as you would expect a very rich man to be. He wanted a wife who was going to devote herself fully to him."

Carly nodded slowly, trying to understand. "So you decided you couldn't be that woman?"

Beth shook her head and smiled ruefully. "I wasn't that smart back then. I was sure that I could be that woman. I was ready to throw away all my years of studying and my plans to be a doctor in order to follow Paul around the world and just be his wife. I might even have been happy. I don't know."

"So what happened?"

"Paul and I started to talk about children. He assumed that we would have a fleet of nannies and then send them all to boarding school. His lifestyle didn't have a lot of room for small children and their incessant demands. That was the first crack in our relationship."

"Did he even want children?" Carly questioned.

"Oh yes, must carry on the family name and all that," Beth grinned. "He wanted a couple, but he didn't want them to bother him especially."

"I think I would have had a problem with that as well," Carly told her, finding it difficult to imagine.

"It was how he was raised," Beth explained. "He survived, so he didn't see any problem with it. It wasn't how I was raised, though."

"Me either," Carly told her.

"Anyway, that was our first argument, and a few days later he dumped me. He said he just didn't think I was ideal for him. I was turning out to be not as much fun as he had expected. I went to cry on my best friend's shoulder," Beth grinned. "Mark was my best friend from the very first day of medical school. He was actually from a small town in the north of England, so we had similar backgrounds. We just gravitated towards each other and became good friends. He wasn't my type at all, and he swore I wasn't his, so we studied together, went out for meals together, and did just about everything together." She paused again, once more lost in her own thoughts.

"You can't stop there," Carly protested. "What happened next?"

Beth laughed. "I told Mark how Paul had dumped me and about our fight about raising children and Mark got really upset. He started talking about studies that have been done about neglected children and the negative effects of boarding school and all sorts of stuff. I started trying to defend Paul for some reason. Suddenly Mark and I were arguing for the first time ever as well. After a while I just slammed out of his apartment and went back across the hall to mine and cried myself to sleep. When I woke up the next morning I realized that I was far more upset about the fight with Mark than I was about the fact that Paul had dumped me. Then I just had to convince Mark to marry me."

Carly laughed. "That couldn't have been hard," she said.

"You'd be surprised," Beth answered. "Mark is shy and somewhat insecure. It took him a long time to believe that I was really attracted to him. But it was totally worth every second that it took. I know I made the right choice. Every day, when I wake up next to him, I still can't believe how lucky I am."

Carly smiled at her. "You make a great couple," she told Beth. "It's obvious that you're very much in love and that you're wonderful parents."

"So what's going on between you and my brother?" Beth asked.

Carly opened her mouth to answer, a hundred different replies springing to mind, but she was interrupted by a small boy in a white uniform.

"Mummy, did you see me? Master Hall said my roundhouse kick is getting really good!" Matthew bounced into his mother's arms for a quick hug before bouncing away.

"Did you watch, Aunt Carly? Did you see me doing my form? I've almost learned all of it, but I keep messing up my stances."

Carly laughed. She had no idea what he was talking about, but she gave him a huge hug and told him how wonderfully he had done. Mostly, she was just grateful for the interruption.

The rest of the week continued in much the same way. Beth picked Carly up every morning and afternoon, providing her with a wonderful packed lunch each day. Carly was mostly finished with the packing, but she found that she loved spending time in Bessie's cottage anyway. She spent hours sorting out Bessie's books, and then spent many more hours reading through the ones that looked the most interesting.

Each afternoon, Carly accompanied Beth and one or more of the children to their daily activities. Carly watched Heather try to learn to swim, watched more Tae Kwon Do with Matthew and got to see Maggie's attempts at ballet. She and Beth talked about anything and everything except Doncan and Carly felt like they were great friends by Friday morning.

Doncan called Carly a couple of times in the evening and was always hugely apologetic for neglecting her. The conversations always felt awkward to Carly, so she kept them short and to the point. She called Granny and her mother once or twice to update them on the packing, but kept those conversations as short as possible as well. She barely even thought about Tom.

Friday was overcast and cool and Carly was mostly happy to finish packing the last of Bessie's books into one last box. By lunchtime she had finished and after she ate the sandwiches that Beth had provided she took a slow stroll around the house. It looked very different now, with everything personal packed away. All that remained were the large furniture pieces that were going into storage at Doncan's home and a couple of neat piles of boxes of things Carly wanted her Granny to see. Most of Bessie's books had ended up in the "storage" pile as well. Carly loved books too much to get rid of many.

Before she had time to get too emotional about the whole subject, she heard a horn honking outside the cottage. She rushed down the stairs and opened the door to a muscularly built man in a dirty T-shirt.

"You must be Carly," the man said. "I'm Jack from Island Movers. Doncan said I could meet him here."

"Oh, yes," Carly answered, feeling flustered. "That is, Doncan isn't here, but I am Carly."

She smiled at the man, feeling a bit lost. She hadn't been expecting a moving company to arrive. She looked past the man at the large white moving van that was now parked in the small driveway. Maybe Doncan knew he wasn't going to make it, so he'd sent professional help?

Another horn honked and Carly was relieved when she recognized Doncan's car as it parked behind the moving van.

"Oy, you've blocked me in," Jack shouted angrily at Doncan as the lawyer stepped out of his car.

"You don't think I'm letting you leave before every last little bit of work is finished, do you?" Doncan shouted back. "If I didn't block you in, you'd probably try to sneak off when we're only half done."

"Aye, I would at that," the man grinned and then gave Doncan a big hug. Doncan was dressed in jeans and a T-shirt and looked less like a lawyer than he usually did, but he still didn't look like the kind of person who would be friends with someone like Jack.

"Carly, I see you've met my cousin Jack," Doncan smiled at Carly and then gave her a quick hug as well.

"Your cousin?" Carly questioned as she was released.

"Yeah, don't let appearances fool you," Doncan told her. "He owns the moving company and he makes four or five times what I make in a year."

"Doesn't matter," the other man replied. "Marcia spends it just as fast as I make it, mostly on those spoiled brats of ours."

"Your kids are wonderful, and only a little spoiled," Doncan answered.

"And I'm sorry we didn't get to meet you at the picnic," Jack told Carly. "The wife insisted that we have a fortnight at Disneyland in Paris and we had to miss the big family gathering this year."

Before Carly could think of a suitable reply, Doncan was giving instructions to Jack and the two men who now appeared from the van. Carly offered to help once or twice and even tried moving a box, but she quickly found that she was just in the way, so she headed outside to watch the sea while the professionals got on with the job.

She was sitting on her favorite large rock watching the tide come in when Doncan found her.

"The guys are just about finished," he said quietly once he reached her side.

"Great," Carly answered as she faced him, her emotions in turmoil.

"It's nice to see you, by the way," Doncan said, resting a hand on her arm.

"You, too." Carly blushed and turned back to look at the sea. "I hope your case is all sorted out," she said formally.

"Pretty much," Doncan answered, moving a step closer to her and slipping an arm around her. "It's chilly down here by the water," he remarked almost as an explanation.

"I feel bad about selling the cottage," Carly blurted out. "Like I'm letting Bessie down somehow."

"Bessie wouldn't feel that way at all," Doncan told her. "She knew that when your Granny inherited the cottage it would have to be sold. We talked a lot about the different options that she had, but she really wanted your Granny to be the beneficiary of her estate. She left a special account just for someone to travel here to deal with the sale mostly because she wanted someone who was family to finalize everything. But if you hadn't wanted to come, she left provisions for that in the will as well."

"Granny didn't like the idea of having everything dealt with by strangers."

Doncan shook his head. "I did tell her that I knew Bessie well and would handle everything with great care, but maybe it was all too much for her to take in at one time. I gave her a lot of information very quickly."

Now Carly shook her head. "No, I'm sure Granny understood perfectly. She just wanted me to come and see the island and get away from Meadville for a while. I think I know what she was thinking."

Doncan looked at her curiously, but she didn't continue. After a moment, he went on. "Bessie knew you would sell the cottage and the furnishings. We used to talk about what might happen to the place after she was gone. There are a lot of options."

"I would love for a little family to buy it and raise their children here," Carly told him.

"Actually, I already have a potential buyer in mind. There's a large construction company that is interested in buying the place, tearing it down and building luxury apartments here instead."

Carly shook her head. "I hate the thought of it being torn down."

Doncan smiled at her and pulled her closer to him. "Carly, I understand that, but your Granny could make a lot of money from the sale. It would be quick because they've already received preliminary planning permission. You should take a look at what they're planning. It would only be two apartments and they would be built to look something like the cottage they're replacing."

"But they would still be tearing the cottage down," Carly replied.

"Even your dream little family might do that," Doncan argued. "It needs so much work, it might be more economical to start over."

"But," Carly tried to argue, but Doncan held up a hand. "Let me get copies of their plans for you to look at," he told her. "I want to have two different appraisals done so that we'll be sure we know the fair market value of the property. Then we can see what the developer offers and you can decide if you want to accept that or put the house on the market and hope someone else wants to buy it. You have to understand, though, that you can't sell it with restrictions. Whoever buys it can tear it down if they want to do so, either right away or ten years from now or whenever."

Carly shrugged and pulled away from Doncan. "I still would rather it was sold to a family, rather than a developer," she said, trying not to sound too angry. It wasn't really Doncan's fault that she felt so miserable about selling the cottage.

"We'll have the appraisals done and I'll get you copies of the plans," Doncan told her, pulling her back towards him. "We can talk some more after that."

"I guess that seems fair," Carly answered, suddenly aware that one of Doncan's hands was rubbing her back. It was hard to think clearly while that was happening.

"Hey, Donny," a voice shouted from behind them. They both spun around and Carly was sure she had a guilty look on her face as she forced herself to smile at Jack.

"We're just about done. You need to move your car," Jack called down to them.

"No problem," Doncan called back. "You can follow us to my place."

Jack nodded and then went back into the cottage. Doncan helped Carly down from her rock and then held her hand as they walked back up the path to the cottage.

"Donny?" she asked teasingly.

"When I was four, everyone called me that," Doncan told her. "I haven't used it since I started school at five."

"Doncan suits you better, I think," she answered appraisingly. "You're too sophisticated to be 'Donny' anymore."

Carly quickly walked through the house again, this time double-checking that nothing had been left behind. "I guess that's everything," she told Doncan when she returned to the kitchen. The movers were loading the last few boxes into the back of the van.

"Let's go, then," Doncan replied. She carefully locked the cottage door behind them, feeling sad but also relieved in some ways that the job was finished. She was silent on the short drive to Doncan's house, but once they turned up the driveway that changed.

"This is your house?" she asked incredulously.

"You don't like it?" Doncan asked.

Carly was momentarily speechless as she studied the huge house that had come into view as they'd driven up the long driveway. It was a massive two-story stone property that must have been built at least a hundred years ago. Carly could see the sea stretching out behind it, so it would have amazing views from inside. Doncan pulled up onto the large circular brick driveway and parked the car.

"Come and see the inside," he invited.

Carly couldn't get out of the car fast enough. She was dying to see the inside of the gorgeous old seaside mansion. Doncan opened the large wooden door and then grinned at Carly.

"Go ahead and take yourself on a tour. I'll stay down here and direct the guys as to where to put Bessie's things."

Carly didn't argue. She spent a happy half hour walking from one spacious and gracious living space to another, delighting in discovering beautiful period features with fabulous modern amenities. The kitchen was enormous, and had obviously been recently remodeled, but the remodeling had been done in keeping with the age of the house, creating a beautiful and ageless kitchen space.

Upstairs, Carly counted six bedrooms, including a master bedroom suite that included a dressing room, two separate walk-in closets, a small sitting room area and a huge master bathroom. Here everything was shiny and modern, from the double whirlpool tub to the immense tiled shower with the rain shower-head and body jets.

There were two other bathrooms on the bedroom level, but they looked like they hadn't been updated since they had been installed. Carly wandered around a second time, inspecting each empty room, mentally filling them with various pieces from Bessie's furniture collection.

"Carly?"

She jumped when Doncan called her name from far away.

"Sorry," she called back, walking towards the central staircase that led up from the entryway. "I'm coming."

She found him in the foyer, laughing with the moving men.

"We're all set," Jack told Carly with a smile. "I'd better get home before Marcia sells the kids to one of the neighbors."

Carly thanked all of the men for their time, hoping that Doncan had paid them well for the service.

"So, what do you think of the house?" Doncan asked Carly once he had shut the front door.

"It's amazing," Carly told him. "I love every bit of it. The kitchen is perfect because it isn't overly modern but it has all the modern appliances. The master bathroom is gorgeous. I just didn't realize you were this rich."

The words were out of her mouth before she'd thought them through and Carly found herself blushing and stammering as soon as she realized what she had said.

Doncan just smiled. "Actually, I bought the house many years ago, when house prices were low. I received a generous inheritance when my grandfather passed away and when I bought the house it was a wreck. It had been standing empty for about ten years and nothing had been done to modernize it since it had been built, so I got a good deal."

Carly nodded, still impressed by the magnificent home.

"And the Quayles are a big family," Doncan continued. "I've done a lot of the work myself and I have plumbers, electricians, and just about everything else somewhere on the family tree. I just call my mother when I need something and she calls around and finds me a convenient cousin who is happy to work for beer and pizza on a Saturday."

Carly nodded again. Even if he was telling the whole truth, the house still had to be worth a fortune.

"Anyway, I have two more bathrooms to finish and then I'll decide whether I want to keep it or sell it."

"Why would you sell it?" Carly asked in surprise.

"It's much too big a house for just one person," Doncan answered. "So if I'm still single when the work is done, I'll probably sell."

Carly didn't answer. She wasn't sure what she even wanted to say. Back in Douglas, the pair grabbed a quick dinner at a small café near the hotel. They kept the conversation to neutral topics until Doncan walked her back to her room.

"I'll call two appraisal companies first thing Monday and see if they can get the cottage done early next week," he told Carly at her door.

"Terrific," Carly answered, distracted by the rush of emotions she was feeling.

"If you agree to sell to the developers, we can have the whole thing sorted out in just a few days," he reminded her. "Your granny can have a check in her hand before the summer is over."

Carly shook her head. "I really don't want to sell to someone who wants to tear the place down," she sighed.

Doncan sighed as well. "You have to think about what's best for your grandmother. Surely a quick sale is better than uncertainty?"

Carly nodded reluctantly. Doncan studied her for a long time and then sighed. "Sorry, but I've really missed you," he told her just before he pulled her close and kissed her thoroughly. Before Carly could do more than enjoy the passionate embrace, he pulled back and smiled at her.

"I needed that," he told her. "I'll call you tomorrow."

Carly opened her mouth to reply, but Doncan was already headed for the lifts.

13

Carly slept in on Saturday, enjoying the feeling of not having to be anywhere at any particular time. She hadn't slept well. Thoughts of Bessie, the cottage, and, of course, Doncan had raced around her brain for most of the night. She finally dragged herself up at ten and took a long hot shower. She had no plans for the day, which left her feeling restless.

Once dressed, she decided to head into the shopping area to do some window-shopping and maybe pick up a few more souvenirs. Still feeling restless, she wandered from shop to shop, ending up in a small grocery store where she entertained herself by trying to figure out how different things like "plain flour" and "icing sugar" were from similar items back home. At noon she grabbed a sandwich at a small café near her hotel.

As she paid for her lunch, she couldn't help but smile at the differently sized and brightly colored currency. While she knew it had real value, it sort of felt like play money to her. She took a long, slow walk along the promenade, watching the waves and letting her mind wander. Except every time it tried to wander off to think about Doncan, she forced herself to focus on Bessie or Beth and her adorable children instead.

It was nearly three o'clock, and she was heading back to her hotel, when her phone rang.

"Carly? It's Doncan. I am so sorry." The instantly recognized voice made Carly's heart race. "Would you believe that I just woke up?"

Carly smiled at the contrite tone. "Just woke up?" she asked. "But it's nearly three o'clock."

"I know," Doncan said. "I was shocked when I saw the clock. I didn't sleep well last week, with all the stress of dealing with that nightmare estate, but I certainly didn't expect to sleep all day today."

"Well, you clearly needed the rest."

"Yes, I guess I did," Doncan agreed. "Anyway, I'm awake now and I'm starving. If I grab a quick shower and throw some clothes on, would you like to have a very early dinner with me?"

Carly laughed. "I had lunch at a fairly normal time," she told him. "But I guess I can manage some dinner. As long as you promise not to get too upset if I don't eat much."

Doncan laughed as well. "I'll tell you what, why don't you come here?" he suggested. "I can start eating as soon as I'm dressed and then fix something for both of us in a few hours when you'll be hungry again."

Carly hesitated, suddenly nervous. "Come to your apartment?" she asked uncertainly.

"I promise to behave like a perfect gentleman," Doncan told her, clearly understanding her tone perfectly. He gave her the address and she agreed to walk over in about an hour. It was only a few minutes' walk away from her hotel and the weather was just about perfect.

Back at the hotel, she combed her hair and added some extra makeup. "He said he's going to be a perfect gentleman," she told her mirror image as she added just a little extra mascara. Her mirror image frowned at her. "Don't look at me like that," she exclaimed. "Of course I want him to behave." Her mirror image looked skeptical, but Carly ignored her.

Carly wasn't sure exactly what she was expecting Doncan's apartment to be like. She thought about it as she walked along the promenade again, this time checking the numbers on the buildings as she made her way along. It will be all glass and stainless steel, the perfect bachelor pad, she decided as she realized she was getting close.

The building itself was one of the larger ones on the seafront. She entered through modern glass doors into a large reception area that looked more like a very expensive hotel lobby than the entrance to an apartment building. There was a uniformed man behind a desk that contributed to the overall hotel effect.

"Can I help you?" he asked, his tone doubtful, as if he was certain that Carly had stumbled into his building by accident.

"I'm here to see Doncan Quayle," she answered, hating how nervous she sounded. The man behind the desk slowly looked her up and down and then frowned as if unimpressed with what he saw.

"I'll ring his home and see if he is expecting you," the man said stiffly. "What is your name?"

"Oh, I'm...."

"Carly," Doncan's voice reached her before she finished. A second later she was being pulled close into a tight hug. When Doncan released her he stared hard at her for a long minute, as if memorizing her features. Carly was sure that he was going to kiss her, and he might have if the desk clerk hadn't coughed loudly behind them.

"I gather you were expecting her," he said dryly, turning away to answer a buzzing telephone.

Doncan just smiled and then tucked his arm around Carly, gently pulling her towards the bank of elevators at the back of the lobby.

Of course he pushed "P" for penthouse. Carly had been expecting nothing less. There was only a short hallway on the top floor, with only four doors leading off of it. Clearly the penthouse apartments were large ones.

Doncan tapped a code into a panel next to his door and a small click told them that it had unlocked. Doncan pushed the door open and motioned for Carly to step inside. She looked around curiously as she entered, but the door opened only into a small entryway. Doncan slipped off his shoes and left them by the door.

"I think it's a European thing," he answered when Carly questioned him. "We always took our shoes off at the door when we were kids and it's really habit now. You can leave yours on if you want."

Carly thought about it and then decided to slip hers off as well. It would be more comfortable as well as being polite.

The entryway had three walls, all of which were lined with shoe cupboards and racks for hanging coats. Now she and Doncan turned right and walked through the large opening that led into the rest of the apartment.

Carly took a few steps around the entry wall and then stopped and simply stared. The huge living room's back wall was entirely made up of windows that showcased the sea below. It was almost the same view as from her hotel room, but seemed a hundred times larger without anything blocking it.

"It's stunning," she breathed, watching the waves and the sand sparkling in the sunshine.

"It's a great view," Doncan agreed. "I have to say, I haven't grown tired of it yet."

"I can't imagine that anyone ever could," Carly told him, walking slowly towards the windows. She could see the entire promenade, from end to end. She watched a ferry pull away from the Sea Terminal and then forced herself to look at the apartment itself.

Again, Doncan had surprised her. Instead of sleek glass and chrome, the apartment had a warm and homey feel. The floors were wood, with several area rugs scattered throughout the space. The couches were large and overstuffed and looked comfortable. There were a few low wooden tables with lamps on them as well. Most of the furniture appeared carefully nondescript, as if deliberately chosen to avoid competing with the view.

The space was huge. One corner contained an open kitchen and there again, the design was warm and comfortable rather than shiny and steel. A large wooden table with half a dozen chairs around it sat between the kitchen and the living room area.

"Want to see the rest?" Doncan asked.

"Oh, yes, please," Carly answered. She was dying to see the rest.

Doncan grinned at her as he showed her around the apartment. There was a small door next to the entryway. Doncan opened it quickly.

"It's just a half-bath," he explained. Carly glanced inside and smiled.

Everything looked brand new and rarely used. On the far side of the living space, opposite the kitchen, was a single door. Now Doncan led her through it.

The short hallway it opened into had three doors leading off of it. Doncan opened the first, revealing a spacious and comfortably furnished guest bedroom.

"There's a small bathroom attached," Doncan told Carly, opening the door to show her.

Again Carly glanced inside. The bathroom was beautifully done and looked like it had never been used.

"Does anyone ever use it?" she blurted out, blushing as she realized how personal the question was.

"Beth lets the kids stay with me once in a while," Doncan told her. "Usually Heather, since she is the oldest, but occasionally Matthew comes for a night or two. I haven't had Maggie yet. Things have been too crazy with work lately for me to have them, though."

"It's all spotless," Carly remarked.

"The building has a cleaning service that you can have come through once or twice a week for a great rate, since they do the whole building," Doncan answered her.

Doncan opened the second door off the hallway to reveal a small office with a built-in desk and walls and walls of bookshelves. Carly was dying to explore the shelves. You could learn a lot about a person by seeing what they read, but it would have been rude to do so.

The third door opened into the master bedroom. Done in masculine dark colors, the room felt warm and inviting, but Carly had to force herself to glance at the furniture before she let her eyes go back to the amazing view. Like the living room, there was a huge wall of windows and Carly loved it.

"Master bathroom," Doncan told her, opening a door inside the room.

Carly glanced at the huge soaking tub and walk-in shower. Here too was an entire wall of windows that showcased the sea.

"I don't think I've ever seen windows like that in a bathroom," she said eventually. "I know you don't have neighbors across from you, but surely people on boats or something could see in?"

❧ Doncan grinned and tapped on a control panel on the wall. The windows began to frost over slowly, getting increasingly opaque as he slid his finger down the panel.

"Wow," Carly gasped. "That is just about the coolest thing I've ever seen," she told him.

Doncan laughed. "It is a neat trick," he agreed. "Now how about some food? I'm starving."

Carly laughed, grateful for a reason to leave the bedroom quickly. The large and comfortable looking bed was making her nervous. She could just imagine Doncan lying there in a tangle of sheets, his always-perfect hair tousled and perfect for running her fingers through. She forced the image from her mind and hurried back into the living space, following Doncan towards the kitchen area.

"Sit anywhere," Doncan suggested. He set out a large loaf of crusty bread with some cheeses and spreads. Carly decided she was hungrier than she realized as she dug into the delicious bread. Doncan opened a bottle of wine and poured them each a glass.

"This is wonderful," Carly spoke around a mouthful of bread, smothered in some soft cheese that she had never seen before.

"I'm glad you like it," Doncan told her with a smile.

Carly perched on a bar stool on one side of the large kitchen island where Doncan had laid out the food. He stood on the opposite side, tearing off large hunks of bread for himself.

"You look like you're feeling better," Carly told him eventually. "You looked really tired yesterday."

"I was exhausted," Doncan admitted. "But the estate is settled now and all of the beneficiaries have formally agreed to the terms, so that's one job done and dusted."

"That's great," Carly told him.

"My next project is getting Bessie's house sold for you, but I think I can do that with one phone call."

Carly grinned. "You think you're that good?" she teased.

"I know I am," he shot back with a wicked grin.

"Oh, please," Carly shook her head.

"Seriously, though," Doncan told her. "I have two appraisers going through the house on Monday. We should have their reports by

Wednesday. Assuming the valuation comes in around where I expect it to, the developers are ready to sign. The house could be off your hands by Friday at the latest."

Carly shook her head. "I haven't agreed to sell to any developers," she reminded Doncan.

"Let's not argue tonight," Doncan told her with a sigh. "Let's just say that we should have everything done by Friday, although you could sign the paperwork as early as Monday, assuming you trust me to sort everything out."

Carly nodded reluctantly. "I suppose I could head for home any time, then. Once I've signed all the paperwork, you don't need me anymore anyway, right? My plane tickets are open-ended. I can fly back any time."

"I'm sure you have a lot to get back to," Doncan replied lightly. "But I think you should plan on staying for the week. Tynwald Day is coming up and it would be a shame for you to miss it by just a few days. Unless you absolutely have to get back?"

"No," Carly said slowly. "I don't have to get back, but my hotel room can't be cheap and I really shouldn't stay if I don't need to be here."

"We're getting a great deal on your room because you're a long-term guest," Doncan waved her concerns away. "Tynwald Day is Thursday and that gives us the whole week to finalize everything. I think you should plan to fly home next Sunday. Of course, you're welcome to stay longer." Doncan's tone was neutral.

"I guess one more week would be okay," Carly said, feeling a million different emotions running through her head. She wanted to get home. She missed Granny and her parents and her little house. But she also wanted to stay and see more of the island and explore whatever was going on with Doncan. She was feeling far too attracted to the man and to his lovely island.

"I'll have Breesha call the airlines on Monday and get your tickets sorted out, then," Doncan told her with a smile. "You'll fly home a week from tomorrow, assuming everything goes smoothly with the house sale."

Carly felt curiously deflated by his words. She took a big drink of her wine and resolutely changed the subject. They talked about favorite television shows, music and books while Doncan cooked chicken in white wine sauce with some secret recipe potato dish and vegetables. After the delicious dinner, eaten casually side-by-side at the kitchen island and accompanied by the rest of the bottle of wine, Doncan suggested a walk.

"I think we both need to walk off some of that dinner," he grinned at her.

"I know I do," Carly groaned. "I'm sure there were a thousand calories in that sauce."

"Probably only nine hundred," Doncan assured her with a smile. They headed down through the lobby and out onto the promenade. It was a lovely evening, and Douglas was bustling with young people, single or in couples, headed into the many bars and clubs that lined the streets around the seafront.

Doncan took Carly's hand and they strolled along the beach as the sunlight faded slowly into sunset.

"Let's get ice cream," Doncan suggested as they neared Carly's hotel.

"Ice cream? After all that rich food?"

"Why not?" Doncan challenged. "It's summer and the perfect night for it."

Carly couldn't really argue, so they stopped and got ice cream cones and ate them sitting on the steps of her hotel.

Doncan walked her to her door and gave her a quick, sticky, sweet good night kiss. For a moment Carly considered pulling him close and deepening the kiss, but she resisted the urge.

"Sleep well," Doncan whispered to her, quickly disappearing down the hall while Carly clamped her lips together to stop herself from calling him back.

• In spite of the turmoil that her emotions were in, Carly did sleep well. All that walking in the fresh sea air must have been good for her, she decided the next morning as she showered and dressed, feeling refreshed.

Doncan hadn't suggested making any plans for Sunday, but Beth called just as Carly was trying to decide what to do.

"Matthew has a Tae Kwon Do tournament today," Beth told her. "I told him you're probably busy, but he insisted that I call and invite you along."

Carly laughed. "I'd love to come," she assured her new friend.

Beth arranged to pick her up in half an hour and they quickly made the short drive to the sports center. Doncan turned up there just before the competition got started and the threesome settled onto the rock hard bleachers to watch the small children doing their thing.

"No Mark?" Carly asked curiously.

"He's watching Heather and Maggie so that I can be here," Beth told her.

"I could have watched the girls if he wanted to come," Carly said, feeling bad that Mark was missing his son's competition.

"It's fine," Beth assured her. "He hates this sort of thing," she confided. "He could watch Matthew all day, but he has no patience for watching all the other kids. He's much happier at home with the girls and this way Matthew gets to tell him all about it when we get back."

Doncan's parents arrived a short time later and joined them in the bleachers. Doncan had chosen to sit behind Carly and as the competition got underway, he rested his hands on her shoulders. Before long, he was gently rubbing her back and Carly found herself shifting uncomfortably as his touch electrified her body.

"Relax," Doncan whispered in her ear, pulling her backwards towards him. She found herself resting against his chest, his arms now encircling her waist. She tried half-heartedly to pull away, but there was virtually no way to do so without causing a scene. At least that's what she told herself as she relaxed into the embrace.

The morning dragged on, with a seemingly endless stream of small children performing set routines that all looked exactly alike to Carly. It was possible, of course, that they were supposed to, but she wasn't sure. Doncan made the odd comment and she chatted briefly with Beth in between competitors, but mostly she just sat still, feeling content in Doncan's arms.

They all got lunch together in the center's café and then returned to the bleachers for the second half of the competition. It was finally Matthew's turn to compete and Doncan sat next to Carly now, ready to cheer on his favorite nephew. In the end, they all cheered loudly for the little boy, who looked to be concentrating fiercely as he worked his way through his form. Another hour later, they cheered again, briefly, before Matthew was soundly beaten by a much larger boy in a round of sparring.

In the end, Matthew got a third place medal for his form, which was enough to make him very happy when he found them in the crowd after the competition finished.

"Well done, big guy," Doncan grabbed him up in a big hug. "I'm so proud of you."

Matthew laughed and then hugged everyone in turn. "I almost forgot step six," he confided to them all. "But then I remembered at the last minute and after that it was easy."

"Everyone needs to come back to ours for pizza," Beth told them all.

"Sounds great," Doncan answered. He grabbed Carly's hand. "We'll stop and get pudding on the way," he said, pulling Carly away with him.

"Hey," she said as they reached the parking lot. "Who says I want to go with you to Beth's?"

"Do you?"

"Well, yeah, but you shouldn't just assume that I'd want to go or that I'd want to ride with you."

Doncan shook his head. "I'm sorry," he said finally. "But I figured you would want to go, and after all that sitting around watching nothing happening for the whole day, I thought you might like a break from Beth and Matthew for the drive to Laxey. If you want I can call my sister and see if you can ride up to her place with her and Matt."

"No," Carly answered sulkily. "It's fine."

Doncan tipped his head and gave her a long look. He took a deep breath and then beeped the car unlocked. "Get in, then," he suggested with a sigh.

Carly climbed into the car, feeling like she was behaving badly. "Does this mean I don't get any chocolate cake?" she asked plaintively after Doncan was seated in the driver's seat.

Doncan laughed and then pulled her close. He gave her a quick kiss on the tip of her nose and then a longer one on her lips. "You can have chocolate cake," he whispered huskily. "As much as you like."

Carly sat back when he released her and licked her lips. Suddenly cake didn't sound nearly as tempting as another of Doncan's kisses.

The impromptu party at Beth's was great fun. After eating way too much pizza and that promised slice of cake, Carly found herself avoiding Doncan, which wasn't all that difficult with three small children underfoot. She played with each of them in turn.

She sat patiently with a table full of stuffed animals while Heather made "tea" for them all, then she chased Matthew around the backyard for half an hour until she was too tired to run anymore. Finally she curled up on a couch with Maggie and read stories to her until neither of them could keep their eyes open any longer. Doncan found them in the sunroom, snuggled up in a chair, both half-asleep.

"It's past your bedtime, Maggie, my love," he said softly, picking up his tiny niece. "Let's get you tucked in."

"Aunt Carly, too," Maggie insisted.

Carly struggled to her feet, feeling exhausted. "I'll come too," she told the sleepy child, shrugging at Doncan. He just grinned at her and led the way up the stairs to the children's bedrooms.

Beth met them at the top of the stairs. "Thanks so much for bringing Maggie up," she told her brother. "The other two are both tucked up and waiting for good night kisses from Uncle Doncan and Aunt Carly."

Carly blushed at the words, but felt she had no choice but to follow Doncan down the hall. He put Maggie gently into her small bed, pulling the covers up around her, and then gave her a kiss. When he stood up to go, Maggie's arms went up.

"Kiss from Aunt Carly," she demanded. Carly was happy to bend down and kiss the little girl good night. Then she followed Doncan into Matthew's room and finally to Heather's where everyone got good night kisses and hugs.

When they got back downstairs, Doncan was quick to suggest that they head back to Douglas.

"Your little monsters have worn both me and Carly out," he told his sister and brother-in-law. "And we both have a busy week ahead, so I think we'll say our goodbyes now."

The drive back was quiet, as Carly was having trouble staying awake on the journey. The day had been a long one. Doncan walked her to her door, but did nothing more than see her safely into her room.

As she washed her face, she scolded her mirror self. "You did not want a good night kiss from Doncan," she told her sternly. "You got kisses from all three children, and that was much nicer than a kiss from Doncan anyway." Her mirror self didn't bother to argue. They both knew she was lying.

Since she was done with packing and sorting at the cottage, Carly didn't have anything she needed to do on Monday. Doncan picked her up at nine anyway, and drove her to Laxey. Instead of taking her to the cottage, however, he dropped her off at the Laxey Wheel. She spent her morning learning a great deal about the mining industry on the island. Doncan met her for lunch at a little restaurant on "Ham and Egg Terrace." Carly was enchanted by the nickname for the short street that used to house a number of small cafés.

After lunch Doncan had to head back to the office, so Carly grabbed a taxi into Ramsey and spent the afternoon wandering through the various shops along the main shopping street. She took a taxi back to Douglas later and had dinner on her own in her hotel. Doncan had told her that he had a dinner meeting and she wouldn't let him call Beth or his parents to suggest that they entertain her.

Carly felt like she was getting far too attached to Doncan and his family. In less than a week she would be heading back to the U.S. and they would be nothing but a pleasant memory. She was planning a further visit to the island with Granny, but that was some way in the future. Anyway, she preferred not to think about that at the moment as she tried to erect barriers to protect her heart. With that in mind, she had told Doncan that she would be fine on her own on Tuesday.

In the morning she took a taxi down to Castletown and enjoyed another tour of Castle Rushen and another visit to Rushen Abbey. She lunched on her own in a small café that she stumbled across while she was walking around the ancient town. In the afternoon she visited the

Old House of Keys, the building where the island's parliament used to meet, and then the Nautical Museum, which housed its own boat. Back in Douglas she took herself out to a small Italian restaurant that was just a few steps away from her hotel.

Wednesday morning she had an early appointment at Doncan's office to finishing going through Bessie's things that were there and to go over the appraisals of Bessie's cottage. Her heart skipped a beat when she saw Doncan pull up outside the hotel to pick her up. She realized suddenly that she had missed him terribly the previous day. He was quiet in the car and at his office he was all business.

"Right, we have two appraisals which have come in only a few thousand pounds apart," he told Carly. "And I have a verbal offer from a potential purchaser for you to consider."

Carly glanced through the two appraisals, skimming page after page of details about the property, focusing on the last page in each report which listed the value the appraiser had estimated for the property. As Doncan said, the two figures were very close together and they were both slightly higher than she had been expecting.

"So tell me about the offer," she told Doncan.

"It comes from the developer I mentioned. He's prepared to offer the average of the two appraisals. He has preliminary planning permission to tear the cottage down and replace it with this." Doncan passed Carly a folder with the plans for the property that the developer wanted to build on the land where Bessie's cottage currently sat.

Carly winced. She hated the thought of Bessie's cottage being torn down. Reluctantly, she opened the folder and flipped through the plans. Doncan was right. The proposed building did resemble the cottage it was replacing, although it would actually be quite a bit larger in order to accommodate two units. Carly sighed. It actually all looked quite lovely, and if they could manage it somehow without tearing down the cottage, she might be tempted to agree.

"I really don't want to sell to a developer," Carly said slowly.

Doncan frowned at her. "As your advocate, I have to recommend that you take some time to seriously consider the offer," he told her. "The developer is offering good money for the property, money that your grandmother would undoubtedly find useful. He's also offering a very quick settlement. We could sign the papers now and it would all be done. Your grandmother would have a check in a month or so."

Carly sighed. "I talked to Granny last night," she told Doncan. "She said that I should do whatever I felt was best."

Doncan smiled encouragingly. "You trust me, right?" he asked.

Carly nodded slowly, wondering if she was right to trust the man.

"I think you should take the offer," he told her. "If we put the house on the market, it could take months or even years to get it sold and we have no idea what price you might end up getting for it. I'd hate to see your grandmother having to wait for ages and then not get a fair price."

Carly sighed again. "I just need to think for a little bit longer," she said eventually. "I can sign everything on Friday, right?"

Doncan looked frustrated. He seemed to be forcing himself to smile at her. "Sure, Friday would be fine," he told her. "Take the plans with you and study them in more depth if you want," he suggested. "They really are great plans."

Carly nodded and picked up the folder. She didn't want to sell to the developer, no matter how good the plans were, but she owed it to Granny to give it serious thought. Maybe taking the money now was the better choice. Doncan certainly seemed to think so.

She spent an hour going back through the boxes of things that Doncan had stored in his office for Bessie, finally deciding to simply take the disks home to look through there. Doncan had already arranged for the suitcases of clothes and papers to be shipped to Granny. The disks and other papers could travel home in an extra suit-case with Carly.

Having finished the sorting, Carly then took herself off to Peel for the rest of the day. She enjoyed another look around the castle and the House of Manannan. She was excited to see all the activity around Tynwald Hill as the preparations for the next day were well underway. Doncan had promised to take her to the ceremony. She hoped he hadn't forgotten. If he had, she would just have to take herself, she decided.

She had just returned to her hotel when Doncan called her.

"I'll pick you up around nine tomorrow morning and we'll head out to St. John's," he told her when she answered.

She did little more than agree before he hung up, obviously busy with something he didn't bother to explain.

As she snuggled down in the large and comfortable hotel bed, Carly wondered if she had made Doncan angry by dragging her feet over the sale. Maybe that was a good thing, she told herself. She was going home soon and their flirtation was going to have to end. It was best to keep things strictly professional from now on, anyway.

She sighed and slid more deeply under the covers. Her brain seemed to be having some difficulty coming to terms with that fact. She tossed and turned, finally falling into a restless sleep filled with dreams that centered on wrecking balls crashing into Bessie's cottage. They came to an abrupt end when her alarm rang at seven. It was Tynwald Day. No matter how tired she was, she was excited about that.

❧ 14 ❧

Doncan was quiet on the drive to St. John's, clearly lost in his own thoughts, and Carly was too focused on the fact that she was leaving soon to make any attempt at conversation. He parked as close to Tynwald Hill as he could get. Many of the area streets were blocked off for the ceremony and street festival. From the parking area, the pair had to walk several blocks in order to get to the ceremony.

They arrived just in time to see the procession of dignitaries and Carly forgot all about being tired as she listened to the new laws of the land being read out in both English and Manx.

"The laws are official now that they've been announced here," Doncan told her.

Carly marveled at the formal uniforms and elaborate wigs that were being worn by the participants.

"I'm so glad that I got to see this," she whispered to Doncan as the formal presentation of petitions for redress began.

"Do they have to submit them in advance?" Carly asked.

"They do. There's an entire process that has to be followed, but anyone who lives on the island is welcome to take part."

"It's an amazing way to run a government," Carly answered.

"It seems to be working," Doncan answered.

After the ceremony finished, the day turned into one big party. Carly was delighted when they ran into Beth and Mark and the girls as they made their way through the crowd.

"Matthew's club is doing a Tae Kwon Do demonstration in about half an hour," Beth told them. "He's beyond excited that he gets to do his form in front of all these people."

"I think I'd be a nervous wreck," Carly admitted.

"I'm nervous enough for him and me," Beth admitted with a laugh.

The little group found a quiet spot in the spectator's area on the large green space between the church and the hill itself. In the center of the space, a section had been roped off for the various performers that were due to entertain the crowds during the day. Carly and Beth chatted about nothing much while Mark and Doncan kept the girls happy by chasing them around in circles.

Matthew and his club did a wonderful job entertaining the crowds. Several small boys and girls performed their forms to much applause and then some of the older children and adults took turns breaking wooden boards, some even doing fantastic flying kicks that amazed Carly.

His group was followed by a group of Manx dancers and Carly was fascinated by the intricate routines they went through, following the music being performed by a small group of talented musicians. After a few minutes, Mark and Beth left with the girls to find Matthew and get the kids home before Maggie's nap time.

"How about some lunch?" Doncan asked as the dancers finished and a different group of musicians began setting up.

"Lunch sounds great." Carly suddenly realized that she was starving. It was nearly two o'clock, so that wasn't surprising.

Doncan took her hand and led her to a huge tent that was full of food vendors. She could only stand and look around in confusion at the variety that was available.

"I hope you'll trust me on this one," Doncan told her as he led her towards the back corner of the tent.

"Absolutely," Carly answered with a grin.

They ate sandwiches and chips and drank sodas, crammed together at a small table that was designed for eight and was being used by ten others when they arrived.

🐌 "We can squeeze together," they were assured by the people at the table who noticed that there was nowhere for Carly and Doncan to sit.

Carly couldn't help but laugh as she and Doncan tried to fit into the tiny space that the big group managed to make for them. Doncan laughed as well and the pair ate quickly in their cramped quarters and escaped back into the sunshine.

Then Doncan took Carly on a tour around the fair. They visited a tent that celebrated Manx businesses. Carly saw the handsome pilot who had flown her to the island, but he was busy talking to a beautiful redhead in a tight air hostess costume and didn't notice her.

In another tent, she was surprised to meet another American. Carly immediately forgot the woman's name, but the other woman was also just visiting the island, doing some research for a book that the Manx History Institute was publishing. It felt strange, but nice, to hear an American accent after the last several weeks of being surrounded by British and Manx ones.

There was a lot to see and an ever-changing schedule of entertainment on the green and Carly didn't have time to get bored. As it got later, Doncan suggested some dinner and again she trusted him to pick something from the huge array of food vendors. Again, she was pleased with his choice, munching her way through fish and chips that were hot, delicious and satisfying.

When they returned to the green space another dance group was setting up and this time they offered to teach the crowd the steps. Carly was one of the first to join in. Doncan followed, seemingly reluctantly. An hour later, Carly was exhausted but happy as she followed the dancers through the last and most intricate dance of the night. Doncan gamely followed along as well, grimacing as one slightly less adept member of the crowd tripped over her feet and stepped all over his.

"That was way too much fun," Carly told Doncan when the last of the music had faded away and the dancers began to pack up.

"I'm glad you enjoyed it," Doncan told her.

"Didn't you enjoy it?" she demanded.

"It's not really my thing," Doncan answered. "But I was happy to do it because it clearly made you very happy."

"Yes, it did," Carly told him. "It was such fun."

Doncan laughed. "I think you need a cold drink," he suggested.

"I'm sure I do. I'm probably a mess as well, all hot and flushed."

Doncan didn't answer. He just led her to a small tent that had only been set up a short time earlier. Now that it was evening, this area was reserved for adults. Doncan found a small table for two at the back of the tent and then went to the bar. He returned with two glasses of crisp and cold white wine.

"Oh, delicious," Carly told him as she sipped her wine.

Back outside, Carly and Doncan watched one of the last bands perform. Carly could feel the excitement growing in the crowd as everyone waited for the fireworks to begin. Most of the families with small children had headed for home hours earlier, but several groups were straggling back now, just in time for the fireworks display.

"Do fireworks ever get boring?" Carly whispered to Doncan, as they stood side-by-side in the middle of the crowd.

"Probably not for you," he answered with a grin. "I'm sure you'll still be finding them exciting when you're ninety."

Carly grinned back. "You think they're boring, don't you?" she challenged.

Doncan chuckled. "Let's just say I would rather be making my own fireworks than watching these," he told her.

Before she had time to process the remark, he pulled her close and kissed her. The kiss started out gentle and Carly sighed as she felt sparks fly and saw the fireworks he'd been teasing her about. As the kiss deepened she stopped thinking and just enjoyed the moment.

When Doncan lifted his head, she sighed and leaned against him. She was starting to enjoy his kisses way too much. Doncan kissed the top of her head and then gently turned her in his arms so that she could lean against him and he could hold her close while they watched the fireworks explode in the sky above them.

The explosions were timed perfectly to go with the music that the final band was playing. The display was long and exciting and Carly "oohed" and "aahed" along with most of the crowd. Doncan remained quiet, holding her close, with one hand gently rubbing her neck. As the last burst faded from the dark sky, the pair began the long walk back to Doncan's car.

Doncan held Carly's hand on the walk back to his car. The streets were crowded with pedestrians trying to find friends, family members and their own vehicles. Carly lost track of how many times she was bumped into by a stroller with a sleeping child in it, being pushed by an exhausted-looking parent as they made their way towards home.

It had been a long day and she was tired and feeling confused. Doncan kept treating her like a girlfriend and she was nothing of the kind. She didn't know how to begin a conversation that challenged him, though, in case she was reading more into it than she should have been. He did kiss her a lot, that was a fact. But maybe most men and women kissed each other all the time and she just didn't know about it because she'd always been with Tom.

The drive back to her hotel was nearly silent. Carly stared out her window, feeling as if she and Doncan were arguing, but not knowing why. Doncan parked in front of the building and wordlessly walked her to her door.

Inside her room, he pushed the door closed and then pulled her close and kissed her thoroughly. Carly was shocked and then overwhelmed by the passion that she felt. After a moment that could have been one minute or twenty, Doncan lifted his head.

"Invite me to stay," he murmured softly.

"What do you mean?" Carly stammered.

Doncan chuckled and ran a hand down her back, pulling her even closer. "I want to stay and make love to you tonight," he replied.

Carly thought for a moment that her heart might have stopped beating. She felt herself blushing and for a second she wasn't sure how to reply.

Doncan's eyes burned into hers as one of his hands brushed a stray hair from her cheek. "What are you thinking?" he asked softly, looking at her curiously.

"I don't know," Carly admitted, confessing to her confusion.

Doncan laughed softly. "Maybe I should just kiss you again," he suggested with a wicked grin.

"NO!" Carly gave him a gentle push and he immediately stepped away from her.

"You want me to leave," he said in a resigned tone.

"I think that's probably best," Carly answered, turning away from him.

"Why?"

Carly took a deep breath. "I'm flying back home on Sunday," she said sadly. "I'm really not the one night stand type."

Doncan chuckled again. "Sunday is three nights away," he told her.

Carly felt a burst of anger. "Three nights, two nights, one night, what difference does it make?" she demanded. "I've been here for less than a month and you've been flirting with me and taking me out and kissing me, but you know as well as I do that we can't possibly have any sort of relationship. And if you think that I'm going to just fall into bed with you just before I leave, you've got another think coming. I am not the sort of person that just leaps about from bed to bed just because a guy is gorgeous and funny and takes me out a few times. You're supposed to be my lawyer, and you keep making me dizzy trying to figure out what you're thinking half the time." Carly paused for a breath, holding up her hand to stop Doncan from speaking.

"I'm not done," she announced. "I really don't know what sort of game you have been playing for the last month, and I don't think I really want to know. I think you should just leave now."

Doncan studied her for a moment, a thoughtful look on his face, before he spoke. "I'm going to leave. You're upset and it's been a long day. But this conversation isn't finished. We have a lot more to talk about before you head home."

Carly swallowed hard. "I'm really tired," she told the man, suddenly feeling like she had overreacted.

Doncan just smiled. "I think we're both tired," he said. "I have to work tomorrow, but you still need to sign the sales paperwork. Maybe we can have dinner somewhere and have that conversation after the papers are signed."

Carly nodded. "That sounds good," she said, not sure that she really agreed.

Doncan left quickly, and Carly sank down into the nearest chair and buried her face in her hands, waiting for a flood of tears. After a moment, she decided that she was too embarrassed by her outburst to feel like crying.

In the bathroom, she washed away the day's makeup while avoiding meeting the eye of her mirror image. In bed she beat her pillows repeatedly, trying to fluff them up and make them comfortable. She lay back against them and stared at the ceiling in the dark.

"Well, I guess I know where I stand now," she said out loud. "He wants to sleep with me. I suppose I should be flattered." She sighed.

Tom had been her first and only lover and she wasn't ready to go to bed with another man. Especially not one who was older and so very sophisticated. He'd probably laugh at her lack of experience. She slid down further under the covers, finally pulling them over her head.

Undoubtedly, Doncan was used to dating beautiful and intelligent women who jumped at the chance to sleep with him after their second date, or whatever number was currently the "right" number.

She sat back up in bed and fluffed her pillows again. Sleep was going to be elusive tonight. There was no doubt about that.

"You'd have slept well wrapped up in Doncan's arms," a little voice suggested.

"I don't think we would have done much sleeping," she told the little voice, blushing as she thought about what they would have been doing instead.

She flipped over in frustration and squeezed her eyes shut. Sternly forbidding herself to think about Doncan, she forced herself to think about Bessie instead.

Many years ago Bessie had been in love and had even been proposed to. Why had she said no? There had to be more diaries somewhere. Carly sighed.

"Poor Bessie, she was probably heartbroken when Peter left, like I'll be when I say goodbye to Doncan."

As soon as the words were out of her mouth, Carly gasped in shock. But they were true. She had fallen in love with the handsome attorney and on Sunday she was going to have to say goodbye.

Now the tears that had threatened earlier began to fall. Eventually, at least, they led her into a deep and dreamless sleep.

❧ 15 ❧

Carly spent Friday wandering around the shops in Douglas yet again. She needed a few more souvenirs for her family and she wanted something special for herself as well. No matter how hard she tried, however, she just couldn't find anything that felt just right to help her remember the island.

"Never mind," she told herself. "You'll be back with Granny some day. You can try to find something then."

Her phone rang around four o'clock.

"Sorry to do this," Doncan told her, "but I can't make dinner tonight. A client is insisting on a late meeting and I can't get out of it."

"That's fine," Carly lied.

"It isn't fine," Doncan replied. "But it can't be helped. I'll have to get you to sign the house paperwork tomorrow. Speaking of tomorrow, I've just hung up the phone with Beth. She's having a big leaving party for you tomorrow."

"A party?" Carly said, dismay obvious in her voice.

"Maybe not a party," Doncan answered. "More of a family picnic with you as guest of honor."

"Great," Carly tried to put some enthusiasm into her voice, but failed.

Doncan laughed. "Don't sound so pleased," he told her. "She's doing it because she really likes you and wants to have a chance to see you again before you go. Apparently the children really want to see you again as well."

"I'd love to see them," Carly admitted. "And Mark and Beth as well. But I'm not sure I feel up to a party."

"It won't be too bad," Doncan assured her. "Just Mark and Beth and the kids and my parents. I think she's invited Uncle Henry as well, but I think that's all."

"That's more than enough," Carly replied.

"So I'll pick you up around ten, if that's okay?"

"Sure," Carly tried to put some enthusiasm into her reply, but she was feeling incredibly sad about leaving and the party plans weren't helping.

"Sleep well," was all that Doncan replied.

Carly ordered room service for dinner, impulsively adding a bottle of wine to her order. She ate looking out at the amazing view from her windows, watching the waves crashing on the sand below.

"I bet if I'd slept with him, he would have found a way to have dinner with me tonight," she told her wavy reflection in the window as she downed a second glass of wine. She felt restless and sad and lonely as she refilled her glass.

She thought about calling Granny, but she didn't want to tell the older woman that Doncan had offered to take her to bed. Even more so, she couldn't admit to Granny that she was now feeling like she should have said yes.

"Maybe I should call Tom," she said angrily to herself. "This is really all his fault anyway. If he hadn't dumped me, I would have been thinking about him all the time and I wouldn't have fallen in love with Doncan."

Carly wondered if that was true. She'd cared deeply for Tom, but what she felt for Doncan was very different. Maybe Tom was right to break up with her. And maybe, even if he hadn't, she still would have fallen in love with Doncan. She just wished that Doncan could understand how she felt about Bessie's cottage.

When she finished the third glass of wine, which was really three more glasses than she was used to, Carly got ready for bed. She tossed and turned for all of a minute before she fell into a deep sleep.

She felt refreshed and incredibly sad the next morning, as she got ready for Beth's picnic. While she had been on the island for only a few weeks, she was going to miss it terribly. Her feelings for Doncan aside, she really liked Beth and Mark and their children. Doncan's parents were incredibly nice as well and they had all gone out of their way to make her feel at home here.

Carly tried to cheer herself up by thinking about her little house back in Pennsylvania. In a few days, she could start doing the painting and decorating that she had put off to make the trip for Granny. Maybe she would get a quote from a builder for putting in some book-cases in the smaller of the spare bedrooms while she was at it. It wasn't like she was going to need a nursery any time soon and she would love to have her own little library.

She was feeling somewhat better as she sat on the steps outside the hotel, waiting for Doncan, but her spirits plummeted again when Doncan arrived. He looked amazingly handsome and her stomach turned itself in knots as he crossed from the car to her side.

He extended a hand to help her up, but she ignored it, afraid of what his touch might do to her. Instead, she busied herself with brushing imaginary dust off her pants, anything to avoid looking at Doncan.

"All set?" he asked quietly.

"Sure," she sighed. "Let's go and get this over with."

Doncan laughed. "I'm sure that Beth would cancel the whole thing if she knew that you felt that way," he told her.

"I don't mean it like that," Carly tried to explain. "I'm just feeling really sad about leaving and I don't really feel like a party."

"I can call Beth and cancel," Doncan offered immediately.

"No, she's trying to do something nice for me. It would be rude to cancel."

"I'm sure she would understand," Doncan told her.

"Maybe, but it would still be rude."

Doncan couldn't argue with that, so they both got into the car and headed out of town.

"I said we could pick up Uncle Henry on the way, okay?"

"Of course it's okay," Carly shrugged.

A few minutes later they pulled up to his retirement home. "You can just wait here if you want," Doncan suggested as he got out of the car.

Carly shrugged again, a gesture lost on Doncan as he was already heading into the home. She sat back and frowned, wishing the day would hurry up and get over with.

In the end, however, she had a much better time than she had expected. Beth made a simple picnic lunch for everyone and Carly spent much of the day chasing the children around and playing games with them. Doncan was similarly occupied, and somehow they managed to avoid spending more than a few moments together throughout the day.

If anyone else noticed that the pair were avoiding each other, no one commented. After several hours of playing with the kids in the hot sun, Carly finally sank down into a chair where the other adults, including Doncan, were gathered.

Doncan's parents were politely interested in Carly's plans for the rest of the summer and Beth was excited to learn that Carly intended to visit the island again, this time with Granny.

"You'll have to bring your Granny to a big family gathering," Beth told Carly.

"If you have one while we're here, of course I will."

"We'll have one because you're here!" Beth told her with a laugh.

"Do you have any idea when you might be coming back?" Mark asked her as he strolled by with Maggie on his back.

"Sorry, I really don't," Carly answered. "Apparently her doctor told her she would be fit to travel around September, but I'll be back to work by then, so it will probably have to wait until I get some time off."

"Christmas!" Beth shouted. "You and your granny can come and spend Christmas with us."

Carly laughed. "I don't know about that," she protested. "My parents might not be too thrilled if Granny and I disappear at Christmas. We have so many family traditions. I don't know. A lot will depend on what Granny wants to do, I guess."

She fell silent as she thought about what she had been planning for the coming Christmas, that perfect holiday wedding that she had been anticipating for years. And then Tom had dumped her instead of proposing and all of her plans had shattered. She still hadn't actually called her friend to cancel the hold on the chapel. Cancelling would be embarrassing, to say the least, even though Michelle was a good friend who wouldn't laugh at her, at least not to her face.

"Carly?" Beth smiled at her. "I think we lost you there for a minute," she said teasingly.

"Sorry, I was just thinking about Christmas," Carly answered. "It's my very favorite holiday of the year. I was hoping that Tom and I might be getting married on Christmas Eve this year."

As soon as the words were out of her mouth, she wanted to take them back. She didn't want to talk about Tom in front of Doncan. And she especially didn't want Doncan to think that she was still unhappy about their breakup.

Heather interrupted the conversation at the perfect time. "Aunt Carly, can you come and play with me now?" she asked. "You said I was next."

Carly couldn't get up fast enough, and she managed to avoid any further adult conversation for the rest of the day. After a delicious dinner of spaghetti, garlic bread and salad, with the same fabulous chocolate cake that always appeared from Doncan's car at family gatherings, the day finally wound down.

"We'd better get you back so you can finish packing," Doncan suggested to Carly as they helped clear away the last of the dinner dishes.

"Absolutely," Carly agreed, even though she had finished packing on Friday. All that remained out were the things that she was still going to need before she left.

Carly hugged Doncan's parents and Uncle Henry. Henry wanted to stay to watch a movie with the kids. Doncan's father would take him home later. Then she hugged Beth and Mark. The three children all swarmed in a massive group hug that saw all four of them dissolving into tears.

"Don't go, Aunt Carly," Heather begged. "You can move into our spare room and stay here forever."

Carly tried to laugh, but she was crying too hard. "I have to go home," she told the children. "I have my own family and my own little house."

"But you'll visit, right?" Matthew asked hopefully.

"I'm hoping to visit soon," Carly assured him.

She climbed into Doncan's car feeling miserable. They were both silent as he drove her back to the hotel, aside from Carly's occasional sniffles as she tried to stop her tears.

Back at her hotel, Doncan walked her silently to her door. Before they could talk, she went into the bathroom and washed away the last of the tear-stained makeup that she had worn. Her eyes were puffy and red and she looked dreadful. She guessed that Doncan would feel less like taking her to bed now.

When she walked back into her room, Doncan studied her for a moment and then smiled. "You look almost exactly like you did when I first saw you," he told her softly. "It doesn't seem possible that I've only known you a month," he continued. "I feel like you've been important to me for a very long time."

Carly sighed. "This isn't really helping," she told the man. "I already feel bad about going home tomorrow. I'm really going to miss your family and the island. You aren't making me feel any better."

Doncan chuckled softly and then closed the distance between them. He studied her anguished face for a moment and then sighed and pulled her close. The hug felt intimate but more friendly than passionate. Carly sighed. This was it, Doncan was going to let her down gently. At least she hoped he was going to be gentle. She pulled away from the embrace and looked up at him.

"You've been great," she said, hoping to preempt him. "I can't thank you enough for everything that you've done to help me with Bessie's cottage and the estate. I don't know what I would have done without all of your help."

Doncan smiled down at her. "I was very glad to help," he told her. "But you still need to sign the papers for the sale."

Carly nodded. "I still don't want to sell to developers," she told Doncan.

"I still think it's your best option, but I'm your advocate, not theirs, so if you want, we can put the house on the market and see what happens."

Carly shrugged. "Maybe we could put it on the market for a while and then, if it doesn't sell, we could sell it to the developers."

Doncan shook his head. "I spoke to someone at the construction office on Friday. If they can't get the place in the next two weeks they are going to pursue a different property further up the coast. You need to agree now or else put it on the market and take your chances with Granny's money."

Carly shuddered at the cold way he was putting it. "I guess I should just sign, then," she sighed.

Doncan gave her the paperwork and she signed where he indicated, approving the sale of the house and authorizing Doncan to act as her agent to finalize everything.

"I'll have the formal sales contract drawn up on Monday for Jason," he told Carly. "Tell your grandmother to expect a big check in a month or so."

"Jason?" Carly asked.

Doncan winced. Clearly, he hadn't meant to say that. "The developer is called Jason. I told you he was someone that I know."

"How well do you know him?" Carly asked, suddenly feeling suspicious.

"He's yet another cousin," Doncan shrugged.

Carly felt all of the swirling emotions inside her turn to anger. "You're selling Granny's cottage to your cousin so he can tear it down?" she demanded.

"He's made a fair offer and is willing to settle quickly," Doncan countered. "Even if he weren't my cousin, I would be suggesting that you accept his offer."

"Just how eager were you to get my signature?" Carly demanded, her suspicions multiplying.

"What do you mean?"

"I mean, how badly did you want me to agree? Badly enough to show me the sights and take me to dinner and romance me? Badly enough to take me to bed?"

Doncan sighed and tried to pull her into his arms. Carly took a step away from him, her eyes blazing with anger.

"At first, I may have been nicer to you than I might have been otherwise," Doncan admitted. "I wanted you to have a great visit, but I also wanted you happy so you would sign the paperwork without any fuss. Jason can send a lot of business my way and he's family. I didn't see any harm in helping him out as long as you got a fair price."

"So you dragged me all over the island and introduced me to your family and everything so that I would trust you enough to just sign on the dotted line and not ask any questions?"

"Carly, you're making far too big a deal out of this." Doncan sighed again and ran a hand over his face. "I started out being nice to you so that we could get the deal done quickly, but I kept being nice to you because I found out that I really wanted to be nice to you."

Carly shook her head. "I don't know if I believe that," she told him softly, her anger turning to sadness.

Doncan frowned. "This isn't going the way I planned," he told Carly. "I don't want to argue about the cottage. That's just business and has nothing to do with how I feel about you."

Carly felt another flash of anger. "The cottage might be just business to you," she told him, "but it's not for me."

Doncan gave her a pained smile. "Look, we aren't ever going to agree about the cottage. We still need to talk about other things."

"Really?" Carly shrugged. "I can't imagine what."

Doncan sighed. "You said the other night that you didn't know what sort of game I was playing," he reminded her.

"Did I?" Carly could hear all of the suppressed emotion in her voice, but she hoped that Doncan couldn't.

"Yes, you did," Doncan answered patiently, pulling her close. "But the thing is, I wasn't playing games, and I wasn't just trying to get your signature, either."

Carly opened her mouth to reply, but she couldn't find the right words for a minute. "What would you call it then?" she finally demanded. "All the flirting and stolen kisses and taking me out?"

Doncan smiled at her. "I'd call it falling in love," he answered her.

Now Carly really couldn't find any words to answer him with. She just stared at him speechlessly for what felt like hours. Finally he spoke again.

"I don't know if I've ever seen you speechless," he chuckled. "But there you are. I've confessed my deepest and darkest secret. I'm madly in love with you. And you know what else? I would be deeply honored if you would agree to become my wife."

Carly's jaw dropped and her knees went weak. She sagged suddenly and would have sat down on the floor if Doncan hadn't tightened his grip. Whatever she had been expecting from him, this certainly wasn't it.

Doncan laughed now as he led her to a chair. "Sit down," he told her. "I didn't mean to scare you silly."

Carly sank into the chair and took a deep breath. And then she took another. She stared out the window at the sea, desperately trying to think.

Doncan sat down in the other chair and watched the sea as well, lost in his own thoughts. "Maybe I should have been more upfront with you all along," he said finally, when she remained silent. "I started falling for you the day you arrived. For a long time, I fought against it. I've always enjoyed being single and never expected to get married. And then you came along and rearranged my plans for the future." He stopped and shook his head.

"It took me a long time to admit to myself that I was interested in more than just a holiday romance," he told her. "Really, Thursday night was my last attempt to convince myself that a fling was all I was interested in. I knew it was the real thing when you turned me down and threw me out and all I could think about was whether I'd upset you or not."

Carly shook her head. "I don't understand any of this," she said plaintively.

"It's pretty simple," Doncan told her. "I love you and I want to marry you. The rest we can work out from there."

"But it isn't that easy," Carly argued. "I live three thousand miles away, remember?"

"You can move," Doncan waved a hand, brushing away a detail that, to Carly, was of critical importance. "We belong together. I've never been more certain of anything in my life. The rest is just details."

Carly felt a flash of anger. "Details?" she demanded, getting to her feet. "You're reducing my entire life to one stupid word? How arrogant can you be? How can you assume that I'll just drop everything and move halfway around the world just because you happened to have fallen in love with me? What about my feelings? What about what I want? You don't understand about the cottage and I don't think you understand me at all."

Doncan opened his mouth to reply, but Carly held up her hand. "Don't say anything, please. As much as I care about you, I just don't think we're going to be able to make this work."

Doncan frowned. "But I want to marry you," he told her, seemingly unable to understand how she could possibly refuse.

Carly stared at him for a long moment, her eyes filling with tears. "I just can't say yes," she finally choked out. "I can't change my whole life for you."

"If this is about the cottage, I can tell Jason he can't have it," Doncan offered, sounding a bit desperate.

"It isn't about the cottage, exactly," Carly told him. "It's about you understanding how I feel about the cottage, my life, everything, really."

Doncan frowned. He looked as if he wanted to argue, but that he didn't know what to say. "We can talk about this," he told her finally.

"We can talk tomorrow," Carly answered vaguely. Right now she didn't feel capable of any further conversation.

"We'll talk tomorrow," he finally agreed, walking to the door. "Meanwhile, remember that I love you and that we can make this work."

He was gone before Carly could reply. She sank back down in her chair and sobbed broken-heartedly. She simply wasn't prepared to give up everything in her life for a man she barely knew, no matter how much she knew she loved him. She knew she was upset about the cottage as well. The whole mess was inextricably tied together in her head and her heart.

Carly was waiting in the lobby with her suitcase when Doncan arrived the next morning, and the atmosphere in the car on the way to the airport was frosty. Doncan may have had a million things he wanted to say, but he didn't seem to know how to start. Carly didn't want to say anything. She was dangerously close to tears already and she didn't want to start crying again.

When they arrived at the airport, Doncan groaned. Beth and the kids were standing at the terminal door, waiting for Carly.

"Carly, we still need to talk," he said as he parked.

"You can call me," Carly suggested, practically running to get away from him and into the safety of a crowd.

Beth and the kids made a huge fuss over Carly as she waited in line to get her boarding passes. Doncan stood out of the way, glaring at all of them.

"My brother seems unhappy this morning," Beth finally commented quietly to Carly.

"I hadn't noticed," Carly lied, deliberately not looking in Doncan's direction.

"I thought you two might have come to some understanding by now," Beth said cautiously.

"We have," Carly answered. "I understand that he is far too used to getting exactly what he wants, and he understands that I'm not prepared to give up everything I have on his whim."

"Oh, Doncan, what did you do?" Beth muttered under her breath as she smiled at Carly. "I think maybe you two need to talk a bit more," she suggested to her friend.

"We don't have time," Carly answered. "I'm going home."

Beth opened her mouth to argue, but Carly wasn't prepared to listen to any further discussion. Instead, she said quick goodbyes to her and to each of the children in turn, and then she turned to Doncan.

"I'll be in touch soon about when Granny might be able to travel over to sort out the furniture and things," she said formally, offering her hand for a goodbye handshake.

Doncan smiled wryly at her. "I'll look forward to meeting her and seeing you again sometime soon, then," he answered as he took her hand. He squeezed it tightly and then covered it with his other one. He rubbed her hand gently, sending sparks up her arm and through her body.

Carly pulled her hand away and grabbed her suitcase. "I guess this is goodbye, then," she said in her most determinedly cheerful voice.

Doncan smiled at her, letting his emotions show in his eyes. "It's only goodbye for now," he told her softly. "This isn't even close to over."

Carly felt her smile falter as she read the intensity of his feelings in his eyes and his words. It took all of the self-control she had to stop herself from dropping her bags and throwing herself into his arms. It just wasn't that simple.

Carly's flight back across the Atlantic was markedly similar to her flight the other way. She spent most of it in floods of tears. After trying and failing to sleep in the uncomfortable airplane seat, she finally pulled out Bessie's final diary and reread page after page.

Bessie's love story seemed even more tragic to Carly now. She reread Bessie's words:

I can't imagine giving up everything in my life to move so far away.

and

I should be the happiest woman in the world, but all I can do is think and cry.

Carly felt new sympathy for the woman whose life now seemed to be spookily similar to Carly's own. She knew that ultimately Bessie had stayed single and that she had remained on the Isle of Man. Now she wondered if Bessie had ever regretted that decision. The flight seemed to take many more hours than it really did, but eventually Carly was home.

❧ 16 ❧

An exhausted Carly staggered off the plane in Pittsburgh, delighted to see her parents waiting for her.

"Mom, Dad," she called as she ran to them. "I missed you both so much," she exclaimed, hugging them each in turn.

"We missed you as well," her mother told her, returning the embrace. "Granny wanted to come as well, but the doctor didn't think it was a good idea. She's just about recovered, but he felt she didn't need the extra exertion. Especially not if she is planning a trip abroad later this year."

Carly tried to smile, but she knew it was more like a grimace. "I'm so tired," she told her mother, trying to cover for the face she had made. "I can't wait to sleep in my own little bed tonight."

"Tom wanted to come as well," Carly's dad told her once they were in the car on their way back to Meadville.

"Tom? Why?" Carly asked cautiously.

Carly's mother laughed. "I think being single didn't exactly work out the way he thought it would," she told her daughter. "I think he's really sorry he broke up with you and is hoping to get you back."

Carly sat back in her seat and tried to give the idea serious consideration. It was no use. There was no way she was even remotely interested in getting back together with Tom. If nothing else, her time with Doncan had shown her that she didn't belong with Tom.

"That's not happening," Carly told her parents. "I'm not going back there."

"Good," Carly's dad said emphatically. "I never did like that man."

"Really?" Carly asked. "You never told me that."

Her father laughed. "I kept waiting, expecting that you would break up eventually. I didn't expect it to take nearly twenty years, but I for one am glad it's over."

Carly shook her head. Her dad had never said anything against Tom in all the years they were together. "Mom, you liked Tom, right?" she asked, curious now.

"Not really," her mom answered.

"Why didn't you ever say anything?" Carly demanded.

"Carly, you and Tom were best friends in third grade, I wasn't about to start discussing the pros and cons of dating the man then. And suddenly it was years later and you were still, stubbornly, sticking to the man in spite of the fact that you were increasingly ill-suited. If I thought you were heading down the aisle, I would have spoken up, but I didn't think you'd make it that far."

"What didn't you like about him?" Carly felt as if her head were spinning from the sudden revelation.

"It wasn't so much that I didn't like him as I didn't think he was good enough for you," her mom replied.

"Exactly," her dad agreed. "He's an okay guy, but he isn't ever going to be anything amazing, and you deserve amazing."

Carly sighed. "What if I don't ever meet anyone amazing?" she asked.

"You will," her mother insisted. She paused for a moment, weighing up her words. "Granny said her lawyer sounded nice on the phone," she said finally.

Carly surprised them all by bursting into tears. "He's amazing," she sobbed. "And he asked me to marry him."

Carly's mom reached into the backseat where Carly was sitting and awkwardly patted her arm. "What did you say?"

"No!" Carly sobbed for a moment longer and then took a deep breath and pulled herself together.

"Sorry," she told her parents as she fought to get her emotions under control. "He really is amazing and I like him a lot, but I still need time to get over Tom and besides, he wasn't totally honest with me about the sale of the cottage. And anyway, I don't want to give up my little house and move halfway around the world for any man. You guys would miss me too much."

Carly's parents exchanged glances before Carly's mom spoke again. "We would miss you," she told her daughter. "But mostly we want you to be happy. What's this about the cottage, though?"

"He kept urging me to sign the paperwork and sell the cottage to a developer who wants to tear it down and build apartments there. I don't want the cottage to be torn down. It was Bessie's home."

"Was the developer going to pay a fair price?"

"Yeah, and the cottage does need a lot of work," Carly admitted. "No one would want to live in it until the kitchen and bathrooms were redone. But he also didn't bother to mention that the developer is his cousin."

"So was he giving his cousin a special price?" Carly's dad asked.

"No, but he did want me to sign fast and not bother to list the cottage."

"So, do you think that Granny could get a better price if she listed the cottage?"

"I don't know," Carly sighed. "The developer is supposed to pay the average of the two independent appraisals that Doncan got. And selling to him will be quick. Granny can have the money in a month or so."

Carly's dad cleared his throat. "It sounds like selling to the developer is a logical choice," he said slowly. "Granny gets a great price and a quick sale. If you take emotions out of it, I can't see that your lawyer fellow did anything wrong."

Carly sighed. "I don't know. I just feel like he didn't tell me everything," she replied. "And I think he was extra nice to me to get me to agree."

"Surely proposing to you goes way beyond being nice?" Carly's mom suggested. "Did you sign the papers?"

"Yes," Carly sighed. "I didn't feel like I had much choice."

"Did he propose before or after you signed?"

"After."

"And you said no because you don't trust him?" Carly's mom asked.

"I said no because he doesn't understand how I feel about the cottage or about my life here. When I said that we lived too far apart, he just waved his hand and said, 'you can move,' like it was no big deal."

Carly's parents exchanged glances. "I think maybe you need to just relax and give yourself some time to think," Carly's mom told her.

"What if he finds someone else while I'm thinking?" Carly fretted as the idea suddenly popped into her head.

"Then you're better off without him," her mom replied. "I'm not suggesting you think about it for the next five years and then call him up. I just think you've been under a lot of stress lately and a lot has happened. Give yourself some time to figure out what you really want. And if you decide that this lawyer can make you happy, then you and he need to figure out a way to make it happen."

Carly nodded sleepily. Her mom gave such great advice. That was her last conscious thought until her parents pulled into her little driveway over an hour later.

✣ 17 ✣

As August came to a close, Carly felt as if she had used up every bit of her energy trying not to think about Doncan. She walked around her tiny house, touching the freshly painted walls in every room. They had all come out almost exactly the way she hoped and she loved her tiny house even more now that it was decorated exactly the way she wanted it.

The smallest bedroom now had two entire walls of bookcases and Carly had delighted in filling the shelves with her enormous book collection. The house was as perfect as it could be, but for some reason it didn't really feel like home to her anymore.

When the phone rang, she worried that it might be Tom again. He had been calling and visiting far too frequently for Carly's liking. He was having a difficult time accepting that their relationship was over.

"Breaking up was your idea, remember?" Carly reminded him.

"But I was wrong," Tom told her, his tone whiny and annoying in a way that Carly realized had always bothered her.

"No, you weren't," Carly answered. "We had great fun together when we were young, but now we need to move on."

Carly finally had to tell him that she'd met someone else to try to convince him that it was really over.

"He's just a rebound guy," Tom had told her. "It won't last and then you'll come crawling back to me. Well, I won't be sitting around waiting for you."

"That's fine," Carly told him. "I won't expect you to be."

The words still bothered her, though. What if he was right? What if she had fallen for Doncan before she was properly recovered from her breakup and the relationship didn't last? Her fears about moving and her doubts about her own feelings nagged at her constantly.

Granny wanted to help, but she could do little besides listen to her granddaughter talking in circles about everything.

"Let's just plan our trip," Granny had finally suggested. "Once I've actually met the man, I'll know a lot more."

After much debate among the family and with Granny's doctors, it was finally decided that they would travel to the island on the 27th of December. Carly didn't have to be back at school after the Christmas break until the 7th of January, so that gave them more than a week to sort out furniture and for Granny to meet Doncan.

Carly headed for the ringing telephone, hoping against hope that it might be Doncan. Her desire to talk to him was a physical ache in her body.

"Carly?" It was Granny. Carly forced down the disappointed sigh that bubbled up inside of her.

"Yes, Granny, what's up?"

"I just wanted to let you know that I just got a check in the mail from the law firm on the island. Apparently the sale went through on the cottage and I've received a huge check. We can certainly book our flights and hotels now."

"That's great, Granny," Carly answered, feeling tears welling up as she thought about the cottage that was about to get torn down. Maybe it was already gone, perhaps Doncan's cousin hadn't wasted any time.

Carly sighed when she hung up the phone, feeling as if nothing was going right in her life. She headed out to get some groceries. School would be starting again the next week and she needed to start planning for that as well.

When she got home the mail had just been delivered, including a medium-sized box with international labels stuck on it. Carly read the customs form and felt her heart skip a beat when she saw that it had come from Doncan's office.

Her hands were shaking as she cut through the seemingly impenetrable layers of tape that sealed the box shut. Once all of the tape was sliced through, she took a deep breath and then slowly opened the box.

There was a letter on top:

"My Dear Carly,

I hope you find the enclosed items of interest.

When we were tidying up the closet in my office we found a couple more of Bessie's diaries that had been forgotten. I know you were fascinated by her story and I hope you enjoy finding out more.

The next item in the box is a book about Manx myths and legends. I've bookmarked a page that I want you to have a look at. Just read it and keep an open mind.

After you've read the book, there is another letter from me in the bottom of the box.

I miss you.

Devotedly yours,

Doncan"

Carly read the letter over and over, dwelling on the "I miss you" as she waited for her heart to stop racing. Tears pooled in her eyes as she thought about the man who had written the note. "I miss you, too," she whispered as she set the letter down and pulled the first items from the box.

There were two more of Bessie's diaries, and Carly quickly opened the first, checking the date. The first entry was dated May, 1945 and Carly frowned. She quickly opened the second book and gasped.

"26ᵗʰ December, 1940

I am afraid I shall be saying no to Peter. I try hard to think about how happy he makes me, but my fear of the unknown is greater than my feelings for him.

I still mourn for Matthew, who was my first love. Perhaps one day I will mourn for the love I have for Peter as well.

It is all just too overwhelming. I've told Peter to go away and leave me to think until the New Year. I do miss him, but it is bearable."

Carly sighed and felt the close to tears yet again. She felt immense sympathy for her relative who had to deal with a situation so similar to her own. Except Bessie couldn't just fly back and forth from the island to Australia whenever she wanted to, if she moved, she might never see her home again.

She was almost reluctant to read any further, knowing what was coming.

"2nd January, 1941

I told Peter that I can't marry him. He took it well. I don't think he was surprised, really. He knows how much I love my little home and how attached I still am to Matthew.

He goes back to Australia next week. I know I shall miss him."

From there the diary switched back to a daily recitation of the weather and what Bessie bought at various shops. Occasionally she mentioned a local news event or even something happening further afield. The next mention of Peter came in February.

"12th February

I've had a letter from Matthew's mother urging me to accept Peter's proposal. I wasted no time in wondering what I might have done differently if this letter had arrived before he left. There is no point."

Carly wasted quite a bit of time wondering what her relative might have done differently if the letter had arrived earlier. She concluded that if Bessie had married Peter she, herself, would never have met Doncan. And that was a terrible thought.

Carly turned page after page of routine diary entries, scanning each page for any additional mention of Peter Quayle. She was finally rewarded many pages later.

"10th March, 1943

I've had a letter from Mr. Peter Quayle. He wrote that he hasn't forgotten me and that he wanted to ask me one more time to consider his offer. If I send him a letter back, he will return to the island to get me and we can be married as soon as is practicable considering what is going on in the world.

He wants to marry and start a family. If he doesn't hear from me by Christmas, he intends to ask a close female friend of his to marry him instead.

He said that he will never love her as much as he loves me, but that he wants a family and will settle for a good woman who will make him happy if he must.

If he were here, I might give a very different reply, but I cannot ask him to return for me. That was the death of Matthew and I couldn't bear to bring about another death in that way.

I've thrown the letter on the fire so that I'm not tempted to reply. I very nearly tried to snatch it back as soon as it lit, but I resisted.

I think that I'm meant to be alone, in my little house, with my books."

Now Carly cried for the relative she had never known and for Peter. It seemed so very sad that she'd ended up alone after having loved two different men. Carly knew lots of people lived alone their whole lives and were happy that way, and she supposed that Bessie must have been happy as well, but it still felt like a sad story to her.

She flipped through the second diary quickly, watching for Peter's name. She was rewarded eventually.

"16ᵗʰ July, 1944

Mr. Doncan Quayle has informed me that his brother is now married. I must confess that I mostly felt relief on hearing of it. I find that my solitude makes me increasingly happy as time goes on.

While it might have been nice to have a husband, I'm not sure that I would have liked sharing my home, wherever it was located, with anyone else.

I adore the small children in my neighbourhood and enjoy having them over to visit, but I'm not certain that I would have been suited to the constant demands of motherhood.

On the whole, I think I have made the best possible choice for myself. I wish Peter and his new wife much joy in the years to come."

Carly sighed. She was fairly certain that her great-aunt was being sincere. Clearly Bessie was happy on her own. But that wasn't the sort of life that Carly was anxious to embrace. She wanted a little family of her own. A quick flip through the rest of the diary revealed nothing further about Peter Quayle.

Instead, Bessie had begun to write notes about books that she had read. Carly was determined to read the notes in more detail when she had a chance. Many of Bessie's books were in boxes at Doncan's house. Maybe she would even bring a few back for her own shelves after her visit with Granny. Unless she decided to marry Doncan and move to the island, a little voice said. Then she could probably keep all of the books.

Carly ignored the little voice and instead pulled the next item out of the box that Doncan had sent. The book was an old one, called *A Guide to Manx Myth and Folklore*, and Carly turned curiously to the item that Doncan had identified.

Carly was surprised to see a portrait of the tour guide she had seen at Castle Rushen at the top of the page. She read the article underneath:

"Charlotte de la Tremouille, wife of the 7th Earl of Derby is said to haunt Castle Rushen. It was there that she received word of the death of her husband from Parliamentarian forces during the final days of the English Civil War. As theirs was a true love match, at a time when such things were generally discouraged, it is said that the Countess can help visitors determine if they have found their true soul mate or not.

The legend states that if a single woman visits Castle Rushen in the company of a single gentleman and that man is, indeed, her true soul mate, the lady will see the ghost of the Countess smiling at her. However, if the man in question is not the right man for her, the woman will see Charlotte's ghost crying.

Many young women on the island swear that they have seen the Countess, but these sorts of stories are impossible to prove."

Carly sat back, stunned. She didn't believe in ghosts. But she had definitely seen the woman in the portrait at the castle when she and Doncan visited. No wonder he had looked so surprised when she talked about seeing the woman, who had definitely smiled at her.

The only thing left in the box now was the second letter from Doncan. Carly pulled it out and opened it with shaking fingers.

"Darling Carly,

No, I don't really believe in ghosts, either. But I have no other explanation for what you saw at Castle Rushen.

Please don't think that I expect you to take the word of a ghost over your own thoughts and feelings. I just wanted you to know about the ghost, as it was a part of my beginning to rethink my feelings for you.

We have a lot we need to discuss. I should have been more upfront with you about the cottage. Even more, I should not have been so dismissive of your concerns when I asked you to marry me. I was so nervous about proposing to you that I could think about nothing else.

Your concerns are valid and I'm not saying that being together will be easy. We will both have to make sacrifices and adjust if we choose to spend the rest of our lives together.

We need to talk. We can work through anything, if we work together. I love you and I will do whatever it takes to make this work.

Yours, always and forever,

Doncan

With tears streaming down her face, Carly put the letter down and tried to decide what to do next. The doorbell interrupted her thoughts.

"I wasn't sure that I gave you enough time to read everything," Doncan told her when she opened her door. "But I couldn't wait any longer to see you. Please tell me we can make this work?"

Carly cried and then laughed and then pulled Doncan close, finally feeling at home in his arms.

CHRISTMAS EVE

arly stood in the back of the tiny chapel and looked out at the small crowd of people who were filling the pews. Everyone that she loved was there. She smiled as she watched her parents fussing over Granny in the very front row. The rest of the "bride's side" of the church was filled with relatives and friends from near and far who were excited about helping Carly celebrate her special day.

Even Tom was there, holding hands with his new girlfriend. Her name was Emily, and for some reason she was proving able to motivate Tom to sort out his life in a way that Carly had never managed. From what she had heard, Tom was now working full-time and back in school part-time and hadn't had a party in at least two months.

The groom's side of the chapel was fuller than might have been expected. Doncan's parents had insisted on footing the bill for anyone and everyone in the family who wanted to attend the wedding. They were able to get group rates for flights and at the local hotel, and Carly was delighted to see Beth and Mark and the kids, as well as Uncle Henry and a handful of other relatives that she remembered from the family picnic. Even Breesha had come along, at Doncan's insistence. She'd been with the law firm for so long that she was really family.

So much had happened in the months since she had opened the door to find Doncan on her doorstep. He had stayed for a month, meeting and winning over her entire family in short order. By the time he'd left, Carly was planning their wedding.

While she was still feeling nervous about giving up her job and moving to the island, it made the most sense under the circumstances. As Doncan pointed out, things had changed since Bessie's day. Carly could fly home to visit her family on a regular basis and they could visit her as well. She and Doncan had agreed to try life on the island for at least a few years. She was going to take some time off from working and write Bessie's life story instead. In the meantime, he was figuring out exactly what he needed to do to get licensed to practice law in Pennsylvania if they eventually decided to move back to the United States.

The music started and Carly took a deep breath, feeling more nervous than she ever had before. As she walked slowly down the short aisle, her eyes met Doncan's and her nerves vanished. Whatever life threw at them, they were going to get through it together. She could see the love in his eyes and she knew that the same expression was reflected in hers.

The ceremony was a blur, and suddenly it was all over and she was a married woman. She laughed as she and Doncan kissed and then everyone was surrounding them and congratulating them and she felt overwhelmed. Doncan held her hand tightly in the crush, providing an anchor in the chaos.

Then they ate and drank and celebrated their new life together with their friends and their families. Carly felt loved and blessed and happier than she had ever been before. Tomorrow was Christmas, which seemed the perfect way to start her new married life.

And the day after that she and Doncan and Granny were heading off to the Isle of Man. It wasn't exactly a honeymoon. That would come later. It was a chance for Granny to see the island and finally sort through all that furniture. Most of it was going to be used to furnish Doncan's huge home in Laxey, they had already decided, but Carly wanted Granny to see it all and, more importantly, to see Carly's new home.

"Aunt Carly, when does Father Christmas come?" Matthew interrupted Carly's thoughts as she sat watching the party as it wound down.

"Oh, any time now," Carly answered with a smile. "You and your sisters better get to bed, hadn't you?"

"Mummy says that Father Christmas is going to leave some of our presents here and some of them back home," Matthew confided as he climbed onto Carly's lap.

"That's very good of him, isn't it?" Carly hugged him tight. "I'm sure you'll get lots of wonderful things here and at home."

"Yes," Matthew said as he snuggled up and rested his head on her shoulder. "But right now I'm awfully tired."

Doncan found Carly sitting exactly where he'd left her twenty minutes earlier when he had gone to check on some arrangements with his father.

"I leave you for a minute and you find another man," he teased as he looked down at his sleeping nephew.

"It wasn't my fault," Carly laughed quietly. "I was just sitting here and he crawled up and went to sleep."

Doncan gently picked up the sleeping boy and carried him over to his father, who was standing nearby.

"Everyone seems to be having a wonderful time," Carly sighed to Doncan when he returned to her side.

"Everything went well and everyone is happy," Doncan agreed.

"I hope you're happy," Carly smiled at her new husband.

"I've never been happier." The love Carly could see in Doncan's eyes made her heart skip a beat.

"I'm getting tired," Carly admitted. It had been a long and exciting day and it was getting late.

"I think everyone is getting tired except your Granny and Uncle Henry," Doncan told her.

Carly looked over at them and laughed. They were dancing together as the band played out the last few songs of the night.

"I think Uncle Henry is quite smitten with your Granny," Doncan told Carly. "I know they were making plans to have dinner together while she's visiting next week."

Carly grinned. "If they get married, Granny can come and live on the island, too. That would be wonderful."

Doncan smiled at her. "Before we go, I just want to give Granny her Christmas present."

Carly followed Doncan across the room and watched curiously as he handed Granny a small wrapped box.

Granny unwrapped it and then pulled back the layers of tissue paper. She looked up at Doncan, confusion written all over her face. "What is this?" she asked.

"It's the deed to Bessie's cottage," Doncan told her. "I thought it should stay in the family."

"But I've had a check for it," Granny said in confusion.

"I bought it," Doncan told her. "I had another lawyer draw up all the paperwork and check that the price was fair," he told Carly with a wink, knowing that she trusted him but wanting to be sure she understood that he deserved that trust.

Carly's eyes filled with tears as she tried to understand. "I don't understand," she said finally, looking at Doncan.

"I know the cottage is important to you," Doncan told her, obviously trying to keep his tone businesslike because everyone in the room was now hanging on his every word. "When it came down to it, I just couldn't let Jason tear it down. I guess, if things hadn't worked out between us, I could have sold it one day and you never would have known the difference. But this way your whole family can use it as a vacation getaway. I've already lined up a bunch of my cousins to start updating the kitchen and bathrooms. It should be habitable some time in the summer."

Carly could only stare at the man she had just married. "Really?" she asked, tears streaming down her face. "You did that for me?"

"I love you," Doncan said simply.

ALSO BY DIANA XARISSA

The Isle of Man Romance Series

Island Escape

Island Inheritance

Island Heritage

Island Christmas

.

ABOUT THE AUTHOR

Diana lived on the glorious Isle of Man for more than ten years before returning to the United States with her family. Now living near Buffalo, New York, she enjoys having the opportunity to write about the island that she loves so much. It truly is an amazing and magical place.

Diana also writes mystery/thrillers set in the not-too-distant future under the pen name "Diana X. Dunn" and fantasy/adventure books for middle grade readers under the pen name "D.X. Dunn."

She would be delighted to know what you think of her work and can be contacted through Facebook, Goodreads or on her website at www.dianaxarissa.com.

Find Diana at:
www.dianaxarissa.com
diana@dianaxarissa.com

Made in United States
Troutdale, OR
06/18/2025